BLOOD HITS THE WALL

Judith Cranswick

© Judith Cranswick 2016
The moral right of the author has been asserted.

All rights reserved. No part of this publication may be reproduced, stored on a retrieval system, or transmitted in any form or by any means, without prior permission of the publisher.

All the characters and institutions in this publication are fictitious. Any resemblance to real persons, living or dead, is purely coincidental.

www.judithcranswick.co.uk

Novels by Judith Cranswick

The Fiona Mason Mysteries
Blood on the Bulb Fields
Blood in the Wine
Blood and Chocolate
Blood Hits the Wall
Blood Across the Divide
Blood Flows South

The Aunt Jessica Mysteries
Murder in Morocco
Undercover Geisha

Standalone Psychological Suspense
All in the Mind
Watcher in the Shadows
A Death too Far

Nonfiction
Fun Creative Writing Workshops for the New Writer

For more information, please visit
www.judithcranswick.co.uk

Prologue

The ear-splitting explosion came first, then the blinding flash. It burst through the tiny observation window from the cab, its reflection bouncing off the solid metal walls and filling the rear of the APC with a painful piercing yellow. She reeled back, burying her face in her raised arms only to be flung sideways as the truck swerved violently before skidding to a halt.

She lay half-stunned on the floor, listening to the rapid gunfire blasting away outside.

At first, she had no idea what was happening, but as the battle raged, she had time to consider the possibilities. Had the convoy run into a loyalist military unit out on patrol? Did they realise she was on board? There was always the possibility that Ukrainian intelligence had discovered she was being moved and had mounted a rescue attempt before the convoy reached the Russian border.

The fighting was still going on when she heard someone at the rear of the vehicle. The doors were thrown open. A man in full combat uniform stood there. Only his dark brown eyes were visible above the chin protector. His black helmet and shoulders were rapidly turning white in the thick falling snow. Friend or foe?

He reached an arm towards her. Instinctively, she recoiled.

'Hurry.'

English!

He half-dragged her as they ran for the cover of the trees beneath the protecting flurry of grenades and continuous gunfire coming from both sides of the road. Several times her feet almost slid from under her on the icy surface. She collapsed into a snow-lined ditch, her heart pounding like a road drill, as she lay breathless and fearful, uncertain of what was going on. Forcing herself to take control, she crawled onto her knees, shook the snow from her hair and pulled up the hood of her thick fur-lined jacket.

It was only when the firing had all but ceased that she dared take a look over the top of the ditch. Peering through the white haze, she could just make out the GAZ Tigr jeep that had been leading the small convoy. It had been thrown on its side by the force of the initial explosion, its undercarriage almost blown away. Two dead bodies, already partially covered by a blanket of snow, lay on the road. Looking back to the way they had come; she couldn't see the third vehicle that had brought up the rear. It lay beyond the bend in the road.

The battle appeared to be over. She sank back down and closed her eyes.

The Historic Cities of the Elbe

Our tour begins in Berlin. Germany's capital is a city with a chequered history, once divided, now reunited. We have two whole days to enjoy its wonderful sites including the Berlin Wall, the Brandenburg Gate and the Reichstag building.

After our day in Potsdam, we travel south through the beautiful Elbe Valley, visiting Martin Luther's home in Wittenberg; Meissen, known throughout the world for the beauty of its porcelain figures and quality china and the historic city of Dresden, home to the Kings of Saxony and now restored to its former glory after World War II left the city centre in ruins.

Our journey along the Elbe ends in Bad Schandau, one of the oldest and most important spa resorts of the Saxon Switzerland region of Germany.

Throughout this wonderful holiday, your expert Tour Manager will be on hand to ensure that you have a truly unforgettable experience.

Super Sun Executive Travel
Specialists in luxury Continental Tours

The Glories of the Elbe Passenger List*

Tour Manager.......Mrs Fiona Mason
Driver............... . Mr Winston Taylor

Mr Peter Adams – *???*
Mrs Sonya Adams – *keeps to herself, chestnut bob.*
Mr Walter Danby – *73, looks older, small, frail, pale completion*
Mrs Elsie Danby – *looks permanently disapproving*
Mr Travis Everest – *red-faced, beer belly, brash, reporter*
Mr Solomon Sachs – *early 80s, Jewish, walrus moustache, cheery*
Mrs Anna Sachs – *outgoing like her husband*
Mr Morris Lucas – *has difficulty with steps*
Mrs Drina Lucas – *impatient with her husband*
Mrs Rose Newsom – *petite, short curly fair hair, talkative*
Mr Gary Peters – *early 40s, tall*
Mrs Loraine Peters – *youngest member of group, friendly*
Mrs Faith Reynolds – *Rose's friend* – *well-endowed, matronly*
Mr Henry Wolf – *late 40s Yorkshire accent. Shy, reserved*
Mrs Barbara Wolf – *dark hair, quiet but not as shy as husband*

* with Fiona's added comments

Day 1

A feeder coach will bring you from your chosen pickup point to Dover where you will board our luxury Imperial-class coach in time for an early-morning ferry crossing to Calais.

New to our fleet this year, Imperial-class is the peak of today's luxury coach travel. Each extra-wide armchair-style seat has its own individually controlled entertainment centre with a choice of recent release and classic films, music and games.

Super Sun Executive Travel

Chapter 1

Fiona helped one of the more elderly passengers onto the coach and turned to face the next person in the queue.

'Peter and Sonya Adams,' said the tall, grey-haired man. She stared at him open-mouthed.

He bent forward over her clipboard and pointed out the names. 'There we are. Right at the top.'

He looked so different in the bright blue bulky padded anorak – she was used to seeing him in a sober three-piece suit – but although it had lost much of its public school crispness, the familiar baritone confirmed his identity.

What was Montgomery-Jones doing here? And posing as someone else! He must be on a case. She felt a moment of panic. Was he on the trail of another terrorist? Could it possibly be one of her other passengers?

She looked at the woman half hidden behind him. Not that she could make out a great deal. Like everyone else, Peter's wife – although Fiona doubted the two were actually married – was bundled up against the unseasonal cold. Her woolly hat was pulled low over her forehead, down to the top of the heavy black-rimmed glasses so that only the striking sapphire-blue eyes were visible, staring over his shoulder above the matching white knitted scarf wrapped around the lower half of her face.

Fiona ticked off the two names and forcing a smile, wished them the customary pleasant holiday and turned to the next person in the queue.

Her mind was racing. She must warn Winston before he

had a chance to see Montgomery-Jones and give away the MI6 chief's identity. She could only hope her driver was still busy loading the last of the cases being transferred from the other feeder coaches by the time she'd finished checking all her passengers on board.

Only those who had decided to travel down the day before and stay at the hotel in Ashford, the last pickup point, had had breakfast, so once the coach had driven onto the ferry, there was a rush to get to the cafeteria.

Fiona waited until Winston had locked the coach. She needed to catch the huge bear-like West Indian before he disappeared towards the drivers' rest area.

'I don't expect you've had time to notice, but Mr Montgomery-Jones is on board as one of our passengers.'

'Your posh chap?'

There was no point in her protesting that the man wasn't *her* anything. Winston always spoke as if she and Montgomery-Jones were a couple. Nothing could be further from the truth! Good-looking he might be, sometimes charming, but much of the time Fiona found him frustratingly distant and enigmatic. What he thought of her was anybody's guess.

'He's calling himself Peter Adams.'

'You know he was comin' on this trip?'

'No. That's why it was such a shock when I saw him. He's travelling with a woman who's supposed to be his wife.'

He turned and looked down at her, a frown puckering his normally smiling countenance. 'You think he's having a naughty getaway with someone else's wife?'

'Hardly! I might know almost nothing about his private life, but I think I can safely say that a coach trip, even a luxury class one such as offered by Super Sun, would be his last choice for a holiday. Let's face it, Winston, he's much more likely to take a mistress to an exclusive villa in Tuscany or more likely a yacht to the Seychelles or the Bahamas. Definitely somewhere extremely expensive and no doubt exotic. No, this trip is clearly work, not pleasure.'

'You any idea what he's up to?'

Fiona shook her head. 'Both his and his supposed wife's passports appear to be genuine which suggests that she is also MI6.'

Fiona always collected all the passengers' passports when they first came aboard the coach. It was company policy to confirm all the details with those on the paperwork she'd been given, and it made it easier when they all checked in to the hotel. She had studied theirs carefully, but they looked much the same as everyone else's, but what did she know about forged papers?

Winston put a massive arm around her shoulders. 'I can see you is worried, sweetheart.'

'Is it any wonder? Whenever he's turned up on any of our previous trips, at least one of my passengers has ended up dead.'

Winston frowned and shook his head. 'But that wasn't his fault.'

'I know that, but why is he travelling incognito?'

'You think it's to keep tabs on one of the other passengers?'

'I have absolutely no idea, Winston. What if I have another killer in the party like last time?'

He shook his head. 'Best not to think about it, sweetheart.'

'I can't help it. I can't afford another disastrous trip. I've had three already. It was hardly my fault we had smugglers on board when we went to Holland or that a passenger was trying to sell secret guidance missile plans to terrorists on the Rhine Valley trip and as for what happened in Belgium . . .'

She stopped and took a deep breath to calm herself down.

'I'm sorry, Winston. The point is I really love this job and I don't want to give the company any excuse to let me go.'

It wasn't just her love of the job. What would she do if she was stuck at home week after week? True, it no longer felt quite like the prison it had seemed immediately after

Bill's death, but the thought still filled her with dread. Those long years spent tied to the bungalow as the motor neuron disease rendered her husband less and less able to do anything for himself, had taken their toll.

Becoming a widow at fifty-four was bad enough, but rather than giving her time to grieve, everyone around appeared to want to control her life for her; telling her she must get out and find something to help her put some meaning back in her life. Their suggestions of working a couple of days in the local charity shop, becoming a hospital visitor or joining some committee for good causes had filled her with horror.

'I can't see that happening, sweetheart. You's taken to the job like a duck to water.' Winston's deep reassuring voice cut into her reverie. 'The passengers always give you glowing reviews when they fill in the forms at the end.'

Fiona gave a deep sigh. 'Those passengers I manage to take back.'

'Come on, sweetheart. No point in worrying about something that mightn't happen. And anyway, you's got me to look after you.' His arm, still protectively around her shoulder, gave a gentle squeeze.

She looked up at him with a wide grin. 'You're a star, Winston. What would I do without you?'

By the time Fiona reached the cafeteria, the place was heaving. She looked around the crowded room, but she could see no sign of Montgomery-Jones and his partner. With so many people milling about, it didn't mean they weren't there of course, but she could hardly patrol up and down the rows of tables looking for them. She would just have to wait until he approached her.

After an early start, she had originally planned to get herself some breakfast on the ferry, but now she had lost her appetite. Just as well, she decided. The thought of battling up and down the aisles with a laden tray in an attempt to find an empty seat was enough to quell any hunger pangs. She limited herself to a cup of coffee and a bar of chocolate she could slip into her pocket for later. Probably a bad idea when she thought of all the calories she would consume in the next two weeks with three irresistible substantial meals a day – Super Sun Tours were not considered the best for no reason. Nonetheless, right now, she needed the sugar rush. The last hour had sapped her energy. Carrying her cup, she eased her way through the throng to one of the windows where she might be able to perch on the sill.

'Are you looking for a spare seat, Fiona? Come and join us.'

She recognised the face. It would be difficult to forget with his bushy triangular sideburns halfway onto his cheek, the walrus moustache and the untidy tuft of a beard on the point of his chin. Anyone looking less like a typical Jewish stereotype would be difficult to imagine.

'Thank you.' She sank down onto the chair next to him. 'It's Mr Sachs, isn't it?'

'Do call me Sol.'

'And I'm Anna.'

Sol proved to be quite a character, a cheerful soul who quickly had Fiona laughing. Anna was equally outgoing. For a couple well into their eighties, they seemed a lively pair. Before long, Fiona had discovered they had a large family with relations scattered all over the country and that most of their holidays were spent visiting them. This was their first holiday by themselves in a long time.

'Though perhaps we should have picked somewhere a bit warmer,' Anna said with a rueful smile. 'Who'd have thought when we booked last October that winter would last right into March?'

'I don't think anywhere in Europe is feeling truly spring-like yet,' Fiona agreed.

'I don't remember it ever snowing in Dorset before,' Anna shook her head, 'But at least the long-term weather forecast for where we're going is dry and sunny. As long as we stay well-wrapped up, I'm sure we'll all have a jolly time.'

Fiona was still smiling as she made her way back to the coach. They may be the oldest couple in the party, but neither seemed to want to make any concessions to their age – Anna's hair was dyed to its original black – and both were clearly ready for anything. It was always good to have passengers who were prepared to make the best of things. Their good humour tended to permeate like the smell of good coffee, spreading warmth and contentment among everyone with whom they came in contact. A definite asset to have in the group.

No matter how hard Fiona tried to push the puzzle to the back of her mind as the coach sped on its way to the Belgian border, it kept returning. If Montgomery-Jones was on some kind of undercover operation on the trail of one of her passengers, he wasn't exactly making much of an effort to socialise. On the coach, he and Sonya had sat towards the back with empty seats around them.

It was pointless to speculate. Even if she did manage to find an opportunity to catch him by himself, she doubted that she'd get a straight answer out of him. She knew from of old that he had the annoying habit of answering nearly all her questions with one of his own.

Their scheduled lunch stop was just off the main road southeast of Bruges. The small hotel, though admittedly not a five-star establishment, provided a more congenial and less frenetic setting than they might otherwise encounter at a motorway services area.

Although the temperature was pleasantly warm inside the coach, few people wanted to make the short journey to the restaurant without a coat, especially as many of them intended to take the opportunity to stretch their legs outside at some point.

Fiona stood at the front door of the coach to provide a helping hand down the steps should anyone require it. Montgomery-Jones and Sonya must have used the side door as Fiona didn't see them until she turned to follow everyone else inside. Sonya appeared to have a bad cold and was clutching a large box of tissues to her chest.

The Super Sun party were the only occupants of the small cosy restaurant. Not surprisingly, the tables nearest the log fire blazing in the large grate were filling fast. Sonya and Peter chose a table a little apart from the others and the constant blowing of her nose kept anyone else from joining them. Best not to approach, Fiona decided.

Fiona couldn't help being curious about Peter's so-called wife. Peter was a very attractive man and the two would be sharing a room for the next two weeks. It was impossible not to wonder about the kind of relationship they might have. What had that to do with anything, Fiona asked herself crossly. Anyone would think she was jealous.

It was impossible to tell much about the woman. Sonya, if that really was her name, was average height, a good three inches taller than Fiona and all Fiona had seen of her features so far was the piercing blue eyes. Even now, Sonya sat facing the wall, so all Fiona could see was the back of her head. Unlike everyone else who had removed their coats, she remained bundled up. In her thick padded jacket, it was impossible to judge her figure. Probably slim, Fiona decided. She had at least removed her hat to reveal the back of a well-cut chestnut bob.

By the end of the meal, Fiona had been so deep in her own thoughts that time had slipped by unnoticed. If she didn't make a move, she would never be back at the coach before everyone else. She jumped up and hurried towards the toilets. It would be just her luck to find herself at the end of a long queue.

As she stood washing her hands, one of the cubicle doors opened and looking up in the long mirror behind the sinks, she saw Sonya's reflection. Her fringe brushed along the top of her glasses and as she leant forward, her hair, cut to just below her ears, swung forward hiding her face. Fiona was tempted to see if she could learn more about what Montgomery-Jones was up to, but she could hardly start pumping the woman straight away.

Fiona turned to her and smiled. Sonya gave a quick nod of acknowledgement and chose the sink furthest away from Fiona.

'How's the cold? I hope you're not feeling too wretched. It's bad enough travelling in a coach all day without feeling under the weather.'

'Umm.' Sonya gave a quick forced smile and turned to the paper towel dispenser.

She was in such a hurry to get out that as she went to pull open the door, she almost collided with someone coming in.

'I'm so sorry.' It was the first time Fiona had heard Sonya speak.

'No problem, my dear. I should have been looking where . . .' Sonya did a quick little dance around the smiling woman and disappeared before Anna Sachs had a chance to finish her sentence.

'Was it something I said?' Anna raised her eyebrows and pulled a face, making Fiona laugh.

'I think she's just trying to stay away from everyone so as not to pass on her germs. I'm sure she didn't mean to be rude.'

Chapter 2

Road works, plus an accident on the Brussels ring road that brought traffic to a virtual standstill, delayed their journey considerably and everyone breathed a sigh of relief when the coach made a brief stop outside Liège. Super Sun was consistently rated the top tour operator in customer polls for comfort; nonetheless, Fiona was grateful for the opportunity to stretch her legs after travelling for three hours. She was a little apprehensive when she saw two large coaches already parked outside the café, but to her relief, Fiona found that there were no major queues at the counter and her passengers would have no problem ordering drinks.

It was warm in the café area. Too hot to sit bundled up in a thick coat in comfort. Choosing not to go to the bother of removing hers, Fiona opted for a takeout cardboard cup of coffee and went outside.

There were tables and benches on the terrace area and all but the furthest away had been cleared of snow, but Fiona decided to stay on her feet. Moving well out of the way of streams of people coming and going through the main doors, she made her way down the length of the building and round to the side.

As she turned the corner, she almost bumped into Travis Everest, a rotund, hunched-up figure with the hood of his thick woollen duffle coat pulled up. He was leaning against the wall, puffing a cigarette.

'Hi, Fiona. Sorry about this. Filthy habit, I know,' he said, looking like a naughty schoolboy caught smoking behind the bike shed. He dropped the half-finished cigarette and ground it out with his heel.

'Don't put it out on my account.'

He shook his head. 'Gave them up three months ago but saw these just now and succumbed to the temptation. They taste foul anyway.'

'Three months is quite an achievement. If you were doing so well, what made you start up again?'

He shrugged his shoulders. 'Oh, you know. Felt in need of a treat. Feeling a bit sorry for myself.'

'I expect you're just tired. Travelling tends to make everyone a bit on edge. Relax. Just think of why you booked the holiday in the first place and all the great places you're going to see.'

He didn't look convinced. 'To tell you the truth, this holiday was a last-minute thing. Just wanted to get away for a bit. Now I'm beginning to wonder if it was such a good idea.'

'When you get back on board, I suggest you take a look through the films on offer on your personal screen. I'll admit it's not as big a choice as on the airlines, but there's everything from recent releases to classics. You're sure to find something you like. You'll be surprised how quickly the time passes when you start watching something.'

He smiled. 'Will you me bring me some popcorn halfway through?'

'No.' She returned his smile. 'But if you fancy another coffee, I can make you one. Though I will let you into a little secret. The stuff you get here tastes a lot better so if you fancy one, I should get it now. If you get one like this with a lid,' she held up her own paper cup, 'you can take it back on the coach with you. I need to make a quick visit before I leave so I'll see you later.'

She stifled a sigh as she made her way back to the main entrance. Travis was the only single passenger, which meant that they would be most likely be sitting together or at least at the same table for most meals. Hopefully, he would cheer up, otherwise things might be hard going.

The Hotel Anker on the outskirts of Cologne was a small family-run establishment, but as the group would be off first thing the next morning, no one was likely to be bothered that it had no swimming pool or fitness room.

'Because of the traffic, we've arrived much later than planned but the restaurant has been kept open for us. I'm going to give you all your keys so that you can go to your rooms for a quick freshen up, but dinner will be served straight away so please make your way back down as soon as you are ready. The restaurant is along that corridor over to the right. Your cases will be delivered to your rooms while we're eating.'

When Peter came to collect his key, he said, 'I'm afraid my wife's cold is taking its toll and she has decided to skip dinner and go straight to bed if that's alright?'

'Of course, Mr Adams. I do hope she feels better soon.'

He smiled. 'Please do call me Peter.'

At least he had kept the same Christian name, she thought as she watched him return to his wife. At least she wouldn't make a mistake if she slipped up in anyone else's hearing when she spoke to him. Not that she was likely to. Though the voice was familiar enough, the cut-glass intonations had gone and the way he spoke was not like the Peter she knew at all. Never before had she heard him say "I'm" instead of "I am" or "wouldn't" and not "would not". He'd never glided over his words in the past. And the old Peter would have said, "I trust that is satisfactory." "Alright" just didn't sound natural coming from him.

Montgomery-Jones switched on the television, sat on the end of his bed and clicked through the channels to find the BBC World News. Sonya tried to settle herself back against the pillows as the announcer talked about further redundancies in the oil industry around the Gulf of Mexico, but soon she was craning forward, hugging her knees, trying to read the tickertape band along the bottom setting out the news headlines. The next item was about the elections for a new leader of a pro-democracy party in some obscure African state she had never heard of. It was almost ten minutes before the announcer moved on to the item they were waiting for.

'Fierce fighting continues in the Ukraine following the capture of the outspoken politician Natalia Shevchenko by pro-Russian rebels a week ago. Miss Shevchenko was travelling with the government delegation on the way to a meeting to negotiate a permanent ceasefire with the separatist leaders when she was abducted.'

A picture of an attractive woman with long fair hair pulled back in a thick plait coiled around her head like a halo appeared on the screen.

'She looks more like a film star than a politician,' said Sonya.

'Natalia Shevchenko was born in Kiev in 1968 at a time when the Ukraine was a republic within the USSR,' continued the announcer. *'During her student days spent at the Moscow Academy, she met and later married Konstantin Belousov, now Colonel Belousov, considered to be one of Russian's major military strategists. After the dissolution of the Soviet Union in 1991, Shevchenko remained in Moscow, supporting her new husband's career. However, the political turmoil in the Ukraine that led to the Orange Revolution in early 2005 brought about a change of allegiance for Shevchenko. Following her divorce in 2008 and opposed to what she saw as Moscow's increasing hold on Ukrainian affairs, Shevchenko returned to the country of her birth. A skilful negotiator with a fluent command of languages, she quickly rose to be a major figure in the Ukrainian parliament as one of the leading advocates of a more Western-looking future for the country.'*

The announcer turned to another camera.

'We go over to our reporter in Hirske just to the north of the rebel-held territories. What are conditions like out there at the moment, James?'

The picture changed to a gloomy outdoor shot of the reporter swaddled in thick coat, fur hat, scarf and gloves in

17

a street of dismal grey buildings many of which showed clear evidence of damage. The picture was made all the more bleak by the thickly falling snow.

'You can probably hear the not-too-distant gunfire in the background. Hirske was re-captured from the rebels some months ago but as you say, the temporary ceasefire came to an abrupt end when Natalia Shevchenko was abducted. Demands for her release in exchange for three separatist leaders held by government forces were met with resistance from many of the hardliners in Kiev.'

'Have there been any more developments?'

'Twelve days ago, the remains of a small convoy of Russian tanks was discovered about twenty miles from here. Although unconfirmed, it is widely believed that the convoy was an armed guard taking Miss Shevchenko from Donetsk to the Russian border. Although the bodies of ten armed fighters, including several in Russian uniform, were recovered from the scene there was no sign of Miss Shevchenko. The initial conclusion was that the convoy had been ambushed by loyal Ukrainian forces; however, as there is still no news as to her current whereabouts, speculation is growing. What we do know is that the immediate result of this incident appears to be a large wave of Russian troops crossing the border.'

After a further brief report of the fighting, the camera returned to the main news desk in London and an item on a rail crash in India.

There was no mention of the Ukraine on CNN. Montgomery-Jones sat and continued to flick through the news channels. Eventually, he switched off the television and stood up.

'No reports elsewhere by the looks of things.'

'Is that good or bad, sir?'

'I have no idea. And do drop the "sir," even in private. Best to keep in character.'

'Yes, si . . . Peter.'

He placed the television controls on the bed within her reach. 'There may be more in the newspapers.'

He picked up his laptop and settled himself into the easy chair by the window. Sonya watched him over the top of the room service menu she was pretending to read. It seemed to take an age for him to log on and scan through the articles. It was impossible to read his reactions. The MI6 chief had never been one to show his emotions.

Eventually, she could wait no longer. 'Are there any other reports about what's happening?'

'A few. They all say much the same thing. The Guardian headline reads, "Ukraine Blames Disappearance of Captured Prominent Ukrainian Politician on Russian Forces." It goes on to mention that a militant group of senior Ukrainian politicians are claiming that the Russians destroyed their own convoy to kill Shevchenko. It gives them an excuse to blame the West for the attack and so justify their invasion of Ukrainian territory. The Ukrainians insist the incursion is a deliberate act of war and they are demanding the West take action.'

'She was a thorn in their side. I don't doubt the Russians would be glad to get rid of her altogether, but would anyone believe that they'd really kill their own forces?' When Sonya received no answer, she asked, 'Any other theories?'

Montgomery-Jones clicked through to another site and began reading. 'The German papers appear to have similar articles with an interesting addition. There is a whole section on her former marriage to Colonel Konstantin Belousov. It implies that her anti-Russian stance was fuelled by their acrimonious divorce.'

'I suppose there is a logic to the idea.'

'There is also mention of her conviction that Russia was attempting to take over the country of her birth might well have been a cause of conflict in the marriage.'

'Are they suggesting that Belousov tried to have her removed?'

'Nothing so provocative, although I doubt the article would have been well received by the Russian powers that be.'

'Do we know where she is now?'

He shook his head. He closed down the laptop and

snapped it shut. 'The last report I had was that the blizzard grounded the helicopter, but on the plus side, they did manage to get across the border undetected. Unfortunately, the weather is not helping. Having to use the back routes only increases the chances of them becoming snowed in. We can only hope that they are able to reach the rendezvous in time.'

'Amen to that,' Sonya muttered to herself as Montgomery-Jones pushed himself from the chair.

'Have you decided what you would like to eat?' He glanced at his watch. 'I will ring room service and then I must go down and join the others.'

Fiona suspected that, like her, many of the passengers were pleased that they didn't have to go to all the effort of having to change and get smartened up for their evening meal. Spending the day cooped up on the coach sapped everyone's energy and enthusiasm and for her, there was the added tension of trying to keep everyone happy and enthused.

As the Super Sun party were the only guests in the restaurant, there was no need for her to stand at the door and indicate their assigned tables. Putting on her brightest smile, she walked over to a table where four people were sitting. She had already spoken to Barbara and Henry Wolf, a quiet couple in their mid-forties from Yorkshire, when they were having lunch, but had not yet had a chance to talk to the two single ladies.

'We were really surprised there were so few people on the tour, weren't we, Faith?' said the lively, petite woman with a pretty heart-shaped face framed with bubbly fair curls sitting next to Fiona who had introduced herself as Rose. In complete contrast, her friend was not only plain but big-boned and particularly well-endowed. Faith's somewhat lank pepper-and-salt hair only served to overemphasise her large nose. 'One of the reasons we like to travel with Super Sun is because they have small groups, but we've never had as few as this.'

'There were quite a few cancellations at the last minute,' Fiona explained. 'I expect it's this really poor weather we've been having. Plus, having only three seats per row rather than the usual four does means that these new Imperial-class coaches take far fewer passengers anyway.'

'Super Sun has always been good, but these extra wide armchair seats are so much more comfortable, and I love the individual screens on the back of the seat in front. We've never travelled in one of these before,' said Rose.

'I'm not surprised,' said Fiona with a laugh. 'They're new this year. I believe Super Sun is the first company to introduce them.'

'You two are seasoned Super Sunners, are you?' Barbara turned to Rose.

'Oh yes. They may be one of the more expensive coach tour companies, but you do get what you pay for,' Rose answered. 'In fact, we met on a Super Sun trip to Switzerland about three years ago, didn't we Faith?' Without waiting for her friend to confirm, Rose hurried on. 'Now we're both widowed, it's nice to have someone to share with. We do a couple of tours a year together. One around Easter in the Spring and one in September, October time. What about you and Henry?'

'This is our first trip with Super Sun,' Barbara replied. 'In fact, it's our first coach tour. To be honest, after today, we were beginning to wonder if we've done the right thing.'

'I'm sure you'll have a wonderful time when we get there,' Fiona said quickly.

'That is the problem with the long-distance trips. Getting there is always a bind.' Rose said sympathetically, 'Perhaps you should have chosen one closer to home to start with. We did a great one to Ireland last year, didn't we Faith? And they do great trips to France and the Netherlands.'

'Henry particularly wanted to go to Berlin, he was born there.' Henry's eyes widened, and he turned to look at his wife, but he didn't correct her. 'Originally, we were going to do a city break. It's only because I fancied seeing some of the other towns that we eventually chose this.'

'You know it well, do you?' Fiona asked, turning to Henry.

'Not at all.' He frowned at his wife. 'My family moved away from the city when I was still a toddler and when my parents died in my late teens, I came to live with my aunt in Yorkshire.' Though he did not have a strong accent, with his short 'a's, it certainly smacked of northern England. No one would have taken him for a German.

People had drifted in while they had been talking. Peter was the last to arrive. He hurried over and took one of the empty seats opposite Fiona.

'Your wife not joining us?' asked Rose.

He shook his head. 'Sonya has taken a cold remedy and decided to have a lie-down. I thought it best to leave her to sleep. If she's hungry when she wakes up, I expect we can get something from room service.'

'Her cold not any better then?' Faith asked.

'I'm sure she'll be better tomorrow,' Peter answered with a smile.

'If she needs any more Beecham's Hot Lemons I brought a couple of packets with me. You never know with this weather, do you?' Rose added.

Comments about the efficacy of hot toddies, stiff brandies and the like continued until the waiter brought their soup.

After dinner, Fiona was halfway across the foyer when Peter caught up with her.

'Thank you for not giving me away.'

'I must confess I was so surprised when I saw you, that I very nearly did.' She looked up at him and added pointedly, 'It might have been a good idea to give me the heads-up before you arrived.'

He raised his eyebrows. 'Believe me, I did not expect to be here at all. That was not the plan. It was all very last minute. The original Peter Adams was involved in a bad car accident only hours before they were due to leave. It was certainly not my choice to replace him, but there was no one else I could send at such short notice. As it was, we only just made the ferry in time. I did try to contact you several times whilst we were in the taxi, but your mobile seemed to be permanently engaged.'

'Things are always a little frantic just before a tour starts.' Damn! Why was she apologising? Montgomery-Jones had the uncanny knack of making her feel she was always the one in the wrong.

'No harm done.' He gave her a beguiling smile, the sort that her mother would have said was enough to make a good girl think bad thoughts. There had been times when his high and mighty attitude had provoked Fiona's fury, but she could not deny that he could ooze charm like a pheromone that made her feel as out of control as a star-struck teenager.

In an attempt to pretend she was immune to his charms, she tried to adopt a superior tone. 'I don't suppose you're going to tell me what you're up to?'

'You know I cannot do that, but I can assure you that this operation has absolutely nothing to do with any of your other passengers and neither are they in any danger. You have no cause for concern.'

'That's a relief. I confess it did cross my mind when I saw you that I might have another terrorist on board.'

'I should have tried to speak to you earlier. For that, I do apologise.'

'I appreciate that it might have been difficult to do so without drawing attention to yourself,' she conceded.

'Is Mr Taylor aware that I am one of the passengers?'

'You have no need to worry on that score. I spoke to Winston before we left Dover. He knows not to let on that he's met you before.'

'Thank you.'

Fiona chuckled. 'Winston's not a great one for names at the best of times. He addresses everyone as 'sir' or 'madam'.

I doubt he knows yours in any case. He always refers to you as my posh chap.'

'Really?' He looked genuinely surprised.

'And you needn't worry that he'll gossip to anyone else. Winston is discretion itself.'

'There is no need to convince me of that. I have absolute confidence in Mr Taylor. You are indeed fortunate to have a man of such estimable qualities as your driver.'

'True. Which is why I always insist that we work as a pair whenever I'm offered a tour.' She smothered a giggle. 'Even if he does have a tendency to wrap me in cotton wool at times.'

'Ahh! But then you do have the tendency to engender the protective instinct in those around you.'

'Are you saying that I can't look after myself?' she said in mock indignation.

'I would not dare to voice such a suggestion, Mrs Mason.'

Day 2

Today we head to Berlin where we will spend the next four nights in the magnificent five-star Hilton Berlin. The hotel is ideally located in the heart of the city – the Mitte district – where many of Berlin's must-see sites are to be found.

The hotel lies at the southern end of one of Berlin's most beautiful squares, the historic Gendarmenmarkt, opposite the Deutscher Dom (the German Cathedral).

Many of the city's major attractions can be found within walking distance of the hotel.

Super Sun Executive Travel

Chapter 3

The modest restaurant on the outskirts of Hanover where they were due to have lunch was well geared to catering for large parties. It was no surprise to see three coaches already lined up in the parking area. Fiona helped the last of her party down the steep steps at the front of the coach.

'Thank you, Fiona. Sorry to be such a nuisance.'

'You're not at all, Morris. The whole reason I'm here is to help so please don't give it another thought.'

Morris Lucas always waited until everyone else had left the coach. His replacement knees made going down steep steps difficult although he had appeared to have no problems walking on the flat.

Once they were inside, Fiona could see that the place was busy. Long trestle tables were arranged in parallel rows, each assigned to a different group. The rest of her Super Sun party had been shown to the table and found their places. His wife Drina had saved Morris a seat at the end of the table. Fiona took the chair opposite him.

They hardly had the time to remove their bulky coats, arrange them on the back of their chairs and settle themselves before waiters arrived holding aloft trays of bowls of steaming soup. Just the thing for a cold day.

Fiona glanced down the table to check that all was well. Sonya sat at the far end against the wall with Peter next to her. Without making a spectacle of herself leaning forward to peer down the line of people on her side of the table, Fiona couldn't see who was sitting opposite the couple. As far as she could tell, Peter was doing most of the talking and Sonya was keeping her head down, concentrating on her soup.

If the woman was trying to make herself inconspicuous, which appeared to be the case, it was having the opposite effect. Her reticence to socialise would soon begin to single her out and cause comment.

'Not quite sure what kind it is, but it's very good,' said Morris, tucking into his soup with gusto.

'Some kind of vegetable, I think,' suggested Sol Sachs who was sitting next to Fiona. 'And just the thing for this weather.'

Fiona pulled herself back from her musings about what Sonya could be up to and gave her attention to the passengers around her and said, 'Nothing like soup to warm you up, is there?'

At least from the outside, the Hilton Berlin was nothing if not impressive, Fiona decided as she gazed across at the warm orange lights that spilled onto the snow-covered pavements from the great archways leading to the main doors. Once inside, she could see that the foyer led into a spacious atrium soaring up to a breath-taking blue glass ceiling. At its far end, a broad central staircase rose half-way, then divided into two curving flights to the first-floor balcony corridors that looked down onto the ground floor below. If the rooms were up to the same high standard, her passengers should find nothing to complain about. It helped that two waiters appeared with trays of welcome drinks.

Fiona ushered everyone to the seating area in front of the reception desk. 'If you'd all like to take a seat for a few minutes, I'll go and sort out the paperwork to check you all in and collect the keys.'

As Fiona approached the reception desk, a short, rather squat man turned and smiled at her.

'Are you from the Super Sun party?' Fiona nodded. He snapped his heels and gave her a quick nod. 'I am Friedrich

Schumacher, but it will be easier for you all to call me Frederick. I am to be your guide while you are here in my beautiful city.'

Fiona tried to hide her surprise. The man might have a full head of iron-grey hair, but he had to be well into his seventies. Much older than she would have expected. Not that there was any reason why he should not be a guide, she told herself. It was his stiff, military manner that made her wonder if he might not be better suited to dealing with soldiers than showing visitors around the city.

'Pleased to meet you. I was not expecting to see you until tomorrow.'

'I thought it might be a good idea to come and meet you all this evening and explain the programme for the next two days.'

'Do you mean now?' Fiona frowned. Her passengers would want to get to their rooms as quickly as possible to get settled in before having to think about anything else.

'After dinner perhaps? If you would be kind enough to introduce me now and then I can ask everyone to meet me for coffee in the lounge when you have finished your meal?'

'I'm sure that won't be a problem.'

By the time Frederick had introduced himself and given his mercifully short spiel, Fiona noticed that with typical German efficiency, their luggage had already been collected from the entrance lobby, loaded onto trollies and whisked away. With luck, if the cases were not already in their rooms, at least her passengers should not have to wait long for them to arrive.

As they all drifted away, Fiona picked up her hand luggage and walked over to the reception desk to return the forms. She didn't mean to listen in to Montgomery-Jones's conversation with one of the other receptionists, but she couldn't help overhearing.

'Do you have anything for Peter Adams?'

'I will take a look for you, sir.'

The receptionist dived under the desk at the far end and

came up holding a white envelope.

'Thank you.' Peter accepted it, put it straight in an inside pocket without opening it and walked swiftly to the stairs.

Fiona stared after him wondering what that was about. He appeared to be in a hurry and probably hadn't even noticed that she was there. She was beginning to find both his and Sonya's presence more and more unsettling. Despite Montgomery-Jones's assertion that his operation would not impact on the group in any way, without the remotest idea of what was going on, their strange behaviour was doing little to reassure her.

Although the general hotel guests at the Berlin Hilton were free to take dinner in the Restaurant Mark Brandenburg throughout the evening, so that the Super Sun party could all eat together, Fiona arranged for tables to be reserved for the group at seven thirty throughout their stay. As there were only fifteen passengers on the tour, two tables of eight had been set aside for the party.

Morris and Drina were the last to arrive.

'Sorry we're so late,' said Morris with an apologetic grin. 'My fault, I'm afraid. I'm a bit of a news addict and I was catching up on the television and forgot the time.'

'Anything special been happening?' asked Faith.

'It was mainly about the arrangements for the Peace Talks with Russia over the Ukrainian situation.'

'Bad business that.' Sol's usual smiling countenance looked grim. 'Did they mention anything about that Ukrainian politician captured by the rebels? There was an article in the Telegraph the day before we left suggesting that she'd been taken to Russia and that's why the Peace Talks had broken down. The Russian-backed rebels claimed she'd being spying for the West. I read a letter in the "From our Foreign Correspondent" section that said that she may have been rescued.'

Morris shook his head. 'There was nothing on the BBC World News. At least not while I was watching.'

'I never watch the news when I'm away on holiday,' Rose said firmly, changing the subject. 'Far too depressing these days.'

'I agree,' said Drina, putting a hand firmly on her husband's arm. 'Let's talk about something more pleasant. I'm looking forward to tomorrow, Fiona. From what we've seen driving through the city, Berlin looks like a fascinating place.'

'I will keep you for a short time only, but I thought you might like to have some idea of what we will all be doing for the next two days. For those of you who have never been to our beautiful city before, you will find Berlin is steeped in history with so much to see that in so short a time I will be able to give you a taster only.'

Frederick Schumacher appeared competent and informative, but Fiona could have wished for their guide to be a little less formal and to sound a little less like an authoritarian teacher instructing a group of students. He was the archetypal German as portrayed in British and American television dramas and old films set in the post-war years. He seemed inordinately proud of the fact that he was from East Germany, which he informed them was where their hotel was located and where they would discover almost all of the city's major sites.

When he had finished, no one had seemed eager to ask any questions, so he made another little click with his heels accompanied by a quick nod of the head. 'Until tomorrow, ladies and gentlemen. We will meet here at 9 o'clock. Please be on time.'

Rose Newman suppressed a giggle as they all watched Frederick walk swiftly to the door. 'Do you think he's going to make us quick march in file when we go on our guided walk in the afternoon?'

Some people began to drift to their rooms straight away. They had spent the best part of two days travelling and it was understandable that several of them were planning on an early night.

Fiona glanced at her watch, then looked around at the remaining passengers. None of her party struck her as late-night revellers that she might need to keep an eye on, so she decided she could take her leave with a clear conscience. It was Sunday and there was something she needed to do. Her sons would be expecting her to call.

'Hello, Adam. How are you all?'

'Hi, Mum. I was beginning to get worried when you didn't phone at the usual time.'

'Sorry about that, love. The reason is that I'm not at home. I'm in Germany, Berlin actually, and this is the first opportunity I've had.'

'But you said you weren't working again until next month. You're not overdoing it are you, Mother?'

Fiona did her best not to grit her teeth.

'Of course not, darling. In fact, according to my boss, this trip should be more like a paid holiday for me. I'm going to have local guides in every city so all I have to do is be there as the company rep. I can just sit back and relax.'

Fat chance of that with Montgomery-Jones and his partner turning up. Not that she had any intention of telling Adam about that. If either of her sons got an inkling of her having any association with someone in MI6 or a hint of the danger she managed to find herself getting into when she became involved in his operations, they would insist she give up the job with Super Sun and put her under some form of house arrest.

'So why didn't you say last Sunday you were going to be away?'

Fiona sighed. Parents were supposed to worry about their children — not the other way around. It would help if Adam stopped treating her like some elderly old dear who wasn't capable of making decisions for herself. Just because Bill, her husband of almost thirty-four years had died eighteen months ago, did not mean she was confined to sitting at home doing nothing. At fifty-five, she still had a life to lead.

'Because I didn't know myself until three days beforehand. Apparently, the tour manager who was supposed to go was taken ill and they needed someone at the last minute.'

'You're supposed to work part-time only. You shouldn't let the company take advantage of you.'

'I'm not. I enjoy it. And this trip should be fantastic. Berlin and all those wonderful towns in the Elbe Valley to the south. I'm really looking forward to it.'

Adam gave a snort of disapproval. 'But you will be home in time for your birthday, won't you?'

She hadn't thought about it before and did a quick calculation. 'Not quite. We get back the day after. When you get to my age, birthdays are something you'd rather forget about.'

'Mum!' He sounded like a whiny twelve-year-old.

'What's wrong with that? I wasn't planning on anything special anyway.' She was finding it harder and harder not to sound irritated. Best to change the subject.

'So how are Kristie and the children? Has Becky recovered from her cough?'

There was a slight pause at the end of the line. 'No. She's been off school all week, so Kristie's made another appointment to see the doctor tomorrow. Poor kid was supposed to go to a classmate's sixth birthday party yesterday. Becky was a bit upset when we said she couldn't go, but all the other children's mums would've been very unhappy if we'd let Becky spread her germs over everyone.'

'Oh, what a shame, poor love.'

'She's up in the bedroom right now watching a DVD feeling very sorry for herself. She wouldn't come down for lunch. Said she wasn't hungry. How much of that is because she's still sulking about yesterday, we're not sure. Our wee lass can be very stubborn and strong-willed when she wants to be. Takes after her grandma,' he added as an afterthought.

'Thank you, darling!'

He had the grace to laugh.

'You still haven't told us what you want for your birthday.'

'I keep telling you, darling, it's far too expensive to keep sending parcels from Canada. Besides, I really don't need anything. Spend it on the children. Just send me a card.'

'But you've just said you won't be home on your birthday.'

'I'll be there a day or so after. Anyway, I must go. Love to you all and give the children a big kiss from Grandma. Bye, Adam.'

She rang off before he had time to fuss about a birthday present. The news about her granddaughter was not good and she resolved to ring again tomorrow night and find out what the doctor had said. Six-year-olds were prey to all sorts of things once they got to school and mixed with other youngsters, but this cough had been going on for over a week now and she couldn't help worrying.

Adam setting up home so far away in Montreal wasn't easy at the best of times, but it was on occasions such as this that Fiona regretted it more than ever. There was absolutely nothing she could do to help.

Day 3

Berlin is a city steeped in history. Capital of the Kingdom of Prussia, the German Empire, the Weimar Republic and latterly the Third Reich, the city was divided after World War II when East Berlin became the capital of East Germany and West Berlin became a walled enclave cut off from the rest of West Germany. When the Wall fell in 1989, German reunification quickly followed with Berlin once more as the capital.

The highlights of our morning panoramic tour include the imposing neo-classical Brandenburg Gate, the Reichstag – home of the German Parliament, the notorious Berlin Wall that divided the city from 1961 to 1989, its East Side Gallery and Checkpoint Charlie.

After lunch, we begin our walking tour in the Gendarmenmarkt, flanked at either end by the Französischer Dom and the Deutscher Dom (the French and German Cathedrals) with the magnificent Konzerthaus (Concert House) in the centre.

In the Bebelplatz, we will see the memorial to the infamous Nazi book burnings that took place in front of Humboldt University, the State Opera building and St Hedwig's Cathedral. Our final destination is the magnificent Berliner Dom which boasts the world's third largest organ.

Super Sun Executive Travel

Chapter 4

Fiona always made it a habit to be down for breakfast early when she was on tour. There was usually so much to be done before the party set off. Normally, that would include a meeting with Winston but today of course, she could leave that to Frederick. For the next two days, she could sit back and let someone else take charge. She had no notes to swot up and no walking routes to commit to memory. Her task was simply to act as rear-end Charlie to ensure no one got lost and that everyone was kept happy. Not that that was always an easy task, but the passengers she'd had the chance to speak to so far all seemed pleasant enough and after last night's smiling faces at dinner, no one had stood out as being potentially difficult.

One advantage of arriving early for breakfast was that the restaurant was not crowded. There were so few people eating that she was able to find herself a table by a window. This was her first opportunity to see the city in daylight and the view brought a smile to her lips. Across the street, she could see the corner of the German Cathedral with its carved pediments supported by a series of columns on each side and the blue dome held aloft by a central tower. She was so intent trying to make out its splendid detail that she did not hear anyone approaching.

'Do you mind if I join you?'

She looked up at the red-faced, portly man smilingly down at her. Even first thing in the morning, Travis Everest looked slightly dishevelled.

'By all means. You certainly look a great deal happier than

when we last spoke.'

Travis put down his plate piled high with sausage, egg, bacon, mushrooms and baked beans, pulled out the chair and dropped heavily onto the seat.

'Yeah. Sorry about that. As you said, it was probably the travelling getting me down. But we're here now and I'm raring to go.'

'Glad to hear it. I was just admiring the cathedral.'

'Is that what it is? Last night when we arrived and saw it all lit up, I thought it was a town hall of some kind, but I can see the cross on top now.'

'The original building was burnt down at the end of the war and although it's been restored, it's now a museum dedicated to democracy.' Fiona laughed. 'You'll have to forgive the lecture. I've just been reading up about it in the guidebook.'

'The whole city looks totally different from the last time I was here. But that was some time ago. Way back in 1989, just after the Wall came down. Back then, the whole city was still a virtual bombsite after the war. Almost everything you see now has been rebuilt or heavily restored.'

'I imagine so,' Fiona said and poured herself another cup of tea.

'That's one of the reasons I was so keen to come back here. See how everything's changed.' He crammed a huge forkful of food into his mouth and began chewing.

'You're travelling on your own?'

'Yep! Never tied the knot. Married to the job, me.'

'What do you do?'

'I'm a journalist. Do you remember the picture of a young woman standing on top of the Wall lowering her kid into the arms of a grey-haired man on the day the Wall came down?' He put down his fork, put up his hands, stretched out from the tips of his thumbs and forefingers and drew his hands apart to outline an imaginary banner headline. 'The headline read, "Man sees Granddaughter for the First Time." It made the front page of The Daily Mail. That was mine.' His face lit up at the memory. 'I won an award for that.'

'To be honest, I can't say I do, but as you say, it was quite a long time ago. So,' she continued brightly, 'Are you still working for the paper?

He shook his head. 'No, I was freelance back then. I tried to get them to take me onto the payroll, but they already had . . .'

The waiter arrived to ask if Travis wanted tea or coffee.

A good time for Fiona to make her getaway.

'I have one or two things to do before we leave so I'll leave you to enjoy the rest of your meal in peace.'

Fiona came down to the reception area a good fifteen minutes before they were due to leave, to find Frederick already waiting. They barely had time to exchange pleasantries before others began to arrive. To judge by the noisy chatter, everyone seemed excited and eager for the off.

Fiona took a copy of the passenger list out of her bag and began ticking off names. Although she hadn't yet had a chance to speak to everyone on the tour, she was reasonably confident that she could put faces to names. She was watching the short corridor from the stairs for new arrivals and noticed Peter and Sonya approaching.

As Sonya glanced across at the assembled group, she gave a sudden start, hesitating in her stride. Turning to look at what had cause Sonya's alarm, Fiona could see nothing out of the ordinary. It appeared that the woman had been staring at Frederick. When Fiona looked back again, Sonya was smiling and talking with Peter. If there had been a problem, it was obviously resolved.

Fiona ticked off their names on her list and looked through to see who was still missing.

Once everyone had arrived, Frederick led them all outside to wait for the coach.

'Before we depart, I would like to show you one of my city's famous buddy bears.' Only a few yards from the hotel doors was a brightly painted, life-size model of a pink bear dressed in pinstriped trousers and black jacket standing on its head. 'The bear is featured on our heraldic shield and is a symbol of peace, understanding and tolerance.'

'Why is he dressed as a waiter?'

'I think it's supposed to be a tailcoat. He's wearing a presentation sash,' Travis ventured.

'It is simply a piece of fun.' Frederick shook away the question as though it were irrelevant. 'You will find bear sculptures all over the city, painted in a variety of colours.'

One of the advantages of escorting small groups was that Fiona frequently had a chance to stand near enough to the local guides to be able to hear their commentaries. On this occasion, because she had moved back to allow the photographers as much room as possible on the narrow strip of pavement that had been cleared, she caught only part of Frederick's explanation of the bear being the symbol of the Duke of Albrecht who founded the city some eight hundred years ago.

'Do mind the snow,' she said quickly to Morris Lucas who was so intent on trying to take a picture that he had only narrowly avoided stepping into the foot-high bank of snow that had been cleared to the edge of the pavement.

'That's all we need,' scolded his wife Drina. 'You falling over and damaging your knees before we even get started.'

Fiona resolved to keep an eye on Morris.

Once they were on the coach, Frederick handed out city maps. He had already marked the location of the hotel on each one.

'You will be able to trace our route as we make our way to our first stop. We will head north through the square and then turn past the Berlin Dom on the way to our first stop. We are now passing the Konzerthaus or Concert Hall on our left.'

'Looks more like a temple with all those great columns and triangular bits on top,' said Morris to his wife sitting in the seat in front of Fiona.

'I will tell you more about this and two more cathedrals this afternoon when we pass them on our walk. We are now in what was East Berlin and it here that you find nearly all of the great historic buildings and monuments. To begin, I would like to tell you a little about the history of our great city.'

For all his stiff, formal, somewhat mirthless persona, Fiona had to admit the man certainly knew his stuff. In preparation for the first stop at the East Side Gallery on an old section of the Berlin Wall, Frederick talked about the post year wars and the building of the notorious Wall and the subsequent reunification of Germany after its fall.

'Life in East Berlin in the Soviet days is often pictured as grey and drear and it is certainly true that there were few luxury goods around, but as an East Berliner, I have to say that it was not as bad as some would like to paint it.'

There were mutterings of surprise throughout the coach.

'So how do you explain the People's Uprising of 1953?' Henry Wolf demanded in a loud voice. Heads turned to look at him. The normally soft-spoken, retiring man sounded almost combative. 'An entire Soviet armored division was brought in to crush the demonstration.'

Frederick's lips thinned, but without emotion he continued, 'That was before my time and under Stalin, things were not good, but I'm talking about the life I remember. About how things were after the wall went up. Some people seem to forget that in the early '60s, our lifestyle began to improve under the communist system. There was full employment. Everyone had a job. Food, housing and basic clothing were cheap. People had access to good healthcare facilities and there was free public transport. Many of us believed that communism was a fairer system for everyone. The rich may have prospered in capitalist West Germany, but the poorest in society were left to fend for themselves.'

'If you believed the rhetoric,' muttered someone a few

seats in front of Fiona.

Fiona had vacated her seat at the front to Frederick and taken a place at the back. It meant that she couldn't see people's faces, but from the odd head shaking and murmurings, it was evident that the majority of people were far from convinced by Frederick's vision of the past. Perhaps it was just as well that they had arrived at their first stop, a remaining section of the old Berlin Wall now covered in a series of colourful paintings.

'In 1989, after the Wall came down, artists from all over the world came here to the East Side and produced an enormous picture wall with over 100 paintings. These were intended to represent a time of change and express the hope for a better, unified future.'

There was a shuffle as everyone reached for coats and gloves before leaving the warm coach to brave the outside. As the group thinned out, moving along the Wall to take a look at the various paintings and taking pictures, Fiona took the opportunity to join them. Listening to the comments people were making as she passed, Henry Wolf was not alone in his skepticism.

'The people may have had the basics, but our illustrious guide seems to have ignored the fact that they lacked basic freedoms such as freedom of speech and the freedom to vote,' muttered Morris Lucas.

'And to travel to the West. What about all those hundreds of people who tried to escape over the Wall?' Drina Lucas added.

Fiona moved on, even if it were not company policy that tour managers should not approve themselves to become involved in discussions concerning politics or religion with clients, she had no wish to become embroiled in what might prove to be an uncomfortable situation.

'I like that one.' Faith Reynolds was standing with her head cocked to one side, admiring a picture of a dozen or so figures sunning themselves on a stretch of beach backed by a high flint wall.

'But they've got no clothes on,' said her friend Rose Newsom in a somewhat shocked tone.

'Yes, but they're all turned away. No naughty bits in sight,' Faith chuckled and catching sight of Fiona who was passing asked, 'What do you think, Fiona?'

'I wonder if that's not the point. The wall is no longer a symbol of oppression and the people are now free not only of their clothes but from all the constraints of the past. I think that's why there's so much orange and red to show a warm future is dawning.'

'You're right! I didn't see that before but now you mention it, it does all make sense.'

Standing next to Rose, Fiona noticed that for once there was someone in the party even shorter than she was, even if only by an inch.

Although the two friends clearly enjoyed travelling together, Fiona mused as they all walked back to the coach, they were very different characters. For a start, they both looked totally unalike. Faith, though only of slightly above average height, was solidly built and tended to plod along, surprisingly keeping pace with her petite friend's dancing steps. According to their passports, Faith was two years younger than her friend but looked a good few years older. In addition, Rose gave the impression that she always blurted out the first thing that came into her head, whereas Faith was more circumspect and gave more thoughtful, measured responses.

As they drove on to their next stopping place, the coach made a short diversion to pass the Jewish Museum. It was a sombre silver-grey block building with featureless walls without windows. The only thing that relieved the solid walls were broken jagged black lines that criss-crossed the surface.

'Here you can see only the end wall of the building,' Frederick informed them. 'The ground plan of the building is very unusual. It looks like a lightning bolt and is intended to represent a broken Star of David. However, it is not a holocaust museum. It tells the story of 2000 years of Jewish history in Berlin. Another unusual feature is that you can only enter the building through an underground tunnel into the basement.'

Although the coach was not allowed to stop, Winston drove past slowly to give everyone the opportunity to take pictures. It was no surprise that Sol Sachs was the last to remain standing, twisting round in his seat trying to catch a last glimpse of the side of the building as they drove on.

'The next area that we will pass is Tempelhof Airport . . .'

Fiona sat back and listened to Fredrick's account of the airport's early Nazi history and then the story of its use in the Berlin Blockade. She felt a little guilty that she wasn't making notes. There was always the possibility that she might be asked to do the actual guiding on a future trip.

She had been reluctant to take on this tour and it had taken all the Tour Director's sweet-talking to get her to agree. It wasn't that she was not interested in visiting such wonderful places – who wouldn't be – especially as they were all new to her, but the thought of two solid days of travel just to get there and return made her hesitate. The unseasonal cold didn't help either.

David Rushworth had been very persuasive. He had promised her that she would have a local guide in every city so no need to prepare any notes, thus flooring her main argument about needing time for essential research. He had even agreed to rearrange Winston's schedule so that he would be the designated driver. After he'd gone to so much trouble, it would have been churlish to refuse.

Quite why he had been so keen that she should manage this particular tour, she hadn't been able to fathom, but now she was beginning to wonder if Montgomery-Jones hadn't had a hand in all this. It would be just like him to manipulate matters behind the scenes. He had before; though quite why he should do so now, she had no idea. Perhaps she was just being fanciful. He was up to something, that was for certain, but what part he intended her to play in the whole affair was a mystery.

Chapter 5

After a brief photo stop at the Reichstag building, they continued to the Brandenburg Gate. Although Fiona had seen pictures of the imposing structure, it was much bigger than she had expected. Frederick gave a brief account of its history and the story of how Napoleon had had the crowning bronze sculpture of Victory in a chariot drawn by four horses removed and taken to Paris only for it to be returned a few years later.

Frederick said he would give them plenty of free time to look at the Gate in more detail, and should they wish, to venture into the Holocaust Memorial a few yards away.

He stood at the door to help everyone off the coach, and with Winston at the side door, Fiona was free to wander around like everyone else. After her first few tours, she had decided that it looked unprofessional if she started snapping photos. This time, with all the rush of last-minute preparations she had forgotten to pack her camera in any case. An oversight she was beginning to regret. It would have been nice to have taken the odd photograph if only to send to the boys. Not that her sons showed a great deal of interest in hearing about her adventures in foreign parts – which was probably just as well, she thought ruefully.

She turned back to retrace her steps to see Anna Sachs trying to take a photograph of the towering columns of the Gate and struggling to keep hold of various bits and pieces at the same time.

'Here, let me help you.'

'Thank you, Fiona.' Anna handed over gloves, map, notebook and pen. 'Sheepskin mittens may keep your hands nice and warm but there's no way you can take a photo in them. And as for the rest of the stuff; I should have left it on the coach, but I didn't think.'

Once Anna had finished taking pictures and had sorted herself out, the two of them walked together back the way they'd come.

'Sol will be wondering where I am. He's gone on to the Memorial. To be honest, neither of us is very religious. We don't go to synagogue or anything, not anymore. Sol did as a boy but I'm only half Jewish anyway. My mother was a Catholic.'

There was no sign of Sol when they reached the stark rows of concrete blocks that composed the Memorial. They stretched almost as far as one could see. Two thousand seven hundred and eleven of them, according to Fiona's guidebook, and they became progressively larger towards the centre.

'Frederick mentioned something about an information centre at the far end. Perhaps that's where your husband's gone.'

Walking through the rows between the tightly packed blocks was no easy task. The snow had compacted to ice and it was difficult to stop their feet from sliding away from under them.

'I'm not sure if this is such a good idea,' Fiona said as Anna sashayed uncontrolled to the next block.

'It'll be easier once we reach the taller blocks. Something to hold onto.'

Anna forged ahead. She and Sol may be the oldest members of the party, but their enthusiasm was undiminished. It was only when Anna skidded precariously and only stopped herself from falling by throwing her arms around one of the blocks that Fiona decided it was time to intervene.

When the two of them had stopped laughing, Fiona urged

that it was time to turn back.

'Shall we try through here,' she suggested, indicating that they move through into another line, 'and see if the ground is any less slippery further over? It might be a bit more protected towards the centre.'

'Okeydokey.'

The route back didn't seem any easier. They both had to concentrate where they were putting their feet, but Fiona could hear loud voices ahead and she looked up to see Sol talking with Frederick back on the main path some distance ahead.

'Yoo-hoo.' Anna waved but the two men didn't appear to notice. The women were too far away to hear what was being said, but the men's body language suggested that Sol, at least, was becoming more agitated.

'Oh dear,' Anna muttered, shaking her head. 'Sol rarely loses his temper but when he does, he can let rip.'

Although the two women struggled to make their way as quickly as possible, Frederick had turned on his heel leaving Sol shaking a fist after him long before they reached the safety of the cleared path. Anna put an arm on Sol's sleeve and pulled him off to one side, pleading with him to calm down.

Fiona, approaching far more gingerly once the blocks became lower and she could no longer propel herself from one to the next, decided to take her time. Frederick was no longer in sight, but she could see that there were half a dozen other people standing around looking either stunned or embarrassed by the incident they had obviously witnessed.

'I think it's time we all headed back towards the coach,' Fiona said brightly. 'We mustn't keep the others waiting.'

Fiona shooed them back towards the parking area in front of the Brandenburg Gate, leaving Anna to deal with Sol without an audience.

Faith and Rose were clearly discussing the incident. Fiona caught odd snatches of their conversation.

'He had no right to upset people like that! That man is so rude.'

'It was a little tactless, but I doubt that he realised that Sol was Jewish,' replied Faith in more reasoned tones.

'That's no excuse. He should never have made such a remark in the first place.'

'The guide was only voicing the opinions of a growing number of people in Berlin. There's an increasing wave of anti-Semitism everywhere these days. He never claimed he felt the same way. And you have to admit, Sol did go over the top.'

Fiona wondered whether she should investigate further or if it would be best to leave well alone and hope it would all blow over. Anna seemed a very level-headed woman; it might be best to have a quiet word with her at some point and see if it was anything she needed to deal with.

Everyone seemed more subdued back on the coach, including Frederick. He said little until they reached the next photo opportunity.

Fiona was a little disappointed with Checkpoint Charlie. She didn't know quite what she was expecting but certainly something a little more spectacular than a small wooden hut that reminded her of a rundown toll booth transplanted into the centre of a very ordinary city street, now dwarfed by towering office blocks. It was difficult to imagine this as the main gateway between East and West Berlin as portrayed in so many spy books and films. No unsmiling border guards, no good guy crossing a great empty space while the audience waited with baited breath, fearful of the shout and sudden rifle fire.

According to her guidebook, the Wall Museum housed in one of the buildings alongside the checkpoint might prove more informative. Fiona made a mental note to tell her passengers if they wanted to learn more about the various ways people tried to escape and their stories, they could return in their free time.

Checkpoint Charlie was the last point of interest on their morning itinerary, and it took only a few minutes to drive the short distance back to their hotel for lunch.

If some of her passengers appeared to be avoiding Frederick when they went into the restaurant, the same could not be said of Travis. He seemed only too eager to talk to the guide and was soon plying him with questions, though what they appeared to be discussing so earnestly, Fiona could not hear as she was sitting at another table with Morris and Drina Lucas and a pleasant, younger couple in their forties, Gary and Loraine Peters.

Fiona turned to Morris, 'Are you coming on the walk this afternoon?'

'Of course. Looking forward to it.' He seemed surprised at the implication that he would think of ducking out.

'Do you know how far we're going?' Drina didn't sound so sure. 'With all this snow around the paths could be quite treacherous.'

'We saw how far this morning,' Morris interrupted before Fiona had a chance to answer. 'It's only to the main Cathedral. And the paths have all been cleared.'

'As I understand it, the walk itself will take about an hour, but there are so many interesting buildings along the way, there will be plenty of stops. Of course, like everything else on the tour, it is optional, but it would be a shame to miss it,' Fiona tried to reassure his overanxious wife.

A burst of laughter came from one of the other tables. Whatever Travis had said to Frederick had certainly amused the normally solemn and taciturn guide. The two men appeared to have become bosom buddies. The other two couples at their table were obviously not included in the conversation but from the snatches Fiona was able to catch, the two men were talking in German anyway.

Though several heads had turned to see what the noise was about, conversation at the various tables was beginning to resume. However, Fiona noticed that Sonya was still staring at the two men with narrowed eyes. It was impossible to read much in the woman's expression, but Fiona had the distinct impression that Sonya was far from happy and that this was something more than mere dislike of Frederick's manner. It seemed to confirm Fiona's earlier suspicion that Sonya had met the man before this morning, although Frederick had given no indication that he had recognised the woman pretending to be Montgomery-Jones's wife.

Chapter 6

Fiona was pleased to see that all her passengers had arrived at the meeting place in the foyer ready for the afternoon's guided walk. She had wondered if the Danbys, the elderly couple who Fiona had judged might have most difficulty, might choose to duck out given the state of the roads. After the comments about Frederick and mutterings of 'Stasi' and the like that she had overheard at lunch, there was also the possibility that one or two of the others might decide they had had enough of their guide for one day.

At least Frederick appeared to be making an effort to be more friendly this afternoon. He was actually smiling. Perhaps it was the effects of the bottle of red wine Travis had bought for them to share over lunch.

'As we all seem to be here, shall we make a start? I see you have come prepared and are all well wrapped up. It is a little cold, but the sun is shining, and we will take our time. Please feel free to ask any questions as we make our way around. Now, if you would all like to follow me.'

As the group started to follow Frederick, Fiona noticed Sonya holding back, talking urgently to Montgomery-Jones. Fiona stood by the main doors waiting. She had the impression that some kind of argument was going on. Not wanting to be thought prying, Fiona decided to leave them to it and went to join the others.

Outside, everyone had already begun to make their way along the pavement to a break in the cleared bank of snow separating pavement and road. Some had already crossed over into the square.

Fiona stood with the last of the party, waiting for a couple of passing cars. By the time the road was clear again, Peter and Sonya had caught up.

Sonya was still muttering. 'I still do not understand why we have to go through this whole charade.'

Fiona caught the look on Peter's Face. She knew him well enough to recognise the narrowed eyes and firmly set jaw indicated his anger. He took Sonya's arm and marched her swiftly across the road, skirting around the stragglers taking her right to the front and out of everyone's earshot.

Fiona wasn't sure what to make of the incident, but any further consideration of what she had witnessed was cut short when someone spoke to her.

'Everywhere looks so pretty covered in a blanket of pure white snow. Back home, it never stays like that for long,' sighed Anna. 'All too soon it's all dirty and grey.'

They walked past an outside café with its tables and chairs covered with two inches of snow like unblemished tablecloths and cushions.

'I do hope you aren't planning to have a coffee stop here, Fiona,' Sol joked.

'That might be a little tricky,' she laughed.

'Is this snow typical in Berlin at this time of year?' Drina asked Frederick as she stamped her feet on the cleared stretch of ground to shake away the loose snow.

'Not at all. I have never known the snow to last so long. But it is the same in your country I believe. Everywhere in Europe, the weather it has been unpredictable. No? Now ladies and gentlemen, if you look at the building in front of us, you will see the Deutscher Dom built for the city's Lutheran community. Today it houses an exhibition illustrating Germany's democratic history. You will notice that all four sides have the same architecture. If you look across to the north end of the square, you will see the Französischer Dom, built for the Huguenot refugees from France, which looks very similar. In fact, only their front towers are identical.'

As everyone walked to the large statue of Germany's great poet and philosopher, Friedrich Schiller, in the centre of the square in front of the Concert House, Fiona attempted to stay close to Morris without making it too obvious. No doubt at his wife's insistence, he had brought a walking stick, but he had no problems keeping up with everyone. As he had said before, walking was no problem, it was steep steps that he found difficult.

Travis joined Frederick at the front as the group followed them both out of the square. Travis said something that caused the guide to let out a loud guffaw.

'Frederick seems a lot more cheerful this afternoon,' Anna said with a grin.

'I'm not surprised,' Elsie Danby retorted primly. 'He drank the better part of a bottle of wine at lunchtime. Anyone would think Travis was trying to get him drunk, the way he kept topping up Frederick's glass.'

'It's certainly put Frederick in a better mood,' said her husband with a twinkle in his eye. 'And give the man his due, Travis did offer everyone else on the table a glass. Not that anyone took him up on it.'

'As I told him, I don't drink,' Elsie said self-righteously, 'and Walter only has the occasional glass and never at lunchtime.'

Walter gave Fiona a sheepish grin. Fiona had little doubt that Walter would have been only too happy to accept Travis's offer had it not been for his wife's swift intervention.

Frederick and Travis were now so engrossed in their conversation that they were beginning to stride ahead. The group was rapidly becoming more spread out.

Fiona made her apologies to the Danbys and made her way to the front, trying to think of a tactful way of suggesting Frederick might like to slow down without arousing the man's hostility.

Some ten minutes later, Frederick attempted to take a shortcut across a deserted car park. He led the group along a cleared track that ran diagonally across to the far corner. Before he and Travis had gone more than a few yards, it became evident that the route was far too treacherous. The cleared path was now covered in a glassy ice. The half dozen people who had already begun to make their way gingerly turned back to the main path and the whole party then trouped right round the outside.

By the time they reached Bebelplatz, another large snow-covered square, Fiona was reassured that all her party, including Morris and the frail looking Danbys, were more than capable of handling the conditions and keeping up. She should stop worrying, enjoy the spectacular buildings, and listen to Frederick's explanations.

Frederick headed over to a patch cleared of snow in the middle of the square. The reason became evident when everyone had joined him and gathered round to peer down through a glass panel set into the cobbled ground to see the rows of empty bookshelves far below in some underground cellar.

'This is a memorial to the infamous book-burning that took place here in 1933 in front of Humboldt University. Here in this square, Joseph Goebbels, Hitler's propaganda minister, ordered the burning of twenty thousand books that were considered to conflict with Nazi ideology.'

'First books and then the Jews,' muttered Morris, shaking his head.

'Too true,' said Sol. 'And my father was one of them.'

Anna put a hand on his shoulder as the big man continued to stare down into the Empty Library, his face heavy with emotion.

'Much the same sentiment is shown over on this plaque,' Frederick's voice broke the silence that had descended over the group.

He walked over to a brass plate. 'These are the prophetic

words of the poet Heinrich Heine in the previous century, translated they read, "Where they start by burning books, they will end by burning people." It was not only Jews the Nazis exterminated; gypsies and homosexuals were also persecuted. Berlin has a Gay Holocaust Memorial to remember the 54,000 people who were convicted under the regime. In 2012, our German Chancellor opened a Gipsy Holocaust Memorial. You can find both memorials over in Tiergarten Park, near the Reichstag.'

As the bulk of the party moved forward to peer at the plaque, Fiona caught Sonya looking at her with such an appraising stare that she felt momentarily disconcerted. Had Peter mentioned that they already knew each other? Exactly what had he told her?

Travis stamped his feet and began slapping his arms around himself in an effort to keep warm as they waited.

'It's bad enough to freeze the unmentionables off a brass monkey,' Travis remarked as Sonya stared at him disapprovingly. 'Aren't you cold?'

For a moment, Fiona thought the aloof woman wasn't going to answer, but eventually Sonya gave him a curt nod and said, 'Yes. But not enough to make a fool of myself dancing about.'

Travis gave a burst of laughter. 'Love you too, darlin'.'

Sonya tossed her head and walked quickly over to the others clustered around the plaque.

Before they left the square, Frederick pointed out a large circular building at the far end covered by an enormous green dome. 'St Hedwig's Cathedral was originally built in the mid-18th century but like so many buildings here in Berlin, it suffered considerable damage during World War II and has been heavily restored. It is the seat of the archbishop of Berlin, the world's youngest cardinal. Now let us move on to see the Berliner Dom.'

'My goodness, another cathedral,' exclaimed Rose. 'That's four almost within spitting distance of each other. For a once-communist city, Berlin seems to have a large Christian population.'

Frederick shook his head. 'As I said, the German and French Doms are now museums, St Hedwig's is a Roman Catholic cathedral, but the Berliner Dom is an Evangelical church rather than a true cathedral as it has no bishop. In Germany if you are registered as Catholic, Protestant or Jewish, you must pay a religious tax on your annual income tax bill, so in Berlin, fifty percent of people are atheists.'

Nearly everyone was busy taking photos, and Fiona found herself standing next to Sonya.

'I'm glad to see your cold is much better.'

Sonya turned sharply, looking a little startled.

'I'm so sorry. I didn't mean to make you jump,' Fiona apologised.

Sonya gave her a somewhat forced smile, which didn't quite reach the grey eyes. 'I was deep in thought.' There was a faint trace of accent that Fiona hadn't noticed before.

'Did you decide not to bring a camera or are you leaving all the photography to Peter?'

'Yes. Peter takes better pictures. I must go and join him.'

Fiona wasn't sure if there was anything personal in the way Sonya hurried to get away from her or if she was simply trying to avoid everyone. The woman certainly wasn't being any more sociable now she had recovered from her cold than before.

Three or four of the keener photographers had decided to walk right to the far end of the square to get a better picture of the cathedral, but the majority began to congregate around Frederick.

'I hadn't heard about the book burnings before,' said Rose, making conversation while they waited.

'It happened all over Germany, not just here in Berlin. Students made great bonfires of any books by authors who did not conform to the idea of German purity. Not just by Jewish authors but any works by communists, socialists, pacifists and any writings on sexuality and pornography.

Great works of philosophy, anything considered at all intellectual, were all consigned to the flames.' Frederick was in his element. 'Fascism tried to eradicate free thought. Things were very different here after the war of course. Life may not have been easy here in East Berlin under socialism, but education was truly valued. Everyone had access to education. Not just schools, but books and equipment were free, and the children were given free meals. Even the nursery places were free.'

'Only so the women would be free to work in the arms factories,' muttered someone behind Fiona.

If he heard the remark, Frederick chose to ignore it.

By now, all the photographers had returned, and the party moved off. Soon they had reached a busy dual carriageway. Once the group had reassembled on the far side, Frederick led the way to the bridge past another large imposing building. 'This is the old armoury which now houses the German History Museum. Now we will cross the River Spree onto Museum Island.'

Peter and Sonya were lagging behind the others deep in conversation as everyone else made their way to the bridge. Fiona was uncertain whether to wait for them. She had no wish to appear to be trying to listen in on what they were saying but had it been any of the others, she would have gently urged them not to get left behind.

Frederick was already halfway through his spiel about the famous Schlossbrücke or Palace Bridge by the time she caught up. Several of the group had already begun to wander across to admire the eight beautiful statues arranged on top of the walls on either side.

In front of them stood the neo-baroque Berliner Dom.

'During your free time tomorrow afternoon, when you will have more time, you may like to return here to visit one of these five famous museums. Tomorrow I will tell you more about each of them and the wonderful treasures they each hold but this is as far as we will go for this afternoon.'

'What's that great modern looking tower over there?'

asked Rose.

Sounding decidedly annoyed at being pre-empted, Frederick said, 'I was about to point out the Fernsehturm. It is the television tower, the tallest building in Berlin. Should you wish, it is possible to go up the tower. There is a revolving café in the sphere section at the top. It gives splendid views of the whole city and beyond. Another possibility for your free time tomorrow that I would like to point out while we are here is the DDR museum just across the river from the Dom. It attempts to show life in East Germany during Soviet times.'

Frederick's comments inevitably resulted in a fair amount of chatter as couples discussed the next day's options.

'We're rather spoilt for choice,' said Morris. 'What would you recommend, Fiona?'

Probably not a good idea to admit this was her first visit to Berlin. 'I think it very much depends on what interests you. I'm sure Frederick will give us lots more information after we've been to Charlottenburg. We should have some time on Wednesday when we get back from Potsdam, so I don't think you need to try and cram too much into tomorrow afternoon.'

Frederick clapped his hands for attention. 'Ladies and gentlemen, I am now going to make my way back for those of you who wish to return to the hotel. However, if any of you would like to spend a little longer here visiting the cathedral or exploring the island, you are welcome. The choice is yours. The route back is not difficult, and you can retrace your steps. If you check your maps, which I hope you all still have with you, the hotel is marked. Can you all find the Berliner Dom?' He held up a map and pointed with a gloved finger to the appropriate spot.

'I wouldn't mind a sit down before we start back,' admitted Elsie Danby. 'Is there anywhere near where we can get a cup of tea?'

'There is a small basement café in the Berliner Dom which is highly recommended,' replied Frederick.

'That sounds like an excellent idea,' Drina said, tucking her arm through Morris's.

Several other couples began to drift off leaving half a dozen or so people who had decided to return with Frederick including Travis.

Travis had been locked to Frederick's side for most of the afternoon engaging him in conversation whenever they moved from one stopping place to the next. The two men now appeared to be firm friends. Fiona was not surprised to see Peter and Sonya amongst those planning to return with Frederick. Sonya had looked decidedly bored for most of the afternoon. For an MI6 operative, she didn't exactly seem to be throwing herself into her undercover role.

Once Fiona had checked that no one was in need of her services, she decided to take the opportunity to visit the cathedral. The rest of the day was her own. She could relax and behave like any other tourist.

Chapter 7

It was already dusk by the time Fiona reached the Gendarmenmarkt. As she waited to cross the road into the hotel, she saw two figures walking back from the other direction. She gave them a wave. Even at a distance, it was easy to recognise the women. Rose prancing along, clearly doing all the talking, alongside the heavier Faith, keeping pace with her more solid step.

'We've just been shopping,' Rose informed Fiona when they caught up.

'So I see,' said Fiona with a laugh, eyeing their laden carrier bags.

'Have you been in the chocolate shop on the corner over there?' Faith turned back and pointed to the end of the block.

'Not yet. I haven't had a chance to look in any of the shops yet.'

'You must go tomorrow,' Rose said. 'Even if you don't buy anything. There are these huge chocolate models of all sorts of things: a church, a ship, a clock tower and an amazing model of the Brandenburg Gate. You should see the sculpture on top, the chariot and the four horses. The detail is unbelievable. And there's a volcano spurting chocolate lava.'

'And the smell! It's fabulous.' Faith closed her eyes and wrinkled her nose. 'We bought lots to take home as presents.'

'Plus a little something for ourselves,' Rose giggled. 'We're going to pop up and have them now with a nice cup of tea.'

'Sounds like an excellent idea. I'll be sure to take a look tomorrow.'

Fiona was so busy talking with the two friends as she pushed through the big glass double doors that she didn't spot the policeman until he stepped in front of her, holding out an arm to prevent all three of them from entering further.

'What on earth's going on?' Rose's question went unanswered.

'Are you ladies staying in the hotel?'

Fiona nodded.

'May I have your names please?'

As the policeman checked off Rose and Faith's names against the list he had on his clipboard, Fiona tried to see what was happening beyond the foyer in the atrium. Something major was clearly going on by the great sweeping staircase. A large area had been roped off with red and white police tape and two men in white paper suits were on their hands and knees presumably collecting evidence of some kind.

'And you, madam?'

'Pardon?'

'Your name please?'

'Oh yes. Mason. Fiona Mason.'

Fiona was still trying to work out what was going on, when she realised the policeman was asking her another question.

'I'm sorry. What did you say?'

He sighed. 'You are the tour manager for the Super Sun party?'

'That's right. Can you tell me what's hap . . .'

'Please wait here a minute. The Inspector. He would like to speak to you.' He turned away and spoke quietly into the phone attached at his shoulder. He was speaking in German, but she heard her name mentioned and presumed he was informing his superior that she was back in the hotel. When he had finished, he turned to Fiona and said, 'He is coming directly.'

'But . . .' Before Fiona had a chance to ask any questions, the policeman was busy stopping someone else who had just come through the doors.

Fiona moved aside to allow him to return to his task. She realised there were at least half a dozen uniformed officers questioning everyone who came in. Most of the incomers were asked their names and then allowed to move to the reception desk or up to their rooms by the lifts or the side stairs. Quite why she had been singled out to wait for a senior officer, she could not fathom.

Fiona removed her gloves, hat and scarf and unzipped her padded jacket, but it was fast becoming unbearably warm. She had been on her feet for over three and a half hours and was tempted to move over to the seating area in front of the reception desk despite the policeman's instruction. Although from there, it would not be possible to see what was going on in the atrium and she had to admit her curiosity was getting the better of her.

Several men in dark suits standing just outside the cordon were deep in conversation. It wasn't only an area on the ground floor that had been marked off. On the first-floor balcony above, there was evidently another no-go area and another paper-suited investigator was conducting tests on the railing.

After ten minutes, the Inspector had still not arrived. Fiona approached the policeman and smiling sweetly, said, 'Would you let the Inspector know that I've gone up to my room. I'm in 407.' He frowned but before he could protest, she added firmly, 'I need to use the bathroom.'

As Fiona stepped out of the lift, an excited group of her passengers rushed up to her.

'Have you heard the news? Someone fell from the first-floor balcony.' Even though she had only been back in the hotel for a few minutes, it was no surprise that Rose was one of the first with the news.

'I heard it was one of our party; that pushy chap who's been sucking up to Frederick all day,' Drina Lucas chipped in.

'Do you mean Travis?' Fiona suddenly felt cold.

Her husband nodded. 'That's the one. The reporter for The Daily Mail.'

'He's hardly a Fleet Street journalist or whatever you call them these days.' Walter Danby was scathing. 'I googled him on the internet. He works on the Swindon Advertiser.'

'Until we know for certain what's happened, perhaps we should . . .' Fiona's attempt to quell the speculation was ignored.

'But it was definitely one of our lot. Why else would the police want to interview us all?' Rose insisted.

'Exactly! They've already made a start. Morris saw one of the policemen knocking on Sol and Anna's door, didn't you?'

Morris nodded enthusiastically.

'I expect the police will be interviewing all the guests staying in the hotel, not just our party,' Fiona said quickly, 'If you'll forgive me everyone, I need to get to my room.'

Feeling guilty for not doing more to quash wild rumours from spreading any further, Fiona hurried to her room. Apart from an urgent call of nature, it would not do to antagonise the Inspector further by not being in her room to answer his call.

Fiona had to wait another half hour before the phone rang.

'Mrs Mason? This is Sergeant Hase. Would it be possible to ask you a few questions?' He spoke with only a faint trace of accent.

'Certainly, Sergeant. Would you like me to meet you downstairs?'

'I will come up to you if that is acceptable. I will bring a female officer with me.'

Fiona did not have to wait long.

The Sergeant was young, early thirties, a big man; almost six-feet tall with broad shoulders and already showing signs of a paunch. He held out his hand and smiled.

Once they had shaken hands, Fiona waved him to the armchair by the window and invited the policewoman to sit on the upright chair that she had already pulled out from beneath the dressing table. The policewoman shook her head and remained standing by the door.

Fiona took the chair herself and turned to the Sergeant. 'How may I help you?'

'I would like to check details.' He took a small notebook and pen from his pocket. 'You are the tour manager for the party from Super Sun Executive Travel and your local guide is Friedrich Schumacher?' Fiona nodded. 'You and your party arrived at the hotel last evening?'

'That is correct.'

'The names of all those on the tour. It is possible to have a list?'

'Certainly,' Fiona stood up and reached for the folder on the dressing table.

'May I take this? I will return . . .'

'No need. Please keep it. I always bring plenty of copies.'

'Thank you.' He read down the list then looked back up and Fiona. 'Herr Schumacher. He has been with you all day?'

She nodded. 'We had a scenic drive this morning around the city, came back here for lunch and then Frederick took us on a short, guided walk to the Berliner Dom.'

'You did not all return together?'

'Some people opted to stay in the area and Frederick walked with the rest back to the hotel.'

'At what time?'

'I didn't look at my watch, but I would guess it would have been around three o'clock or a little after when we all went our separate ways.'

'And Herr Schumacher. That is the last time you saw

him?'

'Yes. I visited the cathedral and then took a stroll around Museum Island. I returned to the hotel a little before five-thirty.'

'Do you have the names of those who returned with Herr Schumacher?'

'I'm not sure. Mr and Mrs Adams, Travis Everest, Mr and Mrs Sachs. I think Mr and Mrs Wolf may have done as well or it may have been Mr and Mrs Peters. To be honest, everyone was bundled up in thick coats, hats and scarves and it was more a question of counting heads and checking no one wanted my help rather than seeing who went where.'

He smiled, 'I understand.' He ticked the appropriate names on his list and added question marks to the ones she hadn't been sure of. 'Herr Schumacher. Were there any problems?'

Fiona licked her lips. After the incident at the Brandenburg Gate, she could hardly say none. After a moment's pause, she said, 'What sort of problems?'

'No conflict, no arguments?'

'Frederick has an unfortunate manner and is not an easy man to warm to, but everyone chose to accompany him on the afternoon walk.'

She desperately wanted to ask why he was asking all these questions about Frederick. Surely, it was Travis he should be asking about. For such a big man, the Sergeant was softly spoken and there was nothing abrasive about his questioning, but she had dealt with enough policemen in the past to know it was not a good idea to ask questions. They rarely answered, and it only made them tetchy.

'You did not know of any disagreements between Herr Schumacher and any members of your group?'

From the steady way he looked at her, Fiona suspected he must already know about the fracas at the Jewish Holocaust Memorial. There was nothing to be gained by trying to pretend it hadn't happened.

'On one occasion, I believe Frederick said something

which upset Sol Sachs; one of those little misunderstandings that sometimes occur. I don't know exactly what was said, but it was all quickly resolved.'

'Were there further incidents? With Sol Sachs or another person.'

'No. Not as far as I am aware.'

'You discussed the occurrence with Herr Schumacher, perhaps?'

'No. I saw no need. Sol said nothing to me and as I said, the matter was resolved.'

'And you, Mrs Mason? Did things go well between you and Herr Schumacher?'

'There were no problems. We only talked very briefly when I first arrived and since then, although we may have exchanged a few words, we haven't had what you could call a proper conversation. As a guide, he certainly knows his stuff, though I admit I could wish him a little less abrasive in his manner, but I have no difficulties with the man.'

'You had no complaint?'

'None whatsoever. He is somewhat brusque, and he doesn't go out of his way to be friendly, but not all guides are necessarily the life and soul of the party.' It flashed through her mind that the Sergeant might not understand such an English cliché, but he gave a quick grin before his expression became serious again.

'There was one time I suggested he might like to slow down a little on the walk. The conditions were such that some of the less able passengers were beginning to drop behind. But that was only because he'd been answering someone's questions at the front and hadn't noticed.'

'He had no cause to feel that you were about to report him to the agency about his conduct?'

'Certainly not! Nothing was further from my mind. I can't claim he is the best local guide I've encountered, but he is far from being the worst. I can think of no reason why he would imagine that I am thinking of complaining about him.'

'What was his mood the last time you saw him?'

'I'm not quite sure what you mean, Sergeant.'

'Was he depressed?'

'Certainly not. He seemed more lively than he'd been all day. I heard him laughing with one of the passengers as they walked away.'

'I see.' He smiled and said, 'One final question, Mrs Mason. Do you know of any reason why Herr Schumacher should be in this hotel at four o'clock?'

Fiona looked at him in surprise. 'No. I assumed he would return to his own home after he'd brought everyone back to the hotel. Unless he stayed to talk to some of them.'

'Do you know who that might be?'

Fiona shook her head. 'I'm sorry, Sergeant. I wasn't here, so I cannot help you I'm afraid.'

The obvious person was Travis, but as she had no proof, she decided that it might be better if the police learnt that from Travis himself.

'No matter.' The Sergeant smiled and folded the copy passenger list and tucked it into his notebook. He eased himself forward in the chair, replaced the notebook in an inside pocket then got to his feet. 'Thank you for your help, Mrs Mason.'

'May I ask what has happened, Sergeant? My passengers are rather worried, and I would like to be able to tell them something. There are all sorts of rumours flying around. Are you saying that Frederick was involved in this incident this afternoon?'

He smiled. 'I am sorry to tell you that Herr Schumacher died this afternoon here in the hotel. He appears to have fallen from the first-floor balcony. We are trying to establish exactly what happened.'

Chapter 8

Fiona sat on the end of her bed. staring into space for some time after the two police officers had left. Did the Sergeant's questions imply that Frederick was suicidal? The idea seemed ridiculously far-fetched but presumably, the police had to consider all possibilities.

It was equally ridiculous to consider that any of her passengers would have cause to deliberately murder the man. They had known him for less than twenty-four hours. But it was bound to have consequences for her tour. Not least, what would happen tomorrow? She needed to speak to Winston.

He answered on the second ring. 'Hello, sweetheart.'

'Winston, are you in the hotel?'

'I's in my room.'

'Have you heard what's happened?'

'Only that someone died in the hotel. I saw all the police cars pullin' into the car park when I was cleanin' the coach.'

'That someone was Frederick, our guide.'

There was silence at the other end. 'Winston? Are you still there?'

'You's kidding me?'

'No. I'm not. It looks like someone may have pushed him from the first-floor balcony. I've just been interviewed by a police Sergeant. I expect they'll want to talk to you sometime. They seem to be talking to all of our passengers.'

'You okay, sweetheart?' He must have heard the break in her voice. 'I's coming round. What room is you in?'

'Room 407.'

'I's on my way.'

Fiona threw her mobile onto the armchair and lay back on the bed feeling utterly drained. She barely had time to pull herself together before she heard a soft knock at the door.

The giant West Indian almost filled the doorway. He took a couple of steps into the room, put out his hands and held her shoulders at arm's length studying her face intently.

'I'm fine, Winston.' She smiled up at him. 'Honestly. Shut the door and come on in. We need to sort out what happens tomorrow.'

'You sure you is all right, sweetheart? It's not like you to let things get you down,' he said gently once they were seated side by side on the bed.

'Do you know what really upset me? When I heard that it was Frederick who had died, my first thought was, thank goodness it wasn't one of my passengers. How dreadful is that?'

He gave one of his deep rumbling laughs and shook his head. 'I 'spose the first thing we need to do is inform Head Office. I'll see to that. No need for you to worry. What do you wanna do about tomorrow?'

'I'm not really sure. Can we manage without a local guide? I know hardly anything about Charlottenburg or the other places we are due to see. The trouble is the police may not have finished with their interviews. They may want us to make ourselves available at any time, so I'm not sure whether it's worth ringing the local agent to ask for a replacement guide in any case. Plus, it would seem very heartless and uncaring to do so.'

Winston looked at her and shook his head.

'I know you think I'm being oversensitive, but there it is,' she said firmly. 'Anyway, thinking about it, I'm sure the police will have already contacted the local agency so, in due course, I expect they will get in touch with me. Even if we cancel tomorrow's tour Frederick was due to go with us to

Potsdam on Wednesday and we will need them to send us someone then.'

They sat talking for a few more minutes and Fiona felt considerably calmer by the time the driver got up to leave.

'We'll leave it at that then, Winston. I'll try and speak to the Inspector after dinner and see what he says. We'll have a breakfast conference and make final decisions before I speak to everyone at 9 o'clock.'

'That's all we can do, sweetheart.' At the door, he turned with a final admonition, 'Now don't you go worrying yourself. Any problems you ring me.'

'I will, Winston. Thank you, and just in case I haven't said it before, you're a treasure.'

He chuckled and closed the door.

Because Frederick Schumacher was known to them all and they must constitute some of the last people to see him alive, it came as no surprise that the police wanted to speak to the members of the Super Sun party as a matter of priority. However, the decision by the police to continue to conduct interviews throughout the evening was making matters difficult for the restaurant staff trying to cope.

Fiona had arrived early and tried to encourage her passengers to fill in the tables as they arrived, but this still left the second table with only three seats taken at the start of the meal.

'Poor Frederick, it's dreadful isn't it?' said Loraine Peters as she sat down. 'It seems so much worse when it's someone you've actually met. I mean it's not something you expect when you go on holiday, is it.'

'Umm,' Fiona replied noncommittally. If only the woman knew!

'The police have already interviewed us,' announced her husband Gary. 'We were among the first. They started with everyone who was in the foyer when poor Frederick fell.'

'So you two saw what happened? How awful for you.'

'No, not really.' Gary shook his head. 'We were just

coming back in when it happened.'

'We heard this screaming and there was a rush of people over to the far end of the atrium by the main stairs. Then someone said a man had fallen from the first-floor balcony. We didn't actually see anyone fall. We didn't even see the body. We stayed back. We had no idea it was Frederick until much later,' Loraine explained.

'We were about to go up to our rooms when the police arrived, and everyone was told to wait until they had taken our names.'

'Were there many people there?' asked Fiona.

'There seemed to be quite a few gathered around the body. Around thirty or so,' suggested Loraine.

'Less than that. I'd say more like twenty,' interrupted her husband. 'Most were in the entrance area like us although a lot of people then rushed forward.'

'We told the policeman we hadn't really seen anything when he took our names, but he asked us to wait anyway.'

'Eventually one of the plainclothes officers came over to talk to us,' said Gary. 'He asked us why we were in the hotel, how long we'd been in Berlin and all that sort of stuff and then if we knew Frederick. That's when we realised it must have been him.'

The waiter came over to the table. 'Would you like to order, now?'

'We're quite happy to wait for a bit until a few more people arrive, if that's all right with you, Fiona,' said Loraine.

'That's fine by me. It's nice having big tables so we can all sit down together and get to know everyone, but it doesn't make for a relaxed meal when people keep coming and going. Not when you're half-way through your main course when the person next to you is only just starting their soup, and the one opposite is finishing their dessert.'

'Exactly,' said her husband. 'And we can always have a drink while we're waiting. Shall we take a look at the wine list?'

It was another ten minutes before Sol and Anna arrived.

'Were you there when it happened?' Loraine asked once the two had sat down.

'No, thank goodness. We came down for a cup of tea in the café when we got back after the walk but were up in our room again by the time it happened,' said Sol.

'The first we heard about it was when we had a phone call from a policeman saying that there had been an incident and that the police wanted to speak to all the guests who were in the hotel at the time.'

'Anna told him we'd been in our room for the past hour and knew nothing about any incident, but it didn't make any difference.'

'Not that they came very promptly. We were getting ready to come down to dinner by the time the two of them arrived,' Anna said indignantly. 'And then the questions! They went on and on. You would think poor Sol had murdered Frederick the way that Inspector kept badgering him. "What was the argument about at the Holocaust memorial?" Never mind Sol explained it wasn't an argument. Sol just took exception to the flippant way Frederick had said in his opinion there was too much fuss made with all these memorial ceremonies the town was planning to mark the seventieth anniversary. Said something about the Jews should stop going on about the horrors of the past and move on.'

'That wasn't very tactful,' said Fiona.

'I agree,' said Loraine, 'and please don't think I'm trying to excuse him, but Frederick probably would not have said it if he'd realised that you were Jewish, Sol.'

The normally placid Sol Sachs did not look appeased. His chin dipped and bright black eyes glared up at her from under shaggy eyebrows, his brow creased in a sullen frown.

Time to change the subject.

'Is anyone else getting hungry?' Fiona cut in. 'Shall we order? I'm not sure if anyone else is going to arrive.'

Just as they all picked up their menus, Travis pushed through the doors and stomped over, his face the colour of an overripe plum.

'They've taken away my laptop!' he roared. Everyone in the restaurant turned to see what was going on. 'You've got to do something, Fiona. I want it back!'

'Are you saying it's been stolen?' Fiona got to her feet.

'No, no. The bloody police. They've taken it away for examination.'

'But why?' she motioned him to sit down.

'I need it,' he pleaded, becoming suddenly almost tearful. 'It's got all my notes on it. I have to get that article off tonight if it's going to make tomorrow's pages. It's no use sending the national papers anything that's not up to date.' Travis plonked himself down on the chair and banged his balled fists on the table.

'Yes, Travis, but why did the police want your laptop?' Fiona repeated, trying to calm the man down.

'Because they think there's something incriminating on it, I suppose. That police Inspector all but accused me of luring Frederick into the hotel specifically to kill him.'

'But why would they think that?' said Loraine. 'You were the one person in the group who seemed to get on well with him. You two seemed great buddies.'

'Hardly,' Travis was scathing. 'Couldn't stand the chap. Right miserable little sod! And so full of his own importance, going on about the medal he'd been given back in the 60s. Mind you, that's what gave him away. The only time the Soviets did anything like that was to reward border guards when they shot people going over the wall. It's such a bloody good story.' He turned back to Fiona. 'I need that laptop, Fiona. You've got to get it back.'

'If it's been taken for evidence, Travis, I hardly think the police will pay any attention to what I have to say.'

'It must be against my human rights or something. I haven't been charged with anything, so how can they do that?' He was getting more and more agitated.

Fiona shook her head. 'I have no idea. Listen, Travis if it would help, I will speak to the Inspector, but you need to calm down and tell me exactly what happened. Why would the Inspector think you murdered Frederick?'

'How the hell would I know? Didn't seem to believe me when I said I invited Frederick up to my room to interview him about his life behind the Wall during the Cold War. That sort of thing would make a great features article and I could do with something to make a bit of a splash. My career's taken something of a dip of late. That Inspector tried to make out that I lured him upstairs so that I could push him over the balcony. Never mind that it happened before Frederick had even got to my room.'

'You didn't see him when he came back to the hotel?' asked Walter.

'Don't you start! That's just what that bloody Inspector said. Frederick rang me when he arrived, but I needed to go to the bathroom, so I gave him my room number and he said he'd make his own way up. I wasn't to know someone was going to chuck him over the bloody balcony, was I? That's what I said to the Inspector. Not that he believed me.'

'Who do you think did it?' asked Walter.

'I don't know, do I?' With a weary sigh, he pushed away the cutlery in front of him, folded his arms on the table, and slumped forward.

Anna, sitting next to him, put out a hand and patted his arm. 'I really don't think you should worry too much. That Inspector all but accused poor Sol of murdering Frederick and I expect he's going to treat everyone else in the same way.'

He pulled away and glared at her. 'That's not the problem. I couldn't care less what the man thinks. He can't prove I pushed him over because I didn't do it. It's my laptop I'm bothered about.'

Fiona was relieved to get away after the meal. Travis had sat in morose silence while they were all eating. Although that was preferable to having to listen to his bad-tempered complaints, it didn't make for a very relaxed atmosphere. Fiona had tried to make light conversation, but the others all seemed too wary of provoking another outburst from Travis to give more than monosyllabic replies, so she soon gave up the effort.

Because it had taken some time before they had ordered their meal, the rest of the party at the other table were long gone by the time Fiona left the restaurant. For that reason, she was surprised to see Montgomery-Jones on the stairs ahead of her when she walked up to her room.

'Peter?'

He turned, his face set in a tight expression.

'Is something wrong?' she asked.

He waited until she had climbed the remaining stairs and they walked together along the corridor.

'I was summoned to speak to Inspector Bauer.'

Fiona had to work hard to hold back the grin that threatened to break out. The thought of anyone daring to *summon* Peter Montgomery-Jones was something of a novelty, but it would hardly improve the imperious man's disgruntled mood if she were to display her amusement.

'I hope he was a little more polite to you than he seems to have been with some of the other members of the party. Both Sol Sachs and Travis Everest seem to think he was accusing them of murdering Frederick.'

'Really?' She could sense that he wasn't paying a great deal of attention to her chatter. He clearly had something on his mind. 'Inspector Bauer requested that I inform Sonya that he wishes to speak with her.'

He made as if to stride away, but Fiona put a restraining hand on his arm. 'Before you do, Peter, can you assure me that you had nothing to do with Frederick's death?'

He stopped and looked down at her incredulously. 'You think *I* killed him?'

She shook her head vigorously. 'Of course not. Not you personally. What I meant was, I need to know that he wasn't killed because of something to do with your mission, whatever that might be.'

The grey eyes narrowed and there was a long pause before he said firmly, 'I can categorically assure you, Fiona, I have no idea who killed Frederick Schumacher or why. At the risk of sounding heartless, the man's death is yet another problem for the operation. The more attention your tour attracts, the more difficult it becomes to complete our mission.'

He strode away before she could detain him further. Peter Montgomery-Jones was not a happy man, but somehow, she did not think that it was because of anything she had said to him.

Day 4

This morning, our tour takes us to the west side of the city and the magnificent Schloss Charlottenburg and gardens. This beautiful palace takes its name from the wife of Elector Friedrich III, Sophie Charlotte, for whom it was built as a summer house. We drive on to Spandau, one of the oldest towns within the greater Berlin area which was spared the worst of the bombing in World War II. After exploring its picturesque market square with its timber-framed houses and surrounding medieval streets, we will return to the hotel for lunch.

In the afternoon, there will be time to explore Berlin at your leisure. Why not visit one of the world-class museums on Museum Island? The Pergamonmuseum is famous for its original friezes from the Pergamon altar; the Altes Museum houses a treasured collection of Greek and Roman art and sculpture; the Neues Museum is home to the iconic head of Nefertiti, or the Bode Museum with its collection of Byzantine Art, housed in a fine historic building at the north-west tip of the island.

If you are interested in finding out more about life in Soviet East Berlin, why not visit the interactive DDR museum. Here you can gain a sense of what it was like going to school, queuing for food, and work and home life under constant Stasi surveillance. Here too you can learn more about the infamous Berlin Wall.

Alongside Checkpoint Charlie you will find the small wall museum with its displays of photos and related documents of successful escape attempts from East Germany, together with the escape apparatus: hot-air balloons, getaway cars, chairlifts, and a mini-U-boat.

Super Sun Executive Travel

Chapter 9

Fiona had spent a restless night. She had lain awake until the small hours, and try as she might, her thoughts kept coming back to the possible consequences of Frederick's murder. It was inconceivable that any of her passengers could be responsible. She might not know them well, but they all appeared to be perfectly pleasant, normal people and it was hard to conceive that any of them might have a possible motive. Travis might be single-minded in his obsession to get the interview that would put his flagging career back on track, but it would serve no purpose to dispose of the man before he had the full story about the East German's time as a border guard, if that was what the man had been. And Sol was far too good-natured to be considered a murderer whatever Inspector Bauer might think. In the end, she had fallen asleep just before dawn, only to be rudely woken by the jangle of her alarm.

It wasn't like Winston to keep her waiting. They had agreed to meet at seven thirty for breakfast as was their custom. In the normal course of events, he was down before her, but he still had not arrived fifteen minutes later.

Fiona toyed with her breakfast roll. She had lost her appetite and excellent though it looked, she could not face the thought of a cooked breakfast.

She stared out of the window, but the elegant columns and fine carved pediment failed to hold her attention. It could have been plain brick wall for all she took in of the view.

'Penny for them, sweetheart.'

'Winston!' She turned her head and looked up into the smiling deep brown eyes.

'I's sorry I's so late. That Inspector chap phoned me just as I was leavin' m' room. Wanted me to see him straight away.' Winston settled himself in the chair opposite.

'At this time in the morning! He doesn't waste much time, does he? He sent a message to say he wants to see me later this morning. Heaven knows why. I told the Sergeant everything I know yesterday.'

'Looks like this morning's trip is right out of the question then?'

Fiona nodded. 'We thought it would be, so it's not exactly a surprise. I only hope the passengers won't be too disappointed. Most of them will realise it's not going to be possible because several of them have been summoned to present themselves at the interview room throughout the morning. I've only spoken to him the once and I appreciate he has a job to do, but Inspector Bauer does come across as somewhat officious.'

Winston gave a broad grin. 'He does have the knack of making you feel guilty. Don't he?'

'That's one way of putting it.' Fiona gave a sigh.

'What's you gonna do with yourself this morning?'

'There's quite a bit to do first thing. I need to check with the local agency about a replacement guide for tomorrow. Then I'm hoping everyone is going to turn up at nine o'clock for the meeting so I can let them know what the situation is. From what I can tell, the Inspector has already spoken to all those who came back to the hotel with Frederick after the walk, so he should be finished with the rest of us by the end of today. With luck, we'll be able to continue with the planned itinerary tomorrow.'

Travis was waiting for her, pacing up and down between the seating area and the reception desk when she arrived downstairs.

'Have you spoken to the Inspector about my laptop?'

Fiona took a deep breath. 'As I told you last evening, Travis, I doubt the Inspector will pay any attention to me. I have no authority to demand he return it to you.'

He ran his fingers through his already untidy hair. He looked as though he was about to argue with her.

Other passengers were arriving. To forestall an unpleasant scene, Fiona said quickly, 'I shall be seeing him later this morning. All I can do is to ask when you might expect to get it back. Now, please sit down and calm yourself.'

As she sat waiting for the remaining passengers to assemble in the foyer, she wondered if her message about the meeting had got round to everyone. It was a relief when she saw Morris and Drina Lucas, the last to arrive, emerge from the lift.

'I'm sorry our tour of Schloss Charlottenburg has had to be cancelled. If anyone is particularly keen to visit on your own, if you'd like to stay behind, I'll see if I can arrange for a taxi to take you over there. If there are several of you, you might even like to share one. For the rest of you, I hope you still have your city maps and as you can see in the Super Sun Programme booklet you were sent, there are plenty of options to keep you busy for today.'

'What about lunch?' Elsie asked.

'Lunch is here in the hotel at one o'clock in the Restaurant Beleatage, the one upstairs where we had lunch yesterday.'

'Where we had breakfast?'

'That's right, Walter. Any more questions?' She looked around, but none came. 'In that case, have a lovely day everyone.'

Several of the group who had arrived already dressed to brave the cold outside made for the exit doors, a few stayed chatting for a few minutes and the rest made their way back up to their rooms.

Morris and Drina Lucas were still sitting on one of the comfortable settees. Morris looked up and smiled at Fiona.

She walked over to join them.

'Have you tried the swimming pool here, Fiona?'

'No. I haven't been down there. Are you thinking of taking a dip?'

'We were wondering what to do. We have to speak to one of the policemen in just over an hour. It's not possible to do very much in that time,' Morris explained.

'I can't say I feel like getting undressed again.' Drina shrank back into her thick knitted polo-necked sweater, hunching her shoulders, 'but it seems such a waste to hang around in our room.'

'Umm, I know what you mean,' agreed Fiona. 'The Inspector wants to interview me later this morning. If you fancy a stroll to the shops, if you turn left when you go out of the hotel, there is a whole street of them at the end of this block, including a very nice chocolate shop. I've been told it's well worth a visit to see the chocolate models, if nothing else.'

They looked at each other. Morris raised his eyebrows and Drina nodded.

'Thank you, Fiona. That sounds like an excellent idea.'

They walked over to the lifts together.

'We might have the same problem after our interview. Would it matter if we decided to skip lunch? Then we've got the rest of the day,' asked Drina. 'We can get something when we're out.'

'That won't be a problem. Like yesterday, it is a buffet meal in any case. Timing isn't crucial. I expect there will be one or two other people who choose to do the same.'

Fiona left the elderly couple at the lift doors and made for the stairs. It sounded a sensible idea she decided, but unfortunately not one open to her. She needed to be in the dining room. Even if none of her passengers had any questions, they would expect her to be there.

It was only as she reached the fourth floor and began walking along the corridor that she remembered. In all the upset last evening, she had completely forgotten about ringing Adam to find out what the doctor had said about Becky's condition.

She looked at her watch. Just gone half past nine, which meant it was still the middle of the night over in Montreal. Why was it that trouble always seemed to come in threes? On top of Frederick's murder and Travis being difficult, she had more than enough to cope with without the worry over the health of her eldest grandchild.

The conference room that the police had taken over as an incident room had a glazed glass panel in the door. As far as Fiona could tell, there were several tables with people working at computers. She gave a tentative knock.

'My name is Mason. Fiona Mason. Inspector Bauer asked to see me at ten fifteen,' she said to the smiling plump-faced woman who stood in the doorway.

'Oh yes.' Closing the door behind her, the woman led the way along the corridor. 'The interview room. It is along here.'

She tapped on the door and without waiting for a reply, opened it sufficiently to put her head around. Fiona didn't speak any German but in the brief conversation she heard the woman say 'Frau Mason' and assumed she was telling the Inspector that she had arrived.

The woman pushed the door wide and stepped back to let Fiona in.

Though Fiona had given little thought to what the man might look like, she had not expected the tall, balding middle-aged man with a pleasant welcoming smile on his long face as he stood to lean across his desk with outstretched hand to shake hers.

'Good morning, Mrs Mason. The investigation has meant that your tour for today has been affected. I apologise.'

His smile disarmed her, but she had seen Montgomery-Jones use similar tactics in the past and she still felt wary.

'My passengers were disappointed, but I am sure they all appreciate why the trip had to be cancelled.'

'It was necessary.' He waved a hand to a chair for her to sit down.

He glanced down at the papers in front of him. 'You have worked for Super Sun for one year?' He looked up, waiting for a reply. She nodded. 'Is this your first visit to Berlin?' The man's English was good but more heavily accented than his Sergeant's.

'Yes.'

'You are leading a tour when you do not know the city?' His tone was pleasant enough but there was a steely glint in his eyes.

'The company needed someone at the last minute.' Deciding that if she were too guarded in her answers. it would sound as if she was holding something back, she added, 'My role is purely to ensure everything runs smoothly. Super Sun has employed local guides for each of the towns we will visit, so it will not be a problem that I haven't been to the area before.'

'I see.' He looked at her thoughtfully for a moment before continuing, 'You told my Sergeant you met Friedrich Schumacher for the first time two days ago?'

'That's right.'

'Did you know the name of your local guide in Berlin before you arrived?'

'No. No one at Super Sun would know. Guides are always organised by the company's local agent.'

'Your passengers. Would they know?'

Fiona shook her head. 'How could they?'

'Herr Schumacher. Did he know anyone in your group?'

'Not as far as I'm aware.'

'Did any member of the party become particularly friendly with Herr Schumacher?'

'He and Travis Everest sat together at lunchtime and the two of them spent a fair amount of time chatting on the afternoon walk, as I believe you already know, Inspector. Other than that, to my knowledge, Frederick had few conversations with anyone in my party.'

'Mr Everest has been to Berlin before. It is possible he met Herr Schumacher on that occasion.'

'If he did, he didn't mention it to me. In fact, I gained rather the opposite impression.'

'Mr Everest is a journalist.'

'So I understand.'

'He intended to write an article for his newspaper about Herr Schumacher. Did he mention that to you?'

'Yes. Frederick told everyone on the coach that he lived in East Berlin during the Cold War and Travis was interested in learning more about what life was like during Soviet times. He thought it would interest his readers. I understand that he had already begun to write it, which is why he is keen to have his laptop returned. I wonder if it would be possible for him to . . .'

'Later.' Fiona detected a momentary flash of annoyance in the Inspector's eyes before he resumed the pleasant demeanour he was attempting to portray. 'Mr Everest invited Herr Schumacher back to the hotel for an interview. Did he tell you his plans?'

'No. As I told your Sergeant yesterday, the last time I saw Frederick was outside the Berliner Dom at the end of the guided walk. Mr Everest was one of several people who returned to the hotel with Frederick, so what happened after that I cannot tell you.'

'Someone reported that Herr Schumacher may have been drunk that afternoon . . .'

'That's ridiculous.' The Inspector's jaw visibly tightened at Fiona's interruption. 'He had a glass of wine at lunch, but I can assure you he was perfectly sober. I would have contacted the agency immediately if I had any concerns at all.'

No guesses as to who may have planted that idea in the Inspector's mind. Travis was definitely not Elsie's favourite person! Fiona had a good mind to give the elderly, sanctimonious woman a piece of her mind.

Fiona was still seething when she left the interview room.

The situation was bad enough without other passengers stirring up more trouble. She felt far too keyed up to want to hang around the hotel for the rest of the morning brooding. With lunch in less than a couple of hours, there was insufficient time to visit any of the city's major attractions, so she decided to spend the time window-shopping. Not an activity that featured high on her list of preferred activities, but there was always the possibility of cheering herself up with some chocolate from the shop Rose and Faith had been so enthusiastic about. A sugar rush might be just the consolation she needed right now.

Chapter 10

Fiona's earlier comment about several of the party deciding to skip lunch in the hotel proved to be correct. There were quite a few empty seats in their reserved section of the restaurant. One of which she realised, with a sudden cold shiver, would have been booked for Frederick.

Most of those who did appear had accompanied the guide back to the hotel after yesterday's walk. Fiona assumed they had already been interviewed by the police last evening.

'Did you have a pleasant morning,' Fiona asked Gary Peters as she took her place at one of the tables.

'Yes, thank you, Fiona. Loraine and I went to the DDR Museum.'

'Was that not depressing? Life must have been very grim,' said Sonya, joining in the conversation.

'Well yes. The furnishings in the living rooms and kitchen were pretty basic. Although, thinking about it, I suppose we are talking fifty years ago and our homes back then would also seem rather basic by today's standards,' said Loraine.

'At least we had something better to drive than a Trabant,' said her husband with a laugh. 'Worst car ever made, that.'

'Then why did we have to wait for fifteen minutes in the queue just so you could sit in it?' his wife demanded jokingly. She shook her head and raised her eyes heavenwards. 'Men and their cars!'

Everyone at the table smiled politely.

'Seriously,' Loraine continued, 'I would think the worst thing must have been the knowledge that you were being spied on all the time.'

The conversation moved on and as Sonya extolled the glories of the Ishtar Gate she and Peter had seen in the Pergamon Museum that morning, Fiona was able to sit back, relax and enjoy the cold salmon and salad she had chosen from the buffet.

'The sheer size! And the impact of those rich blue tiles quite takes the breath away.'

'I hope you don't think me rude, but your accent, is it Polish?' asked Loraine.

Sonya smiled. 'You are right. I am British now of course, but I came from Poland five years ago.'

'Was that for work?' asked Loraine.

'Back in Poland, I was a teacher.'

'Faith used to be a maths teacher,' Rose volunteered from the far side of the table. 'What subject did you teach?'

'History.'

'I would imagine that's a little difficult in England,' Faith said with a smile. 'The British history syllabus must be very different to the one you were used to. When I was at St Joseph's, I always had problems with surnames I couldn't pronounce. We had lots of Polish children but then you'd expect that wouldn't you?'

'Oh?' Sonya tucked the swinging ends of her bob behind her ears.

'I mean you'd expect them all to go to the catholic school. It's such a deeply catholic country. Are you teaching now?'

Peter put a hand over hers and said, 'She's a kept woman now, aren't you dear?'

'Kept woman?'

He laughed, 'It means that you gave up working when we got married. And what did you do this morning, Fiona?' he said, smoothly changing the subject.

'Not a great deal, I'm afraid. Unlike you four, I had to wait around for my interview with Inspector Bauer.'

Fiona told herself that Peter's seemingly affectionate clasp of Sonya's hand probably had more to do with stopping her from putting her foot in it than anything else. Though quite why she had felt a sudden pang by the gesture she could not explain. It wasn't as if Peter was anything to her despite what Winston liked to suggest. Half the time she didn't even like the man.

Apart from the few odd words they had exchanged in passing, Fiona realised this was the first time she had had the opportunity to speak with Sonya – the first time she had the chance to study her. Fiona sat quietly observing the woman sitting opposite. Now that Sonya had recovered from the bad cold that had kept her more or less isolated from the group for the first couple of days, she appeared confident and outgoing. According to the ages given in their passports, she was a good ten years younger than her so-called husband, although for a woman supposedly in her early forties, she could have passed for someone quite a bit younger.

Fiona was still musing when she realised Peter had asked her a question.

'I'm so sorry, I was miles away. What did you say?'

Peter smiled. 'I only asked about your plans for the afternoon.'

'To be honest, I haven't made up my mind. Spoilt for choice really. Rather like that selection of delicious desserts over there. I was trying to decide whether to be good and restrict myself to a coffee or give in to temptation. I know if I wander over just to take a look, I shall succumb.'

'Do let's!' Rose clapped her hands together. 'We are on holiday.'

Before making any decisions on how to spend her time this afternoon, Fiona had an important job to do. As soon as she left the restaurant and got back to her room, she sat on the bed and pulled out her mobile. She let the phone ring for some time before giving up. Perhaps Kristie was out for the morning. She had hoped to catch her daughter-in-law before she began her day. Fiona did a quick calculation.

Allowing for European summer time, Montreal was now six hours behind Germany, so it should be almost ten o'clock. There was always the possibility that Becky had recovered, and Kristie had taken her to school and hadn't got back yet. Young children do bounce back very quickly, she tried to console herself. Adam's number was programmed into her mobile and she could always ring him, but unless it was an emergency, she didn't like phoning him at work. She would have to try again before she went to bed when they would all be home again.

The day's planned itinerary may have been abandoned but given the smiling faces and general buzz at dinner, everyone seemed to have spent and an enjoyable day doing their own thing.

Morris and Drina had been to the top of the Television Tower.

'The views from the top were amazing.'

'We had great views too when we went up to the dome in the Reichstag. You're supposed to book in advance but when we got there, they had some free places. We had to wait for a bit, but it was well worth it.'

Rose's excited chatter made up for the almost monosyllabic Henry Wolf who was sitting on Fiona's right. Fiona made a few attempts to bring him into the general conversation and although he was pleasant enough, he was far from being the talkative kind.

'What about you, Fiona? Where did you get to this afternoon?' asked Morris.

'Loraine and Gary were telling me about the DDR museum over lunch. They said how fascinating it was, so I decided to pay it a visit too. After all, it's not the sort of thing you can do anywhere else. It was interesting to see what life was like in Soviet times.'

'I'd have thought that would interest you too, Henry. I mean, you being born here in Berlin,' said Rose.

Henry shook his head and frowned. 'The last thing I need

is to be reminded of those times, thank you very much.'

To cover his rudeness, Barbara said quickly, 'We went to the Neues Museum. I really wanted to see that head of Nefertiti. You know, the famous one you see lots of pictures of, with long neck and tall hat.'

'The iconic one! It's gorgeous,' Faith enthused. 'I wouldn't have minded seeing that. I didn't realise it was here in Berlin.'

'It was very special, wasn't it, love?' She turned to Henry, but he sat silent and grim-faced. Barbara hurried on, 'We went on a Nile cruise several years ago and the souvenir shops are full of plaster copies. Since then we've always been fascinated by all things Egyptian.'

Fiona was puzzled. It was understandable that Henry should be upset about what had happened to the city of his birth. From the vehemence of his answer, it was almost as though Henry had personally experienced the hard life of East Berliners in that era. She would have liked to ask him if he had any family members who had remained here, but the conversation had moved on.

Fiona was surprised to see that everyone in the party had decided to gather for coffee in the lounge after they had eaten. Even Elsie and Walter who frequently went straight up to their rooms after dinner were there. Perhaps they were all hoping to get more news. Although they all sat in one large group, conversation was in small clusters. From what Fiona could make out, the majority seemed to be talking about Frederick's death. There was a great deal of speculation, some of it wild and verging on the absurd, based on the questions they'd had to answer during their individual interviews.

Fiona went to refill her cup at the coffee station set up on a side table. As she went to pick up the milk jug, someone beat her to it and held it ready to pour for her.

'Thank you, Peter.'

'My pleasure.'

The two of them were alone. This was a good chance to ask the question that had been troubling her for the last hour or so.

'I was wondering,' she said tentatively. 'Before you left England, did you do any background checks on the passengers on this trip?'

He looked at her for a moment or two before answering. 'A very brief one only. There was no need. Why are you asking?'

'No particular reason.'

He gave a low chuckle. 'There are no convicted murderers in the party if that is what you are concerned about. A couple of passengers may well have points on their driving licences, but no one has a criminal record.'

Any further discussion on the subject had to be dropped as others wandered over for refills.

Morris Lucas was not the only member of the party interested in finding out the latest news on the coming Peace Talks on the television. Peter Montgomery-Jones sat on the end of the bed, clicking through every news channel available in each of the five languages in which he was fluent, plus a couple more with which he was sufficiently familiar to be able to glean the gist of what was being said. His face was expressionless.

Sonya stood at the side of the bed staring at the screen, hands on hips, jaw firmly clenched.

Montgomery-Jones clicked back to the BBC World News.

'The Foreign Office have strongly denied the assertion by the Russian Leader that the Ukrainian politician, Natalia Shevchenko, who disappeared over two weeks ago is a British spy or that she is now in Britain.' The announcer's voice sounded oddly dispassionate.

Once he had exhausted all he could find, Peter switched off before moving over to the armchair. He picked up his laptop lying on the table beside him. Having looked at every broadcasting news station, he turned his attention to every newspaper that carried any reference to the possible plight of the Ukrainian politician Natalia Shevchenko now believed to be in the hands of the Pro-Russia rebels.

'Adam, it's me.'

'Hi Mum, what's up?'

'I was phoning to see what the doctor said on Monday. I'm so sorry I didn't ring last night. We had a spot of bother in the evening and it put it right out of my mind.'

'Nothing serious, I hope.'

'No darling. Nothing to bother you with. Someone lost their laptop.' That at least was true. She could hardly tell him about Frederick. 'What was the doctor's verdict?'

'He's not overly concerned. He said coughs can last for weeks, but Becky's temperature has shot up since we got back, and she's completely lost her appetite.'

'Perhaps you should contact him again.'

'Kristie rang the surgery again this morning, but he just said keep her quiet and make sure she gets plenty to drink. She spent most of the day lying on the settee half asleep.'

'That doesn't sound like Becky.'

'Exactly. She's normally such a livewire. We're trying not to show Adam Junior that we're worried but he can sense something's wrong, so he's playing up. We've been trying to keep the two of them apart as much as we can, just in case Becky's infectious. Poor Kristie's taken the brunt of it all and she's run ragged.'

'I wish there was something I could do.'

'Kristie's mother's already said she'll come over and help but Kristie keeps putting her off.'

'Do let me know how things go, won't you? And give everyone my love.'

'Thanks, Mum. You too.'

Fiona rang off and put her mobile on the bedside table. She picked up her book and settled back against the pillows. After re-reading the same passage three times, she gave up the effort and switched off the light. Switching off her mind was another matter, but she would have another full day to cope with tomorrow. Worrying about her granddaughter would help no one.

Day 5

Today our visit takes us through the western suburbs of Berlin to Potsdam, first settled by Slavs in the 10th century. It survives as an independent city and the capital of Brandenburg within the Greater Berlin area.

As we make our way through the city, we will have a further opportunity for a photo stop at the home of Germany's parliament, the Reichstag and see the Bundeskanzleramt or German Chancellery building, locally nicknamed the Washing Machine because of the round window at the front of the building. From there, we will drive through the attractive parkland of the Tiergarten which began life as a hunting ground for the Royal family.

Potsdam owes its importance to the Great Electors. Despite considerable damage in World War II, Potsdam remains one of Germany's most attractive cities.

The highlight of this morning will be a tour of Schloss Sanssouci, the magnificent summer residence of Frederick the Great, said to be Germany's rival to Versailles.

After lunch, we will visit Cecilienhof built by the last of the Hohenzollern family for Crown Prince William and his wife Cecilie as a summer palace. It played an important role in history when it served as the venue for the 1945 Potsdam Conference at which the partition of Germany was decided between Churchill, Truman and Stalin

Super Sun Executive Travel

Chapter 11

Fiona approached the man behind the reception desk.

Before she had a chance to give her name or explain why she had come, he said, 'Good morning, Mrs Mason. The gentleman you are expecting is sitting over there.'

It never ceased to amaze Fiona how so many of the staff working at reception desks in hotels appeared to remember one's name so easily. True, he was probably the one who had phoned her two minutes ago to let her know the guide for this morning's tour had arrived, but even before guests had said a word, staff appeared to be able to judge the nationality of new arrivals simply by their general demeanour.

She fervently wished she had their skill to remember names. She was getting better, but it took a great deal of time and effort. When she took in everyone's passport at the start of every trip, it often took the best part of the ferry crossing studying the photos in order to put names to faces, adding a few notes to a passenger list as an aide-mémoire. Though she had to admit, some passport photographs left a great deal to be desired.

As she walked over towards the person indicated by the receptionist, the young man snapped shut the book he'd been reading and jumped up from his seat.

'Mrs Mason? I am Klaus. Klaus Fischer.' He shook her hand vigorously.

He was average height and very young but Fiona reflected she had reached the age when so many young people seemed more like sixth formers than professionals these days. If he were not proficient at his job, the agency would never have sent him.

'It is good of you to be here so early. The group will not be down for another half hour or so.'

'I thought it best to check with you and the driver before we set off. Find out if there is anything special that you would like me to do.' His accent was less guttural, more pleasing than Frederick's had been.

'Winston should be here in a moment or two. I rang him when I heard you had arrived.'

'I have the proposed itinerary here.' Klaus picked up the small rucksack and clutching the book he'd been reading under one arm, attempted to open it.

'May I take that for you?'

He handed Fiona the relatively weighty tome and sank back down onto the well-padded bench, balancing the frameless rucksack on his knees. While he went about his task, Fiona glanced at the book she was now holding. Nothing to do with today's visit she judged. It looked more like a textbook. Perhaps he was a student, and this was a holiday job. Guiding was probably a good deal more interesting way of supplementing his grant than serving in some bar.

Klaus pulled out a clipboard with a sheaf of papers attached, retrieved his book from Fiona and stuffed it into the rucksack. Fiona sat down next to him.

'I have the proposed itinerary here.' They went through it together. 'That is what you were expecting?'

'Yes,' replied Fiona. 'That is what we agreed with Frederick.'

'Poor Frederick,' sighed the young man. 'I did not know him well, but I went out on a few jobs with him when I was first training. Such a dreadful accident.'

Fiona did not disabuse him about Frederick's fate, and to his credit, Klaus did not pry.

'It's a pity we had to miss the trip out to Charlottenburg Palace yesterday,' she said. 'But I'm sure everyone is looking forward to Sanssouci.'

'We could make a diversion to see the outside of the

schloss if you would like. We have to drive through that part of the city to get to the autobahn in any case. It would only add five or ten minutes.'

'I'm sure everyone would appreciate that.' Her smile was only exceeded by his own obvious delight at pleasing her. 'I will have to ask Winston, obviously, and talk of the devil!'

'I heard that, sweetheart. What have you let me in for now?'

'I'll let Klaus explain.' She introduced them to each other then added, 'If you two don't need me anymore, I will leave you both to discuss matters. There are a couple of things I need to see to before we leave.'

Hurrying back up the stairs to her room, she felt more positive than she had done since she'd learnt of Frederick's death. Klaus may lack the deceased guide's experience and possibly his expertise, but he had a natural charm that would bring out the mothering instinct in every woman on the tour. His obvious desire to please could not fail to be appreciated by everyone.

Klaus proved to be a great hit. Not only did everyone warm to him as Fiona knew they would, his considerable knowledge and obvious enthusiasm made him the perfect travelling companion. Nothing appeared to be too much trouble.

As they travelled through the Tiergarten, he was happy to make a quick unscheduled photo stop for those who wanted to take pictures of the gold-plated winged figure crowning the sixty-nine feet Victory Column.

'Strictly speaking,' he said conspiratorially, 'we are not supposed to stop, so I'm relying on you to hurry back or I shall be for the chop.'

From the way Frederick had responded to the request which Gary Peters – one of the keenest photographers – had made a couple of days earlier, Klaus's jest was not without a certain amount of truth.

As they sped along the E51 motorway to Potsdam, Klaus

continued to regale them with stories of the Electors and the soldier king, Frederick I and his conflict with his art-loving son.

Klaus was happy to answer any questions, although as he was clearly in his early twenties at most, it would have been pointless to ask about life in Soviet times. Any judgements that the group may have had from their dealings with Frederick and Inspector Bauer that Germans were largely a dour, mirthless people were rapidly being dispelled.

Fiona glanced at her watch as they reached the outskirts of Potsdam. She took the itinerary sheet out of her tote bag to check the details and felt a momentary pang of alarm. With the diversion and the extra photo stops, according to the timing on the sheet, they were over half an hour later than scheduled. When the coach stopped, Fiona quickly made her way to the side door and managed to catch Klaus before he began helping passengers down the steps at the front.

Taking him to one side she asked, 'Lunch is booked for one, is it?'

'I checked with the restaurant first thing.'

If he thought she was fussing, he didn't show it. Nonetheless, he was young and presumably inexperienced. In his desire to please, had he forgotten about the timings? She could think of no more tactful way of saying it without seeming too critical, so she blurted out, 'It's just I was a little concerned about the time.'

'All in hand,' he assured her with a disarming grin. 'Our trip to Charlottenburg and the other stops has made life a great deal easier. Normally, we give everyone at least an hour to explore the gardens at Sanssouci. In the spring and summer, they are magnificent, but with all the snow, there really is not that much to see, plus I don't want anyone to get cold.'

The sun was shining in a cloudless blue sky, but the air had a decided chill and everywhere was under a deep carpet of snow. They stopped to look up at the elegant yellow-gold Rococo façade, the sunlight glinting on the solid wall of tall arched windows reaching almost to the top of the single storied building. Klaus pointed up to the words "Sans Souci" written in large letters at the base of the green copper dome in the centre.

'Without a care, or carefree,' translated Morris. 'But why is it in French not German?'

'Good question.' Looking even more like a mischievous schoolboy in the bobble hat and knitted woolly scarf, Klaus's face lit up in a wide grin. 'It is said that King Frederick spoke better French than German. Back in the 18th century, French was often spoken at court throughout Europe, even in St Petersburg. When we get to the library inside you will see the majority of the books are in French. Sanssouci was Frederick's summer retreat, his country cottage, away from the pressures of affairs of state at court, but still as sumptuous a building as befits one of the world's great kings.'

'What a wonderful view,' exclaimed Drina, as she turned round to look down onto the great banks of terraces stretching below them.

After a few minutes, Klaus clapped his hands for their attention. 'Now, if the photographers have had their fill, let us move into the warm.'

He led the way around the building to the back. It was a surprise to find that they had to pass through a small insignificant gate in the high, neatly trimmed hedge to reach the palace entrance. Fiona had expected something much grander.

'We are going in through what was the back door,' Klaus explained.

As they proceeded through the gardens, the vast parkland came into view, but few people stopped long as they all sought refuge from the cold.

Fiona was bringing up the rear as they wandered through

the corridor of rooms. She allowed herself to hang back a little to better take in the sheer beauty of the place. The pale green of the walls and soft mauve of the silk padded sofas were pleasantly restful. Frederick the Great wasn't the only one who felt the need to get away from the pressure of work, she joked to herself.

Her smile quickly faded when she turned back and noticed Anna Sachs looking all around with a worried frown. Fiona hurried over.

'Is there anything wrong?'

'I was just wondering where Travis had got to. I haven't seen him all morning and he doesn't seem to be here. We didn't leave him behind anywhere, did we?'

Fiona smiled. 'No. Well, we haven't lost him, if that's what you mean. He's staying in the hotel today.'

'He's not ill, is he, or has that horrid Inspector demanded to interview him again?' Anna's jaw tightened. 'I saw Travis talking to him after breakfast this morning.'

'No nothing like that. Apparently, he was asking about his laptop. You know the police took it away. The Inspector said that their lab technicians had finished going through the files and that it would be returned to the incident room later in the morning. That's why Travis decided to stay behind. He's keen to get it back as soon as possible.'

'So he can finish this article of his?'

Fiona nodded. 'I expect so. He does seem to be obsessed with it.'

'That's one word for it. If you ask me, I can't see how one article on a man who happened to be a border guard nearly thirty years ago is exactly hot news. Surely it could wait till this evening, or the end of the holiday come to that? There aren't exactly a flock of paparazzi clamouring around the hotel to get the story out.' Anna shook her head in disbelief.

'Exactly.'

'If it was some shock revelation about a prominent politician or a celebrity trading on a blameless past, I could perhaps understand it, but Frederick was only a tour guide.

No disrespect to you Fiona, but you know what I mean.'

Fiona laughed. 'No offence taken. I agree with you. Perhaps we ought to catch up with the others. We're missing all Klaus has to say.'

After the last room on their tour of the house – the Voltaire Room, with its shiny yellow walls and copious plaster flower garlands – Klaus led everyone outside and around to the side of the palace.

'Frederick is said to have died sitting in his chair in the study. It was his dearest wish to be buried here in the grounds of Sanssouci alongside his beloved dogs. He wanted no great pomp. As you can see, his grave is a very simple affair. A single flat piece of stone. Unlike Louis IV who claimed, "I am the State", Frederick is reputed to have said, "I am the first servant of the State".'

'Why are there potatoes on it?' asked Rose, ever curious.

'The population was growing rapidly in Frederick's time and he is said to have introduced the potato to feed them all. That is why he was nicknamed the Potato King. Now, if there are no more questions, you are free to explore the grounds and we will all meet back at the coach at twelve thirty. Half past twelve.'

'It's a pity we can't keep him as a guide when we move on,' Elsie confided to Fiona as they made their way into the restaurant for lunch.

If even the critical Elsie Danby had been wooed by the young man's charms, then things were definitely looking up. It was inevitable that the ladies would quiz Klaus and it didn't take long to discover that as Fiona had suspected, he was a student in his final year of a history degree and guiding was a holiday and weekend activity.

'My finals are coming up in a couple of months and I was planning on spending the Easter break getting down to some serious revision. When the agency telephoned me yesterday and asked if I could step in at the last minute, I was happy to do so. I love guiding. It is such a great opportunity to meet people and to practise my English. Besides, it is good to have a break from studying now and again,' he finished in a conspiratorial whisper that made everyone laugh.

'Have you been doing it for long?' asked Rose.

'Almost three years now.'

'Do you cover just the Greater Berlin area, or do you go further afield?' Fiona asked.

'The first year or so I only did the tours in the city centre, but now I am more experienced, my bosses are happy for me to do more of the day trips from the city. The agency provides guides for much longer three and four-day tours, but I have not done the training for those. Potsdam is one of my favourite tours. Apart from being two of the most impressive and beautiful buildings in the whole area, Sanssouci and Cecilienhof are steeped in history, which is my subject. That is why I could not say no when the agency said they needed a last-minute replacement.'

Inevitably, Frederick's name came up in the conversation. At first, Klaus seemed a little guarded in his answers as to how well he knew the deceased guide.

'He wasn't exactly someone we all warmed to,' said Rose in her usual forthright style. 'I don't know why he became a guide at all. He didn't seem to like people very much.'

Klaus's lips twitched and then he said, 'He was fine once you got to know him, and he was very experienced.'

'Just because you've been doing it a long time doesn't make you good at the job. If I'd have been his boss, I would have pensioned him off long ago. He was very rude to poor Sol.' Rose's assessment was met with several nods of agreement.

'Frederick and the boss go back a long way.'

'Was he an East German border guard too?' asked Loraine.

'Sorry?' Klaus's eyes widened as he stared at her.

'Isn't that what Travis said Frederick had told him?'

Loraine looked around the group. There were several surprised looks. If the story hadn't got round before, it was now common knowledge.

'I don't think that's quite what Travis was saying,' Fiona said quickly. 'He was only thinking out loud. Just an idea he had. As far as I know, Frederick didn't claim anything of the sort.'

Klaus shook his head. 'I never heard anything like that. I know he has always lived in East Berlin and that he believed passionately in communism in the old Soviet times, but he is . . .' He paused, then corrected himself, 'was, no longer a paid-up member of the party.'

'I know we shouldn't speak ill of the dead,' Drina said with pursed lips before Fiona could continue. 'But we all thought he must have been in the Stasi.'

'Come on now,' Fiona said brightly. 'What will poor Klaus think of us all? Let's talk about something more pleasant. There look to be some very tempting cakes and puddings over on the buffet. Shall we go and help ourselves?'

Chapter 12

Fiona had thoroughly enjoyed her day in Potsdam and to judge from the smiles and the comments she had overheard, so too had her passengers. The two palaces had been spectacular, and she could not have wished for a better guide than Klaus. Nonetheless, as she climbed the final flight of stairs to her floor, she was more than ready for a quiet sit-down with a cup of tea.

She pushed open the door of her room and saw a folded sheet of paper on the floor. Someone had slipped a note under the door while she had been out. It was from Sergeant Hase. A request to ring him when she returned to the hotel. Fiona sighed. Things had been going so well.

She struggled out of her coat and pulled off the thick sweater. With the multiple layers beneath, it was not an easy task. By the time she had taken off her boots, removed the extra-long woollen socks and put everything away, she had made up her mind. She picked up the kettle and marched to the bathroom. If the matter was urgent, the Sergeant would have rung her mobile, so he could wait another ten minutes until she'd had her tea.

Fiona's knock was answered by a shout, which she assumed meant that she should go in. Tentatively she pushed on the door and peered round. Sergeant Hase looked up from his desk in the corner and smiled. He walked over, pulled the door fully open and stepped out into the corridor.

'Shall we go to another room? We can be a little more private.' It wasn't really a question, so Fiona simply fell into step until they came to the interview room.

Once they were settled one on either side of the desk, Hase said, 'Thank you for coming. This is not an interview; I wanted to pass on a message from Inspector Bauer. I understand that you and your party were planning to move on tomorrow morning.'

'That is correct.'

From the way he hesitated, then licked his lips, she knew he was the bearer of bad news. 'Inspector Bauer would like you all to stay here in Berlin for the time being.'

Fiona stared at him in disbelief for some time. 'Why?'

'The investigation into the death of Friedrich Schumacher is still ongoing.' His words became more clipped and the German accent more pronounced.

'But your team have already interviewed every one of my passengers. At length!'

'Inspector Bauer may need to speak to them again.'

There was little point in railing against the Sergeant about the Inspector's decision, however unreasonable. She changed tack. 'But our accommodation for tomorrow night is booked at the Hotel Luther in Wittenberg. We don't have anywhere to stay in Berlin.'

'It is low season. You are a small party. You will have no difficulty finding rooms here.'

Fiona wasn't at all sure about that, but that was hardly the main problem. How would her passengers react to the news?

'Have you any idea how long the Inspector intends to keep us here.'

'Not more than a day or so, I am sure. He is waiting for some information to arrive.'

After a pause, Fiona asked, 'Where is the Inspector? I need to speak to him.'

'I am sorry, but he is no longer in the hotel. He will be back first thing in the morning.'

'What a surprise!' She pretended to look at her watch. 'It has gone five o'clock. We can't expect the boss man to work more than an eight-hour day, now can we?'

'He was called to a meeting at the station, otherwise I am sure he would have spoken to you personally.' Hase took one look at her expression and hurried on, 'If he does return here this evening, I will let him know you would like to speak to him.'

The Sergeant was so uncomfortable at being the bearer of such unwelcome news that she felt guilty. It was hardly his fault and further protests would get her nowhere.

'Better still, let *me* know.' Chances were, even if he did return, the Inspector would be much too busy to make time for her. She would need to seek him out.

He grinned and nodded. The poor man probably suffered more at the hands of his irascible, high-handed boss than anyone.

The shared moment of fellow feeling as she and the Sergeant walked back along the corridor was not enough to lift her spirits and this was hardly the time to wallow in a sense of injustice, Fiona told herself sharply as she made her way back to the central atrium. There were things to be done. Complaining to the Inspector was unlikely to change matters. First off, she would need to check if the hotel could accommodate them all for an extra night. Then, speaking to Winston had to be her priority.

Fiona had already ordered a pot of tea for them both in the few minutes it took for Winston to arrive in the small café on the ground floor.

'It's not the end of the world, sweetheart.'

'It feels pretty much like it! Oh, Winston, there are times when I wonder if I'm not jinxed in this job. If things can go wrong, they do. I really don't know how I'm going to face the passengers tonight. They are not going to be happy about the delay and what on earth am I going to do with them for the day? They've already had extra free time when Tuesday's trip was cancelled.'

Winston leant across the small table and put a hand on hers. 'I's been thinking. We could still go ahead with tomorrow's programme. It'd take a couple of hours or so to get back but it's doable. We'd be back in time for dinner, no problem.'

Fiona managed a weak smile. 'I think everyone would prefer that. But what about Friday? Our tour of the porcelain factory in Meissen is booked for eleven o'clock.'

He patted her hand and smiled. 'It's not that far. If we go across country instead of following the river, it shouldn't take more than two and a half hours. We might need to leave here early, but we can look at the programme and work out the details.'

'I dare say the factory would be prepared to give us a later slot if needs be. That's one advantage of coming in the low season. That is assuming the Inspector is prepared to let us leave by then. He can't keep us here indefinitely.'

'We'll worry about Friday later. Let's get tomorrow organised first.'

'You're right, Winston. If we're going to have to come back here tomorrow evening, I wonder if I should ring the local agent and see if I can arrange for Klaus to come with us for the day.'

'Good idea. Have you spoken to Head Office yet?'

Fiona shook her head. 'I thought it best to work out what we're going to do first. They aren't going to be happy. It's going to involve them in a great deal more expense. The Berlin Hilton must cost a bomb. And that's on top of the cancellation fee to the little place we were booked into in Wittenberg, never mind the increased fuel costs all this extra travelling is going to entail. Do you think they'll complain if I book an extra day's guiding?'

Winston's deep rumbling laugh caused a few turned heads. 'It's peanuts in the great scheme of things, sweetheart. Every tour has an extra contingency budget. Unforeseen things happen. All part of business. This is a mere hiccup compared with some disasters they've had to pay out for. The boss man ain't gonna hold you personally responsible, you know.'

'Hmm. Let's hope so.'

'Is it true we're not moving on tomorrow; that our trip to the Worlitz Gardens and Wittenberg has been cancelled?' Rose collared Fiona before she managed to get inside the restaurant doors.

'Not exactly,' Fiona tried to reassure the excited woman.

'But Travis said the Inspector told him . . .'

Fiona held up her hands to ward off Faith, who for once looked as agitated as her friend.

'It's true we will be spending another night in this hotel, but we will be following tomorrow's programme, so you are not going to miss out on anything. Shall we go in and sit down? We're blocking the doorway.'

It was inevitable that the news would get out, Fiona realised. She would have preferred to tell them all at the same time at their after-dinner meeting when she could put a positive spin on the situation, but bad news always travels fast.

All eyes turned to Fiona as she and the two women made their way across to the tables reserved for the Super Sun party. She was surprised to see so many of them already there. No doubt, they were as anxious to find out what was going on as Rose and Faith had been.

Fiona positioned herself where they would all be able to hear her and then announced, 'Whatever you may have heard, ladies and gentlemen, tomorrow's itinerary has not been changed. We will be visiting the gardens in the morning, and in the afternoon, we will have a tour of Martin Luther's house followed by a guided tour of Wittenberg.'

'But what about…'

Fiona held up a warning hand. 'I will give you all the details after dinner when we meet for coffee in the lounge when everyone is here. I will answer all your questions then. Although one other piece of good news I will tell you now. We are going to have the pleasure of Klaus's company for another day. In the meantime, enjoy your meal, everyone.'

A buzz of conversation broke out, but from the smiling faces, Fiona was able to sink into her chair without the sense of dread she'd been feeling for the last few minutes.

Travis was the last of the group to come into dinner. He took the empty chair at the table next to Rose. She quickly filled him in on Fiona's announcement.

Fiona continued her conversation with Sol and Anna and did not hear everything that was said on the far side of the table, but it was evident that Travis was getting a good roasting from Rose and Faith. Whether that was because he had obviously been drinking, his ruddy face was more flushed than usual, or for upsetting them by spreading false rumours about the cancellation of the next day's activities, she couldn't tell. Travis sat slumped in his seat, saying nothing, seemingly oblivious of everything that was going on around him.

'Are you all right, Travis?'

He looked up at her with an empty expression. She tried to give him a reassuring smile which he acknowledged albeit with a grimace before picking up the menu card and staring at it. She could hardly cross-examine him across the dinner table, so she let it drop.

If anyone else noticed his totally defeated demeanour, they didn't show it and the conversation carried on around him. They probably put it down to the drink or perhaps they thought he was sulking after the way he'd been taken to task, but Fiona sensed that the problem went much deeper.

It was only as she was savouring the last mouthful of chicken in a particularly tasty sauce that it occurred to her what might be troubling him.

'Travis.' He looked up. 'Did you manage to retrieve your laptop from the Inspector's clutches this morning?'

He shook his head.

'Then you should have come with us,' Rose said without a trace of sympathy. 'You missed a really fabulous day.'

There were murmurs of agreement all round.

'Sanssouci was absolutely exquisite and Cecilienhof was so interesting,' Anna said.

'Now you could certainly have made a story out of that, Travis,' Gary said. 'Klaus's account of the differences between the Yalta and Potsdam conferences was fascinating. How Stalin had been able to get his own way at Yalta with a gravely ill President Roosevelt and Churchill thought to be past his prime.'

Fiona expected Travis to make some scathing remark about how could he be expected to make a news-breaking story about events that happened seventy years ago, but he said nothing.

'Klaus was quite tactful, but he did sort of suggest that Churchill was going a bit gaga. Or was that just me?' Faith asked.

'Oh yes,' agreed Gary. 'It's common knowledge the old man's mind was going towards the end.'

'Really? I didn't know that.'

'Anyway,' Gary was keen to get back to the point he'd been making. 'According to Klaus, and the lad is reading history at university, things were very different when it got to the Potsdam Conference five months later. For a start, the war was now over and with Germany defeated, there was no longer any need for the three allies to unite against a common enemy. Talks proved very stormy. Stalin fell out bigtime with President Truman who had replaced Roosevelt and the conservative defeat at the election halfway through meant that Attlee eventually took over from Churchill.'

'I thought the palace itself was beautiful. From the outside, it looked more like an English National Trust Tudor house than a German Palace with all that half-timbering,' said Anna, changing the subject. It was clear that whatever interest the post-war politics the visit may have stirred in Gary had left little impression upon her.

'Oh yes, it was beautiful, wasn't it . . .'

As the women raved about the quaint architecture, Fiona studied Travis. He was clearly deeply troubled. Was there something on that laptop he hadn't wanted the police to see?

Fiona waited until the meal was finished and fell into step with Travis as they left the restaurant.

'I'm sorry you had a wasted day. Did the Inspector say when he was going to return your laptop?'

Travis gave a great sigh and shook his head. 'That's the least of my problems.'

'Can I do anything to help?'

'I doubt it. I spent nearly all afternoon incarcerated with that bloody man. He's convinced I murdered Frederick.'

'But why, Travis? What evidence does he have?'

'It's my own silly fault. I wrote these stupid notes for an imaginary article after we heard that Frederick had died. At the time, we all thought it was an accident. I was just doodling and made up a series of bullet points but that was all, just make-believe. A "what if" scenario. What if Frederick really had been a border guard but was keeping his past a great secret. Maybe, he thought it was all about to be revealed, and because he couldn't face the shame and scandal, he decided to end it all by jumping off the balcony.'

'That's a pretty wild story, Travis.'

'I know, but it was all just a flight of fancy. I never intended to write it properly let alone submit it anywhere.'

'The Inspector didn't believe you.'

'Did he hell! Said it was in pretty poor taste, considering the man I was supposed to have made a friend of had just died.'

'Hmm. Perhaps he had a point.'

'Don't you start.'

'I can see why he might want to give you a hard time over it, Travis, but it's hardly sufficient evidence to charge you with murder.'

'He kept going on about how I'd been boasting about having a breakthrough article. I couldn't make him understand that it wasn't anything to do with how it looked in those notes.'

By now, everyone else had disappeared into the lounge and would be waiting for her. 'I need to let folks know the arrangements for tomorrow. Come and have some coffee and we can talk after the meeting.'

Thanks to the promise of another day with Klaus, the group accepted the rearrangements for the following day with good grace. The prospect of the extra travelling time was met with the inevitable groans, but everyone accepted that it was far better than missing out on the visit to Wittenberg altogether. Morris raised the question of what would happen on the day after, but Fiona managed to sidestep the question, at least for the time being.

Once the questions had all been answered, everyone drifted away to fetch coffee from the side table. Elsie Danby and Drina Lucas appeared to have struck up a friendship, which Fiona did not find surprising, given that both women appeared to have the same somewhat disapproving air of anyone who did not concur with their way of thinking. She had little doubt that the two would take the opportunity for a good whinge at the changes to the published programme. The two women settled themselves at one of the smaller tables. She couldn't help noticing the look of disappointment on Morris's face when he and Walter returned, each carrying two cups of coffee.

She heard him say, 'Aren't we going to join the others?' She didn't catch his wife's reply but felt a pang of sympathy for the man as he settled himself resignedly into the chair next to Drina.

Fiona wondered if Anna and Sol would join them, given that the three couples constituted the oldest members of the party; however, they chose to sit in the larger circle where the conversation could be guaranteed to be more lively.

Travis was looking marginally less agitated and it was a relief to see he had decided to join the group. He was already sipping his coffee and chatting with Barbara Wolf, so Fiona decided the promised chat could wait till later.

When she got back from the coffee station, Gary was talking about his visit to the DDR museum and how much life must have changed in Berlin since those times. Before long, the conversation moved on to how much life for everyone had changed since the days of their childhood.

'Look how we all tend to have foreign holidays these days. Nobody went abroad much when I was a child,' said Rose. 'My first foreign holiday was to France and even that was in a tent.'

'It's not just that. Look at the jobs we do. My dad was a farm worker and my grandad before him. We've had so many more opportunities,' said Gary.

'Too true,' said Travis, throwing back the last of his double whiskey. 'All the men in my family went straight into the railway works. Mind you, there wasn't much option back then. Swindon was a railway town. In its heyday, the carriage and wagon works employed 14,000 men, but I got a scholarship and went to grammar school, so my mum insisted I got a job with prospects. She had visions of me being a doctor or a lawyer.'

'What did she say when you told her you wanted to be a reporter?' asked Sol.

Travis had the grace to laugh. 'I started off in banking. She was happy enough with that. Sad to say, she passed away not long after that. What I really wanted to do was to become a novelist. I hated banking, so when a job came up with the local paper, I jacked in the bank and took the job.'

'What happened to the novel?' asked Henry.

'One day,' Travis laughed. 'What about you? Did you follow in your father's footsteps?'

Henry looked wary. 'No. I work in IT. Not much call for that back in the 60s when he started work.'

'True enough. What did your dad do?'

Peter shifted forward in his chair. 'I'm going to get myself a drink. Would anyone else like one?'

'Not for me, thank you,' Fiona said as he stopped by her

chair.

As she watched Peter join the queue at the bar, Fiona decided to get herself another coffee. It was easy to see why Peter felt the need to get away. No doubt he had a good cover story, but did it go back as far as his father's occupation and a full family history?

She had to ask one of the waiting staff to fetch more milk and it was several minutes before she returned. The young man had filled her cup to the brim, so she was concentrating so hard on not spilling it that she almost bumped into Henry Wolf as he strode to the door. Barbara was looking flustered. She got to her feet, her barely touched glass of wine in her hand. She put it on the table and hurried out after her husband.

'What was that all about? Did I miss something?' asked Fiona.

There were several bemused faces and much shrugging of shoulders.

'He didn't like that question, did he?' said Travis with a laugh. 'Remind me, Fiona. What exactly are we going to see in Wittenberg, tomorrow?'

As the group began to split up, Sol and Anna came over to ask a question and by the time she had finished chatting with them, she realised Travis was already on his feet and heading for the door. She hurried to follow him. Although she could sympathise with his problems, it was no excuse for upsetting other passengers.

He was already halfway across the atrium by the time she reached the door. She was about to call his name when she realised that she was not the only one intent on tracking him down. Inspector Bauer was striding towards Travis, a grim expression on his face. Whatever the man wanted; it was not to return the confiscated laptop.

'Inspector.' Fiona hurried to the two men.

'Not now, Frau Mason,' he growled, waving her away with the back of his hand. He did not even turn his head to look at her. He put a hand under Travis's elbow and marched him towards his temporary office.

Fiona stood watching the two retreating figures, feeling helpless.

At twenty past nine, there was still no news. Sergeant Hase had promised to get back to her. Could she use that as an excuse to make enquiries at the incident room?

There was only one other person besides the Sergeant still there and he seemed to be packing piles of files into a large box. Fiona's mouth went dry as she looked around the room and realised that most of the desks had been cleared. Perhaps she was jumping to conclusions.

She turned to the Sergeant who was looking at her expectantly.

'I was wondering if you had any more information for me as to when we might be free to leave Berlin.'

'I apologise, Mrs Mason. I have not had an opportunity to speak to you. At this moment, I do not have an answer,' he gave her a weak smile presumably intended to be reassuring, 'but unofficially I think that very soon there will be no further need to detain all of you.'

His precise choice of words did not go unnoticed.

'Are you saying the case is closed?'

'No. But we will be moving the base of operations back to the station.'

'May I speak to the Inspector? Is he still interviewing Travis?'

There was a pause before he answered. 'The Inspector has taken Mr Everest to the station.'

'He's been arrested?'

He smiled, evidently trying to soften the blow. 'What is it they say in your English television dramas? Mr Everest is helping with enquiries.'

She wanted to protest, demand to speak to the Inspector, but what would be the point?

Chapter 13

Travis looked at his watch for the third time in less than five minutes, tapping his foot impatiently under the table. The Inspector was taking his time. If the man thought he was going to intimidate him by keeping him waiting, he was wrong.

Ignoring the silent young police constable sitting across the small table, Travis folded his arms across his chest and sat back in the chair, staring up at the ceiling.

The door opened and Inspector Bauer marched in and sat down. He put down the buff card folder he'd been carrying and opened it.

'Mr Everest. Your statement concerning your relationship with Friedrich Schumacher.'

'There was no relationship. I'd only met him that Monday morning.'

'You were at the briefing the night before?'

'Well yes, but it was for ten minutes or so. I didn't speak to him personally.'

The Inspector took a small black notebook from his inside jacket pocket, flicked it open and scribbled some notes.

'You claim Sunday evening is the first time you met him.'

'I've just said so.'

'But this is not your first visit to Berlin?'

'No. I was here in November 1989. I reported on the Wall coming down.'

'But on that occasion, you did not see Friedrich

Schumacher or speak to him?'

'No.'

'Before you came to Berlin, what did you find out about Friedrich Schumacher?'

'I'm not sure what you're getting at. If you mean, did I look into his past history or check any records relating to the man, the answer's a definite no. How could I? I had no idea he would be the local guide.'

'After your meeting on Sunday evening, you tried to find out more about him?'

Travis shook his head. 'No. Why would I?'

'Then why, Mr Everest, would you believe that Friedrich Schumacher served in the Grenztruppen der DDR – as a member of the Border Troops of the German Democratic Republic?'

'I didn't. I...' Travis sat stunned.

The Inspector turned over the top few sheets of paper in the folder until he found what he was looking for. He picked up the sheet, turned it round, and pushed it across the table so that Travis could read it. It was a printout of one of his own laptop files.

'According to this,' the Inspector leant across to jab a finger on the paper, 'you claim he served in the military as part of the border patrol. Also, he was responsible for shooting a man attempting to flee over the wall.'

'But that's just some stupid jottings I made up.'

The Inspector's disbelief was evident both in the expression on his face and in his voice when he asked, 'Do you often make up such stories accusing strangers of killing people?'

'Yes. No. I mean, I think up all sorts of different scenarios about people I meet to amuse myself. Especially self-important types like a local councillor standing for re-election. I imagine him with some dark secret, like having a love child with the wife of his opponent. Just for a laugh, I might map out an exposé article. It may be a childish way of poking fun at people who annoy me but it's hardly criminal.

I never intend to publish it or even show it to anyone else.'

'You had no evidence to suspect Friedrich Schumacher. Yet you tell your fellow travellers that Frederick was a border guard during Soviet occupation. Also, he shot a man trying to escape over the wall.'

'I didn't.' His head was beginning to spin. He desperately needed a drink.

The Inspector sat back and folded his arms. 'We have evidence that you did, Mr Everest. From several of your party.'

'I may have joked about it to one or two people. Frederick hadn't exactly made himself popular with anyone and I may have made some throwaway remark about not being surprised if he turned out to have this terrible past. I probably went on about how it would make a fantastic angle for a story.'

'But you say you had no evidence that Friedrich Schumacher was a border guard or that he had shot at anyone.'

'No,' Travis admitted. 'But I felt he had some secret he wanted to cover up. That's why I was keen to speak to him again privately.'

'You intended to force him to admit to something incriminating about his past?'

'No of course not,' Travis protested. 'I don't deny I thought a few drinks might soften him up a little.'

Inspector Bauer's lips tightened.

'Frederick was a great talker. He liked to boast,' Travis said quickly.

'You think he would tell you such a secret?'

Travis shook his head and stared down at his hands clenched on the table.

'If Friedrich Schumacher shot and killed a man, even if as part of his duty, why would he tell you? A journalist. You would be the last person he would tell. If such a story was printed, even if he escaped prosecution, his reputation would be ruined. He would lose his job, his friends and he would be ostracised by the whole community.'

Travis hung his head.

'Well! Would he not?' demanded the Inspector.

'If you put it like that, I suppose so.'

'Yet you plied him with drink to make him talk?'

'Hardly! We shared a bottle of wine over lunch, that's all. I'll admit the more he drank, the more garrulous he became. He was easy to flatter, and he liked to boast. That was when he said he had been awarded a medal.'

'Did he say for what?'

Travis shook his head. 'I asked him of course but he was pretty cagey.'

'Cagey?'

'Wary, guarded. He wouldn't tell me. That's what got me thinking. I knew that border guards were awarded medals for exemplary service including shooting East Germans trying to escape to the West.'

'Did you ask him outright if he had been a guard?'

Travis hung his head. 'There was no point. He would never admit it.'

The Inspector gave a derisive snort. 'Mr Everest. You have slim evidence on which to base your theory. Herr Schumacher may have received a medal for all sorts of reasons. Not enough for you to spread rumours or to begin writing your article.'

Inspector Bauer put his hands on the desk, pushed himself back in his chair and turned to his colleague sat next to him. 'Do you not agree, Detective Constable?'

The constable nodded.

Travis ran his tongue over his dry lips.

'Why would Schumacher agree to go with you to your hotel room?' The Inspector fired at him. 'What did you promise him?'

'It wasn't like that.' Travis gulped. 'We chatted together throughout the afternoon walk. He was evasive about his past, but as I said, I knew if I was ever going to get any kind of story out of him, I'd have to get him on his own. When we got back to the hotel, I suggested we went to the bar and I'd buy him a drink. I told him I was a journalist and all we hear back home is how dreadful it all was in Berlin during the occupation. I said how fascinating it would be to read the other side of the story from someone who'd actually lived through it all. He seemed interested in the idea, especially when I said there might be money in it for him, but first he had to report back to his office or some such, so we arranged he'd come back to the hotel later.'

'Did you fix a definite time?'

'No. He didn't know how long he'd be, so I gave him my room number. I assumed when he got back to the hotel, he'd get reception to ring me and I'd come down and we'd find a quiet corner in one of the bars.'

'You claim you never intended that the two of you would be alone in your room.'

'No. I never saw Frederick after we parted at the hotel entrance at around four o'clock.'

The Inspector leant forward until his face was inches from Travis's. 'Can you prove that?'

Travis shook his head and stared down at his clenched hands.

Silence settled over the room.

Travis ran his tongue over his parched lips. 'May I have some water?'

'The constable will see that you get something to drink and a meal. I am not satisfied with your answers, Mr Everest, and I still have many questions. We will talk again. Tomorrow.'

Day 6

This morning we begin our tour along the unspoilt Elbe valley. Our first stop will be at the Wörlitz Gardens created by Prince Franz, duke of Anhalt-Dessau. He also extended and altered the old Dutch-style gardens of Oranienbaum Palace and together, these gardens form one of the first and largest English parks in continental Europe. Prince Franz also redesigned the 17th century Oranienbaum Palace with a Chinese-style teahouse and a pagoda in the gardens. The palace also has one of the largest orangeries in Europe which still houses a wide collection of citrus plants.

After lunch, we continue our journey to Wittenberg. A significant trading centre from the 12th century onwards, the town became an important political and cultural centre in the 15th century when the Great Elector Frederick the Wise founded the University of Wittenberg. The University became home to many progressive thinkers including the town's most famous son, Martin Luther, who was a professor of theology. Another noted teacher at the university was Philipp Melanchthon, professor of Greek.

We will visit the Augustinian monastery where Luther lived, first as a monk and then as the owner with his wife, the former nun Katharina von Bora, and family. Here we will walk through Luther's sitting room and the lecture room where we will find his famous pulpit.

We will end our visit with a walk through the town. We will pass the home of Philipp Melanchthon and his statue together with that of Martin Luther in the market square. On the south side of the square is the house of their friend, the painter Lucas Cranach. Before leaving the square, we will have time to admire the Renaissance town hall and the Gothic church of St Mary where Luther was married and where he regularly preached. We end our walk at the door of the Palace Church on which Luther nailed his 95 Theses which marked the beginning of the spread of the Reformation throughout Germany.

Super Sun Executive Travel

Chapter 14

Fiona woke to the strident jangle of her alarm, feeling anything but rested. She had lain awake for hours and it must have been sheer exhaustion that made her fall asleep at all. She stood under the shower for some time, her face raised to the full force of the water. She felt marginally more invigorated as she wrapped herself in the large fluffy bath sheet and scrubbed at her wet hair with one end.

Why were hotel hairdryers so much less powerful than one's own? She gave up twirling locks of hair around the brush and fluffed up her hair with her fingers. It would have to do. She didn't have the patience to stand in front of the mirror any longer. Besides, filling her mind with such silly, petty things didn't take away the real problem.

She rang Travis's room but there was no answer. Not that she'd expected any. Not after what the Sergeant had said last night.

What was going to happen if Travis had been arrested? Brash, self-obsessed and arrogant he might be, but surely not a murderer. She needed to speak to the Inspector.

If the whole investigation had been moved to the police station, there was little chance of the man ever returning to the hotel. She wasn't sure she would find any of the police team in the hotel at such an early hour, but as she turned the corner, she saw the Inspector coming out of the incident room and walking towards the one he had commandeered as his office.

'Inspector.'

He glanced at her over his shoulder as he went in, leaving the door open behind him.

'I can only spare you a couple of minutes, Mrs Mason,' he said with his back to her.

'I do appreciate that you are a busy man, Inspector,' she said in a voice that she hoped didn't sound too sycophantic but there was no point in antagonising him by being confrontational. 'However, I need to know what has happened to Travis Everest. Has he been arrested?'

He turned and frowned at her. 'As my Sergeant has already informed you, Mr Everest is still answering questions.'

He walked round the table, sat down and began shuffling through the papers in front of him. When he realised that Fiona was still standing there, he looked up.

'Was there anything else, Mrs Mason?'

If reasonableness wasn't going to get her anywhere, she would play it his way. 'Only that I wanted to inform you that my party will be leaving Berlin first thing tomorrow morning.' He opened his mouth to protest, but before he could speak, she continued, 'And unless you are in a position to charge him, Travis will be leaving with us.'

'That will not be possible.'

He threw her a look that might have made a lesser woman quail. Nine years spent battling with self-important bureaucrats to ensure the correct treatment for her terminally ill husband had taught her not to back down. Refusing to let the man's dismissal provoke her, Fiona said calmly, 'I fail to see why, Inspector. As I understand it, you can only hold a suspect for twenty-four hours before charging them.'

'You are wrong, Mrs Mason. In cases of serious crime, we may detain an individual for four days.' His lips tightened. 'Also, Mrs Mason, I am not happy with the Super Sun party leaving Berlin until an arrest has been made.'

'Inspector, we have already acceded to your request,' she pointedly stressed the word, 'to stay an additional night, at considerable inconvenience, not to mention expense I might add, but in order to continue with our planned programme we need to be in Dresden tomorrow evening.'

'That is not my problem.' He looked down and picked up his papers again.

'It is mine, Inspector. You have no reason to keep the rest of us here.'

'As you are aware, Mrs Mason, we are in the middle of a murder investigation and in the light of new evidence, other Super Sun passengers are now under suspicion. Not solely Mr Everest.'

'Who else, for goodness' sake?'

'That I am not at liberty to say.'

'I can only presume you are talking about Sol Sachs. I hardly think a minor disagreement at the Holocaust Memorial constitutes sufficient motive for murder, Inspector.'

His eyes narrowed, 'He is not the only other suspect and believe me, madam, we have far more compelling evidence which includes information we have recently received from our British colleagues.'

'Really!' She ought to have known better than to ask, but not to be deterred, she continued, 'My party had known Frederick for barely eight hours. Shouldn't you be looking for his murderer amongst those who knew him well?'

'Naturally the investigation has considered all Herr Schumacher's associates, but it is a fact that the man was murdered here in the hotel. How would an outsider know Herr Schumacher was in the hotel at that particular time?'

'That, Inspector, is *your* problem. Not mine,' she snapped, echoing the same injunction he had given her. 'You have had three whole days in which to question my party. I have spoken to my company's legal department and as I understand it, you may be able to prevent us from leaving Germany for the time being, but unless you intend to arrest Mr Everest or anyone else in my party, we are all free to continue our tour of the Elbe Valley until we reach the

Czech border.'

She turned quickly and marched to the door. It was all she could do to prevent herself from slamming it closed behind her.

It had been a Pyrrhic victory. She could only hope that her lie about consulting the legal department was true. It would help her cause if the Inspector thought she had the weight of the company behind her. She was fairly confident that he couldn't prevent the group from moving on, but whether Travis would be with them as they moved south was yet to be seen.

Her stomach was still churning by the time she reached the restaurant. She glanced at her watch. Her confrontation with the Inspector meant that she had less than a quarter of an hour before her meeting with Klaus and Winston. There was no time for what her mother would have called a proper breakfast, not that she felt like eating anyway. But she needed a sit-down and a cup of tea at least to regain her calm. She forced herself to take a croissant. It was vaguely warm but not as she liked them – piping hot and straight from the oven.

Klaus had already arrived by the time Fiona reached the foyer. He and Winston were sitting on one of the bench seats near the front doors.

'I'm so sorry. Have you been waiting long?'

'Please don't concern yourself, Fiona. I was early.'

'Shall we move into the atrium? It's a little less like Clapham Junction and we will be able to talk more easily.

He looked at her quizzically. 'Clapham Junction?'

She laughed. 'Less busy. Fewer people milling around.'

The two men got up and followed her up the two or three steps into the enormous atrium where they settled themselves in the armchairs arranged around a small low table.

She glanced around but there was nothing to indicate that

only three days ago, a man had died only a few feet from where they were now sitting and this whole area had been a crime scene. As far as the hotel and the rest of its occupants were concerned, bad things happen but life goes on. Fiona pushed such melancholy thoughts from her mind and tried to focus on what Klaus was saying.

He was looking through the details of the day's itinerary with Winston. The two men began to discuss whether to take the shortest route, which would take them past Potsdam along the same roads as the day before, or directly southwards through a different part of the city, adding another quarter of an hour to the journey.

Winston turned to Fiona. 'Your decision, sweetheart.'

'The passengers might find that more interesting. We only had a fleeting glimpse of the Jewish museum on our first day and that was from the other direction, but will that give us enough time?'

'We should arrive at Wörlitz Gardens around midmorning and if lunch is at one o'clock, we will have a couple of hours,' Klaus said.

'We will need a comfort stop as soon as we arrive,' said Fiona with a frown.

Klaus looked up and gave her a charming smile. 'Of course, Fiona. Our first stop will be at the café where we will also have coffee before we begin.'

She might have known Klaus would have everything in hand. He must have done this trip countless times, so there was no need for her momentary qualm.

'In the summer months we would spend much longer here but this time of year, the Gardens are not at their best and given the weather situation, we will make a relatively short stop before we move on to Oranienbaum Palace.'

They discussed the arrangements for lunch and Klaus double-checked the travel timings with Winston.

'When we arrive in Wittenberg, we can go straight to the old monastery and the Lutherhalle,' said Klaus.

'Super Sun has already arranged for one of the museum

volunteers to act as guide for us when we visit the Luther House but not for the walk through the town afterwards,' she said.

'No problem, I can see to that.'

'I do have some maps with me with the main sites clearly marked for everyone,' she said, pulling a copy from her tote bag.

He gave it a quick glance. 'Excellent. As you see, everything is more or less either side of the main street ending up at the Schlosskirche. There is parking behind the church by the café where everyone can use the facilities before we board the coach at, shall we say,' Klaus did a quick calculation, 'at four o'clock?'

Winston looked at his map and nodded. 'Allowing for the evening traffic, we should be back here at the hotel at half six at the latest.'

'That sounds fine,' agreed Fiona. 'It still gives everyone an hour before dinner.'

'So, is there anything else you would like me to do?' Klaus asked.

Fiona shook her head. 'You seem to have covered everything. I'll double-check with the restaurant about lunch before we leave.'

Winston stood up, looking at his watch. 'Time I went to see to the coach.' He nodded to Fiona and Klaus and left.

'I'm sorry, but I'm going to have to leave you too, Klaus. I will see you in ten minutes.'

'That is no problem. I have plenty of reading to do.' He pulled his rucksack towards him.

Everyone began to assemble at the bench seats between the main doors and the reception area. No one asked about Travis. There was every possibility that no one would notice until they were on the coach. Fiona still hadn't decided whether or not she should make some announcement. Until she had been told that he had officially been charged, it seemed best not to, but someone was bound to ask where he was eventually.

Once the journey began, she sat back and listened to Klaus's comments on the places they were passing as the coach travelled through the southern outskirts of the city. She even took out her notebook to add to her notes for any future visits she might make.

Whether it was the movement of the coach or because she had had so little sleep the night before, she drifted into a doze. When she woke and looked around the coach, she realised she wasn't the only one to drift off despite the early hour. Klaus gently tapped the microphone and the last of the sleepers began to stir.

'In a short while we will be arriving at Wörlitz Gardens. In the early 18th century, most royal gardens in Europe were still very formal, laid out along the lines of France's most famous garden at Versailles with geometric flower beds, ornate fountains, and water features. However, when he visited England, Prince Franz was impressed by the natural appearance of English country house gardens with their expansive lawns, clusters of trees and artificial lakes such as those designed by your Capability Brown. When he returned home, Prince Franz decided to create his own park from what was an old fishing village. He wanted to provide a restful natural environment for all his subjects to enjoy whilst making full use of the existing small lakes and creeks in this low-lying area alongside the River Elbe.'

Klaus was a natural raconteur and after explaining about Franz's numerous reforms and how he made Anhalt-Dessau one of the most modern and prosperous of the small German states, he regaled them with tales of the duke's many mistresses. As the coach drew into the car park and his stories came to an end, someone started clapping and the rest of the coach joined in.

'Travis not with us again today.' Elsie's comment sounded more like a criticism than an observation.

Fiona had still not worked out how she was going to explain his absence and before she could think of what to say, Drina said, 'That Inspector took him to the police station.'

'Has he been arrested?' Loraine stopped walking and turned round to face them, causing the whole of the rear of the group to come to an abrupt stop.

They all looked to Fiona.

'Not as far as I know. If he had been, I'm sure I would have been informed. Shall we move on everyone? We'll miss what Klaus has to say.'

'He is such a lovely boy, isn't he?' Loraine said. 'It's such a pity we can't take him with us for the rest of the tour.'

As the tail-enders quickened their pace, Loraine hung back. 'Sorry about that, Fiona. I didn't mean to encourage the gossip and drop you in it. It was just such a surprise.'

'Don't worry. You made up for it by helping to change the subject.'

The Chinese room was everything Klaus had promised it would be. Truly spectacular.

'Take a look at the ceiling, everyone.' There were oohs and aahs of approval as everyone looked up.

'Wow! That's certainly different,' said Morris.

'The sunburst in the centre is a symbol of the German Enlightenment. You will remember I told you how Prince Franz was a great supporter of the movement. The four golden dragons show the Chinese theme, as do the rather lovely lanterns painted with Chinese figures.'

Everyone lingered, inspecting the various treasures in the room and Klaus had difficulty attempting to move the party on into the next room. Fiona ushered the last of the stragglers after him. Henry and Barbara Wolf were still looking at the china on one of the small corner stands. Even then, as his wife left the room, Henry hung back.

'Fiona, I overheard someone say that Travis has been

arrested. Is that true?'

'Not as far as I know,' said Fiona, moving towards the door so that he had no option but to follow.

'But if the police haven't made an arrest, why are they winding up the investigation?'

Fiona stopped and turned round to look at him. 'That's news to me. Who told you they had?'

'They have moved out of the hotel. Barbara saw them carrying out all their stuff last night.'

'As I understand it,' Fiona said firmly, 'they have moved a number of the staff working on the case in the hotel back to the police station, but there were several people there this morning. Including the Inspector. I spoke to him myself. If they had made an arrest, I'm sure he would have told me. Now, shall we join the others?'

Without giving him a chance to ask any more questions, she turned and hurried to the door.

Chapter 15

By lunchtime, the news about Travis had spread throughout the group. Fiona overheard snatches of conversation at the neighbouring tables.

'Why would the police think Travis had anything to do with it?'

'They must have some evidence. The police wouldn't be keeping him all this time otherwise.' Though she couldn't turn round to check without making it obvious, Fiona was fairly certain that despite the slightly hushed tones, it was Drina making the accusations. She had made little secret of her disapproval of Travis from the time, as she insisted, he had tried to get Frederick drunk at lunch on their first day in Berlin.

'I don't buy it. It doesn't make sense. What possible motive could Travis have? He wanted to interview Frederick for his scoop story. He was the last person to want him dead.'

There were murmurs of assent.

'In most murder cases, it's usually one of the family,' came another voice.

'Much more likely to be someone . . .'

Fiona tried to ignore what was being said. There was little she could do about it anyway. The only good thing seemed to be that apart from Drina, none of Travis's fellow passengers appeared to consider him guilty. Travis had not gone out of his way to make himself popular, so their support was something of a relief as far as Fiona was concerned. Fiona turned to the person sitting next to her and asked, 'Did you enjoy **Oranienbaum Palace**?'

'Oh yes,' said Barbara enthusiastically. 'Beautiful wasn't it? Especially the Chinese room. All those lovely wall paintings.'

'I loved the ones with the birds with the simple sprays of greenery above,' said Sol who was sitting next to Fiona. 'They were all the more striking for being less fussy than some of the others. I took a photo on my phone. I was surprised, it came out really well.'

He pulled out his mobile, found the picture and showed it to Fiona.

'That's excellent. I think that picture was my favourite too,' Fiona agreed. 'That pale background really sets off the wonderful detail in that long, colourful tail. Do you think it's meant to be a peacock? Do they have peacocks in China?'

'No idea.' Sol shrugged his shoulders. 'They're a native Indian bird.'

If Fiona thought she had managed to steer the conversation away from Travis, she did not manage it for long. On the far side of the table, Anna was talking with Sonya and Peter.

'But what will happen to Travis if he's still in custody when we leave tomorrow morning?'

'Perhaps that is a question you should put to Fiona,' suggested Sonya.

Everyone looked at Fiona expectantly.

'As I said earlier,' she said firmly, 'Travis is helping the police with their enquiries . . .'

'Yes, but we all know what that means,' interrupted Henry Wolf crossly, 'what happens if the police want to keep him at the station?'

'Let's hope it doesn't come to that,' Fiona said quickly. 'We may find he has already been released and in the hotel, when we get back, and we'll all be able to continue tomorrow.'

She knew she'd said the wrong thing when she saw the shocked expressions.

'Are you saying the Inspector could stop us all going to Meissen?' asked Barbara.

'I have already told Inspector Bauer that we are leaving first thing tomorrow.'

Henry was still frowning.

Sol shook his head. 'The Inspector said the other day, after my interview, that we none of us were leaving Berlin until the murderer had been arrested. According to him, it could only be one of our party.'

'Then perhaps we should all hope the Inspector formally arrests Travis so the rest of us can continue to enjoy our holiday.'

Sonya's remark was met with shocked silence.

Fiona caught an intense angry glare flash across Montgomery-Jones's normally impassive face before he began to laugh. 'You must forgive my wife's sense of humour, everyone. Her command of English is not always all it should be.'

Her return look was no less hostile, but before she could make any comment, he put his hand over Sonya's in a seemingly affectionate gesture. Fiona had little doubt that the squeeze he was giving it was far from gentle.

Not for the first time, Fiona decided that her original assessment that Sonya was an MI6 operative was way off the mark. So quite what she was doing travelling with the enigmatic Peter Montgomery-Jones, Fiona could not begin to fathom.

Feeling the need to fill the embarrassed hiatus, Fiona said, 'Klaus will be expecting us back on the coach in ten minutes so if you'll forgive me, everyone.'

'In which case, it's time I paid a quick visit to the Ladies,' said Anna, jumping to her feet with a speed that belied her age. Barbara followed in quick succession.

As she pushed her chair back under the table, Henry appeared at her elbow. 'May I have a word, Fiona?'

'Certainly, Henry.' She went to sit back down again but he shook his head.

He looked around almost furtively. 'Can we go somewhere a little more private?'

As most of the others had already left the table, it seemed an unnecessary precaution, but she followed him to the door.

Her mobile started ringing before they were even outside.

'I'm sorry, Henry, I must answer this. I will catch you later, I promise.' She didn't give him a chance to respond. 'Adam. Is everything alright?'

'Wittenberg means white mountain but the official name for the town is Lutherstadt Wittenberg in honour of its most famous son. During the post-war era, religion was discouraged in East Germany, but after the fall of Communism, because of Luther and his historical importance, Wittenberg has become a much-visited town. Born in Eisleben, Saxony, he came here as an Augustinian monk to teach in the newly founded university. His home, the Lutherhaus, is now a museum and that is where we will go now. We are going to leave the coach here but when we come out of the museum, we will go straight to our guided walk through the town, so please make sure you bring your hats and gloves and scarves. The sun is shining but as you know from this morning, it is a very cold day.'

As Klaus gathered everyone together, Fiona stood at the door ready to help the last of the passengers out of the coach.

'Would you like me to take your stick, Morris, and then you'll have both hands to hold on?'

'Thank you, Fiona.'

She waved goodbye to Winston as he moved off to park the coach at the far side of town. She followed the rest of the slowly moving group to their first stopping point in the old monastery courtyard. Klaus never began his talk until the whole party were assembled nor did he ever betray the slightest impatience as he stood chatting with people until the stragglers had arrived.

'As you see Katherina van Bora is coming to welcome you.' Klaus pointed to the larger-than-life black statue of a woman in medieval costume apparently striding towards them. 'Now this lady is the real power behind the Luther throne. Without her, Luther would have been lost. He was pretty hopeless with money and business affairs by all accounts, but unusually for women in those days, Katherina could both read and write and was an exceptionally shrewd businesswoman. She was only twenty-six when they married, and he was forty-three.'

'I thought Luther married a nun,' said Morris.

'Indeed, she was,' Klaus agreed. 'However, inspired by the growing Reformation, she and several other nuns ran away from their Cistercian monastery and asked Luther for help.'

As the party followed Klaus towards the entrance, Fiona noticed Peter was holding back with Sonya. His face was as impassive as ever, but whatever he was saying clearly did not please Sonya. Fiona could hear the anger in her retort halfway across the courtyard though the actual words were incomprehensible as they were talking in what Fiona could only assume was Polish. Though his voice remained low and steady, his face impassive, it was evident that Peter was having none of it. Probably, this was the first opportunity he had in private to let her know that her comments at the lunch table were unacceptable. In times past, Fiona had been on the receiving end of Montgomery-Jones's cold disapproval and she felt a momentary pang of sympathy for the woman. Sonya might not be MI6, but there was little doubt who was in charge in the relationship.

Fiona went inside and left them to it. This was not the time to urge them not to be left behind.

'I'm not sure quite what I expected,' said Anna as the group made its way along the Collegienstrasse sometime later, 'but certainly not that huge ornate silver altar affair in the main hall. I thought he objected to all that kind of ostentation.'

Fiona laughed. 'It surprised me too.'

'I can just see old Luther gloating at the prospect of turning his old monastery into his home,' said Sol with a mischievous grin. 'And seeing his wife turn the rest of the place into a paying guest house must have been like putting two fingers up at the old establishment.'

'Solomon! What a thing to say.' Anna's shocked response didn't last for long as she broke into a girlish giggle. 'You shouldn't judge others by your own low standards. He was a deeply religious man and I'm sure he would never have entertained such uncharitable thoughts.'

She tucked her arm through her husband's, and they strolled away chatting together, their mutual affection clear for all to see.

The same could not be said of another couple in the group. Peter and Sonya were also walking arm in arm but the sullen expression on her face suggested she would have preferred to be somewhere else entirely. To Fiona's eyes, Peter's hold spoke more about control, keeping Sonya in line, than a gesture of fondness. Or was that merely wishful thinking on her part, she wondered? Not that she had any interest in Peter of course she told herself, but she found it hard to warm to his supposed wife and felt he deserved much, much better.

'And this,' said Klaus, pointing up at the building they were now all facing, 'is the home of Philipp Melanchthon. You will remember I told you all about Luther's good friend who helped him translate his bible from Greek and Hebrew.'

Some ten minutes later as Klaus led the way from the market square to the next stopping point, Fiona tried to round up the last of the photographers which to her surprise included Peter Montgomery-Jones. She noticed with a wry smile that Sonya had used the opportunity to get away from him.

Now was as good a time as any. She fell into step

alongside him.

'Peter, I need your help.'

'Oh?' He gave her a decidedly wary look.

'I'm very concerned about Travis. I wondered if there was any chance that you could have a word with Inspector…'

He put up a hand to stop her. 'I am not in a position to do anything, Fiona. It is not that I do not wish to, it is simply that I can do nothing that might draw attention to me or my mission in any way.'

'I'm not asking you to reveal your true identity but surely you could do something? Pull a few strings behind the scenes.'

'Are you so convinced that the man is innocent?'

'Of course, I am,' she snapped. 'How can you ask such a thing? Travis is an obnoxious, self-obsessed fantasist but he's hardly a murderer.'

Peter attempted to suppress a laugh but failed, shaking his head. 'I can see the man has won your heart.'

'Stop being facetious. Travis can't help playacting. He likes to pretend he's this hard-bitten, world-weary journalist even to himself, but deep down he's painfully insecure. You may not agree with my assessment, but either way, Travis deserves justice and I'm convinced he's being used as a scapegoat. Inspector Bauer wants to clear up this case quickly and he's determined to . . .'

'You may not like the man's manner but that is hardly a good reason to doubt his ability to lead the investigation or to accuse him of corruption.'

'That's not what I'm saying,' she said crossly.

Montgomery-Jones glanced down the street. 'We are getting left behind. Let us keep walking.'

'The problem is that the Inspector seems hell-bent on keeping us all in Berlin for the foreseeable future. I appreciate that you don't want to do anything that might jeopardize whatever it is you are up to, but surely it isn't in your interests to be stuck in Berlin?'

They were fast catching up the rest of the party, so Peter

slowed his pace, letting them move ahead just far enough to ensure that he and Fiona could not be overheard.

'Has he said he intends to detain us?'

'Not categorically,' she admitted. 'But he implied as much.'

'Did he give a reason why that might be the case?'

Fiona sighed and shook her head. 'Apart from the fact that he seems convinced that one of the Super Sun party is responsible for Frederick's death. Last night Sergeant Hase said that the Inspector was waiting for information from the British police. What that involves I really don't know. Background checks, I presume. Isn't that what you would do?'

She looked across at him and saw a deep frown flash across his forehead.

'Background checks on Travis Everest or on everyone in the group?'

'I can't say for certain, but I got the impression that it was more than just Travis. Though why he is so fixated on this ridiculous idea that Frederick was murdered by one of the Super Sun Party, I have no idea. You wouldn't be able to cast any light on that, I suppose?'

'We have already had this conversation, Fiona,' he said sharply. 'I have no idea who murdered Frederick Schumacher or why, and in all honesty, at the moment that is not my principal concern. I would be a great deal happier if there was nothing to draw attention to this tour in any shape or form. The sooner we can leave Berlin, the better.'

'In which case, you should try to pull a few strings to make the Inspector let us go.'

'For the very reasons I have just explained, I cannot. Any attempt at outside pressure, however subtle, might arouse suspicion. I would have thought that you of all people would have understood that.'

She stopped walking and glared up at him. 'For goodness' sake, I'm not asking you to reveal your cover. But don't tell me you can't make a few phone calls to someone who could exert some pressure. You've just admitted that it's in your best interest for us all to leave, so for your sake as well as Travis and everyone else's, it's up to you.'

She stomped off to join the others. There were times when the man made her want to scream. Why was he being so unreasonable?

As if she didn't have enough on her mind after that earlier phone call from Kristie. The poor girl had sounded at the end of her tether. Becky didn't appear to be getting any better and Kristie had wanted her mother-in-law's advice as to whether she should insist that they get a second opinion from another doctor. Fiona had had enough experience of overanxious mothers in her nursing days, but how could she possibly advise her when she was half a world away? It didn't help that Kristie had always seemed to be the level-headed, capable type. Not given to overreacting like Adam was prone to do. Had she said the right thing by suggesting that Kristie ring the surgery and ask to speak to their doctor again and as the child was not making any improvement, ask for another appointment?

Chapter 16

Klaus waited patiently, letting everyone take their time looking at the church and taking photos of the famous door on which Luther was reputed to have nailed his revolutionary 95 Theses.

Fiona was still annoyed with Peter. She could hardly make a show of ignoring him but that didn't mean that she had to stand next to him. Instead, she went to speak to Faith who was waiting for Rose to finish taking her photos.

After the two women had been chatting for a couple of minutes, Sonya's strident voice could be heard saying, 'I do wish the stragglers would hurry. My feet are getting cold.'

Faith turned to her with a smile. 'I think they must have heard you. They're coming now.'

Undeterred by the withering look she received in reply, Faith said brightly, 'You know, Sonya, as I was saying to Rose yesterday, you remind me of someone, but for the life of me I can't think who. The hair's different I know, but there is something. Perhaps it's the shape of your face. Someone famous perhaps. It'll come to me. I'm good at faces.'

'It's getting a little chilly standing here,' Fiona said quickly.

Sonya scowled then turned away and stomped towards the path that led around the church to the car park.

Before Faith could pursue the subject, Fiona cut in, 'If we make a move back to the coach, perhaps the others will follow.'

Fiona stood at the side door of the coach ready to help.

'How long is the journey back?' asked Drina.

'About an hour and three-quarters give or take.' Fiona gave her a reassuring smile.

'At least it will give us time to watch a complete film.' Morris was always ready to see the positives.

'Knowing you, you'll be sound asleep before they've got through the opening credits,' said Drina.

Morris laughed. 'More than likely.'

Fiona followed them up the steps and walked down the aisle, double-checking everyone was on board before making her way to take her place at the back of the coach.

As Drina had predicted, within half an hour, Morris was asleep as were the majority of the passengers. As far as Fiona could see, there were very few flickering lights emanating from the personal video screens.

Although her anger and frustration levels had lowered considerably, her conversation with Montgomery-Jones was still on her mind. There was no point even bothering to switch on her screen and find the earphones. She knew she wouldn't be able to concentrate.

Perhaps if she knew what Montgomery-Jones was up to, it would help to understand why he was being so difficult? It was disconcerting not knowing anything at all about his mission. It wasn't as though she expected him to give her details. In their previous encounters, she had had some idea of his end goal, tracking down a smuggling syndicate, thwarting the attempt to pass on military plans to a revolutionary terrorist group or catching the murderer of a British politician, but this time she hadn't the remotest idea what he could be up to.

What bothered her most was that his operation was keeping him at a distance. There may have been the occasional friction between them, and she had lost her temper with him more than once, but Peter had been such an ally in the past.

Winston was always supportive of course, but it wasn't

the same. He couldn't exert the influence that Montgomery-Jones was capable of.

The small stark interview room with its bare walls, single high window, table and four upright chairs was as claustrophobic as the cell where he had spent most of the last twenty-four hours.

Travis sat slumped at the table staring at the small black box at the wall end that was recording his every word. Over and over again. The same questions.

'You did not have a high opinion of Friedrich Schumacher, did you?' Inspector Bauer snapped.

Travis shrugged his shoulders. 'I didn't exactly like the man.'

'Come now, a little more than that, I think. Your computer files make interesting reading.' The Inspector pulled a sheet of paper from the folder in front of him and ran his finger down the list. 'You called him "a big-headed braggart with only two brain cells," "a petty Napoleon who loved the sound of his own voice," "a total nincompoop with notions of grandeur," "a mouse who thought himself a lion," plus several choice phrases considerably less complimentary and probably best not repeated in polite society.'

There was nothing Travis could say.

'Explain to me why, when you clearly had such little respect for the man, did you attempt to befriend him? You even bought him a bottle of wine at lunch and invited him for a drink at the end of the afternoon.'

Travis bit back the temptation to protest that the bottle of wine was for everyone on the table.

'From the very beginning, Frederick made no secret of the fact that he was a supporter of the Soviet occupation during the cold war. There have been lots of features about the horrors of living under that regime, but I wondered if there was any mileage for an article about what life was like from the opposite point of view. He'd talked about the benefits of having full employment, housing, free education and health care and a sense of security. I spoke to him a couple of times in the morning and over lunch we had a long conversation about those times.'

'You claim you feigned friendship in order to obtain information for a story?'

Travis nodded and mumbled, 'That's one way of putting it.'

'The only way, I think.' The Inspector did nothing to hide the sneer in his voice.

'It's how journalists work.'

'But there is no evidence of such a story on your laptop.'

'That's because I never got the chance to interview him as I keep telling you.'

'And yet you wrote here that Schumacher had no respect for others!' the Inspector shook his head in disbelief.

'He upset Sol Sachs,' Travis protested.

'Whereas you intended to malign Schumacher in print!'

'No! I never intended to make those insults public.'

'Then why write them down on your computer?'

'I was just letting off steam. Letting rip on the page helps fire me up, gets the creative juices flowing, psyching myself up so as to write a good article.'

The Inspector looked unconvinced. The harsh Teutonic voice continued relentlessly. 'Let us talk about your notes for this article.'

'I've told you, just part of the process – stupid jottings to amuse myself while I was waiting for Frederick to arrive.'

'What made you think Schumacher had been a border guard?'

Travis put his head in his hands. 'We've been over this.'

'Tell me again.'

For what seemed like the tenth time, Travis talked about Frederick's admiration of the communist system, the security and stability it gave the people, his love of all things military and his pride in the medal.

'Oh yes. The medal.' The Inspector smiled. 'It might interest you to know that Friedrich Schumacher was never a border guard. He was not in any of the Soviet military forces throughout the occupation. He worked in the Trabant factory on the assembly line. Like all his fellow workers, he was given a medal to mark the celebration of the millionth car to come off the production line.'

Travis stared at him wide-eyed. 'But Frederick said . . .'

The door was suddenly thrown open.

'Not now!' growled the Inspector, not taking his eyes from Travis.

'Very much now, Inspector. I would like a private word with my client.'

All eyes turned to the commanding figure who had entered.

'Herr Jäger! This is a surprise.' The Inspector was on his feet. 'I was unaware that Mr Everest here required a solicitor. He has yet to be formally charged.'

'So I understand. Nonetheless, Mr Everest is entitled to the benefit of my services and that is why I am here. As I understand it, he has been in your custody for some considerable time.'

He took the empty chair alongside Travis and turned to the bewildered reporter with a smile. 'I hope they have been treating you well?'

Travis was too stunned to answer with anything other than a nod.

'Good, good. Now Inspector, perhaps before I have a private word with my client, you might care to briefly run through the evidence you have against him with me.'

Chapter 17

Fiona wasn't much in the mood to be sociable after dinner. She sat with some of the others for nearly half an hour in the lounge, but once she had finished her coffee, she made her apologies and left.

She had only just got back to her room when her mobile started bleeping.

Her first thought was that it might be Adam. She felt a moment of panic. Had something happened to Becky? She opened her handbag and unceremoniously flung the contents onto the bed, snapping on her mobile without stopping to read the caller's name.

'Hello.'

'Mrs Mason. This is Detective Inspector Bauer. We have decided to release Mr Everest . . .'

'Thank goodness for that,' she said, sinking down onto the bed.

'There are conditions, Mrs Mason.' The voice was tart. The Inspector was clearly not a happy man. The decision was clearly not one of his choosing.

'Oh?'

There was a pause. 'Would you come to the police station and we can discuss them?'

'I'll get a taxi straight away.'

'That will not be necessary. I will send a car to pick you up.'

'Thank you.'

Before she had a chance to ask any questions, he had rung

off.

Hurriedly she returned her things to her bag, ran a comb through her hair, pulled on her boots, wrapped her scarf around her neck and put on her coat and hat. She would have to keep her fingers crossed that no one saw her on her way downstairs. It didn't bear contemplating what the rest of the Super Sun party might think if she was seen driving away from the hotel in a police car at that time of the evening.

As soon as she arrived at the station – thankfully in an unmarked car driven by a pleasant young officer in plain clothes – she was led through the corridors and shown into a small office where Inspector Bauer, Travis and a smartly dressed middle-aged man whom she had never seen before were waiting.

The stranger got to his feet, smiled and put out his hand to shake hers. 'May I introduce myself? I am Dieter Jäger. I am here to represent Mr Everest's interests.'

Fiona tried to hide her surprise as she sat down on the empty chair next to the Inspector. Things must be bad if the police had given him a solicitor. She glanced across the table at Travis who was the last to resume his seat. His normally ruddy face was now ashen.

'After some discussion,' Dieter Jäger continued, 'Inspector Bauer has agreed to release Mr Everest from custody.'

'You're free to go?' Fiona turned to Travis. 'That is good news.'

'Not quite,' snapped the Inspector. 'As I mentioned on the telephone, there are conditions.'

'Oh?'

'I am by no means convinced of Mr Everest's innocence and he remains a suspect in our murder investigation. However, until all our inquiries are complete, and I have conclusive evidence, Mr Everest will no longer be detained in custody. In normal circumstances, I do have the right to insist that he does not leave Berlin, but at Herr Jäger's request, I am prepared to release him into your custody and allow him to return to the tour group.'

'What does that entail exactly?'

'It means, Mrs Mason, that you are responsible for ensuring that Mr Everest does not leave Germany and that he does not abscond before reaching the German border.'

'But what happens when we leave to go home next Tuesday?'

'I am sure the investigation will be concluded long before. I would have preferred that the whole party remain here in Berlin. Although Mr Everest remains our chief suspect, we are still examining documentation recently received from England about several other of your passengers. Nonetheless, I appreciate the difficulties such a demand would place upon the arrangements already in place for the next three days. Consequently, as I said, I am prepared to allow the whole of your party, including Mr Everest to continue with your planned itinerary at least as far as the border on condition that you assume responsibility for them all.'

'I see.'

'In addition, I insist you report to me by telephone every day and ensure that Mr Everest reports in person at a police station each evening along your route.

'Naturally, I am happy to . . .'

Inspector Bauer held up a hand and continued, 'Before you agree, Mrs Mason, I need you to consider the consequences for you and your company should any of your passengers abscond.'

Fiona's eyes widened.

'Inspector,' Jäger interrupted, 'May I request that my client and I have a private conversation with Mrs Mason before she gives you her answer?'

It was a rhetorical question. The Inspector had little choice as evidenced by his scowl as he pushed himself up from the table and strode to the door.

'I appreciate that all this is all somewhat overwhelming, Mrs Mason.' Dieter Jäger smiled at her encouragingly once the door was closed.

'You could say that.' She turned to Travis. 'It's not that I don't trust you, Travis, but I have no idea exactly how I can be expected to stop you from disappearing off into the night as soon as we leave the station let alone Berlin. Or anyone else in the group for that matter.'

'Exactly.' It was Jäger who answered her. 'You have only known your passengers for a few short days. Hardly long enough to vouch for their characters. Inspector Bauer tried to insist that he retain Mr Everest's passport but as I pointed out, he will need that to book into each hotel every evening. I suggest that you take charge of Mr Everest's passport plus those belonging to the whole group. It might not physically prevent anyone absconding, but it will make it extremely difficult for them to leave Germany and to return home to England without it.'

Ten minutes later, Fiona was left alone in the interview room with Inspector Bauer whilst Dieter Jäger accompanied Travis to collect his belongings and sign the appropriate paperwork.

The Inspector picked up the loose sheets of paper lying in front of him, tapped the edges together on the table and placed them in his folder. He got to his feet and turned to her.

'That was a very astute move of yours, Mrs Mason, to hire the city's most expensive lawyer.' The glower he threw her was as much an indication of his annoyance as his tone of voice. 'I only hope your company thinks the same when it receives the bill for his services when I eventually make an arrest.'

With that, he stormed from the room before she had a chance to reply.

If Travis had been formally charged, then she might have thought to ask if there was any possibility of consulting their legal team, but it had never occurred to her to ask Head Office to consider such a move. They were aware that Travis was "helping the police with their enquiries". She had informed them when she had explained why the group was being made to stay an extra night at the Berlin Hilton. At the time, they had said nothing to her about providing Travis with a solicitor.

There was a knock on the door and Dieter Jäger entered.

'All the paperwork is now complete and Mr Everest will be with you any minute. Inspector Bauer is arranging for a car to return you both to your hotel, so I will take my leave. Before I do, may I give you my card? Should you encounter any difficulties in the next few days, please feel free to give me a call, Mrs Mason.'

She took his business card and asked with a frown, 'Are you anticipating any?'

He smiled and shook his head. 'Are you?'

'I would dearly love to know why the Inspector is so fixated on the idea that one of my party murdered Frederick. Apparently, he has other passengers on his suspect list.'

'So, I understand.'

'It just doesn't seem logical to me. We knew him for less than a day. Surely, the most obvious suspects must be someone he'd known for much longer. His family, his friends or colleagues or someone from his past.'

'I cannot comment on that, Mrs Mason, but I can assure you Inspector Bauer is a good officer and a fair one. If he is focussing on the Super Sun passengers, I am sure he has good reasons for doing so.' He put out a hand to shake hers. 'As I said Mrs Mason, please call me if you should encounter any problems with which I can help. Good day.'

Fiona watched him go, then slumped back in the chair. She should be elated. The party was now free to move on and Travis had been released albeit under restriction. All she could feel at the moment was exhaustion and bewilderment. Dieter Jäger had said that Inspector Bauer was a good officer, but she wasn't so sure. Highly intelligent and able, yes. The accent was still there but it was interesting how the fluency of his English had improved over the last few days. Presumably because of all the practice he was getting. However, if he was so fair, why did he seem to have it in for her group?

Travis was unusually quiet in the car on the way back to the hotel. He sat in the back seat alongside Fiona, clutching his laptop to his chest as though it was the most precious object he possessed.

'Everyone will be pleased to have you back with us again.'

Travis continued to look straight ahead as though in some sort of trance.

'Travis?'

He turned to her. 'Sorry, Fiona. I was miles away.'

'Are you feeling alright? You're very pale.'

He managed a wan smile. 'I'm fine. Just a bit shell-shocked. Nothing a good night's sleep won't put right.'

'Hopefully we'll be able to sneak in without being besieged by the others when we get back, so you can go straight up to your room.'

'That'd be good. I don't think I could face a barrage of questions right now.'

'No, I'm sure. Still you can put all this behind you now and tomorrow we can move on and forget about it all.'

'If only,' he said with a great sigh. 'I've still got to report into a police station every night. That Inspector won't rest until he has me up in court.'

She patted his hand. 'I shouldn't lose any sleep over Inspector Bauer, if I were you. If he had anything at all, he wouldn't have let you go, now would he? I think he was just trying not to lose face in front of Dieter Jäger.'

'I'd still be locked up in the cells if it wasn't for him.' He turned to face her. 'I can't thank you enough for contacting him.'

'I can't take the credit. It was someone at Super Sun Head Office.'

The car drew up outside the hotel. 'Let me go in first and see if the coast is clear.'

Once she had seen Travis back to his room, Fiona went up to her own on the floor above. She sat down on the bed, feeling utterly drained. It wasn't that late, just gone eleven o'clock, but there was an early start tomorrow.

She kicked off her shoes and rested back on the pillow. Not a good idea, she told herself. If she fell asleep now without bothering to get undressed, she wasn't likely to get a good night's rest. Besides there were things she needed to do before calling it a day.

First, she must ring Winston. With luck, he would still be awake.

'That's great news, sweetheart. Didn't I tell you not to worry?' he said after she had recounted the evening's events.

'I know we told everyone last night that we were off at eight o'clock tomorrow, but I wasn't convinced the Inspector would let us go. Having Travis back with us is a great weight off my mind.'

'There's no reason for you to worry anymore. You get a good night's sleep, sweetheart and I'll see you at breakfast around sevenish. Okay?'

'Good night, Winston.'

Just hearing Winston's reassuring lilt was enough to calm her. Even though the things she'd said to Travis about the Inspector letting him go were more to bolster his spirits, there was no reason not to believe them herself. She doubted the policeman would find anything to justify arresting Travis again for all the man's bravado. Besides, she had every confidence in Dieter Jäger.

Thinking of the lawyer reminded her that she needed to ring Head Office. There would be no one manning the office at this time of night, but she could leave a message on the answerphone. It wouldn't hurt to thank them for engaging Dieter Jäger either.

It was only as she was brushing her teeth some ten minutes later, that she remembered about Becky. She spat out the toothpaste, swilled the brush perfunctorily under the tap, and hurried back into the room to find her mobile.

Much to her surprise, there was no answer on the house phone. She checked her watch. Had she made a mistake? Surely it would be teatime over in Montreal. She wouldn't have expected Adam to be home yet, but Kristie liked to give the children their tea around now, so they had time to digest it before they went to bed. There could be all sorts of reasons. There was no point in leaping to the wrong conclusions. She put her phone back in her bag before she was tempted to try Adam's mobile. Even if he wasn't still working, he'd be driving home, and he'd have his phone switched off anyway.

If anything was wrong, Adam would have let her know, she tried to convince herself.

Day 7

Today we will enjoy the delights of Meissen, the "cradle" of Saxony, and one of its most famous cities. In 929, King Henry I established the town as the centre of German rule. His son, Emperor Otto the Great, founded a bishopric. In 1471, construction began on Albrechtsburg, the first German castle to be used as a royal residence.

Meissen's claim to fame is its porcelain. By 1710, the king had established the first porcelain factory in Europe in the castle. Production continued here until 1865 when it moved to a new site in the Triebisch river valley. It is here that we will make our first stop. We will see live demonstrations of the various stages of production and take a guided tour through the exhibition rooms.

After lunch, we will take a guided walk through the city. Meissen is built on hills, and many paths are steep and cobbled so be sure to wear stout footwear.

In the market square, we will see many well-preserved Renaissance-era buildings. The carillon of the Frauenkirche (Church of Our Lady) is composed of a beautiful set of porcelain bells set in a spectacular 175-foot-high tower rising over the square. Building work on the recently restored Rathaus began in 1471, making it one of the oldest town halls in Saxony. Its towers, woodwork and tiles combine to display a perfect example of mediaeval architecture.

Our walk then climbs up towards the castle and the cathedral where we will be rewarded with magnificent views. We will return to the centre down the charming Burgstrasse, a narrow cobblestone street lined with tiny shops selling local crafts.

We end our day in Meissen with a visit to a brewery where after a tour of the premises to see the various stages in the process, we will enjoy a beer tasting.

Super Sun Executive Travel

Chapter 18

Fiona sat stirring her coffee, deep in thought.

'Penny for them, sweetheart.' Winston settled himself in the chair opposite. For once, she was down to breakfast before him.

'Nothing really. Just daydreaming.'

'Did you check with the brewery how long your tour and the tasting are likely to be? The coach park is a good quarter of an hour away, so it would help to have an idea.'

'I'm so sorry! It went right out of my head.'

'Tha's not like you, sweetheart. You's usually so on the ball.'

'Well I've dropped it this time. I've had a lot on my mind just lately. I'll give them a ring before we leave.'

'Your posh chap been giving you grief?'

Fiona shook her head. 'No. Though having Peter Montgomery-Jones around never makes life easy.'

She picked up her cup and drank the last of her coffee.

'So, what's worrying you. Tell your Uncle Winston.'

She sat back stifling a giggle. Though he always acted with all the concern of a protective elderly relative, Winston was probably no more than a year a two older than Adam. Plus, more than anyone else she knew, he had the unerring ability to lighten her gloom. 'Travis is back and at long last we can leave Berlin and carry on with the tour as normal. What's there to worry about?'

'So why isn't you full of the joys of spring?'

Fiona sighed. It was no good. Winston would never let

go. 'I was thinking about my granddaughter, Becky.'

'Her cough no better?'

'That's just it, I've no idea. I tried to phone last night but there was no reply.'

Winston shook his head slowly and smiled. 'So you're busy telling yourself she's been taken real bad and they've rushed her off to hospital.'

She gave him a sheepish grin. 'Something like that. I know how foolish it is, but I can't help it.'

'My mammie's just the same about my sister's kiddies. She always says, "Worryin' is a mother's privilege." I reckon you're just like her. If you ain't got something to worry about, you worry even more.'

'I'm not that bad!' Fiona protested with a laugh.

'Then just you look on the bright side. If you ain't heard from your boy, then things are fine. He'd ring you soon enough if there was real crisis.'

'Point taken.'

'So off to that buffet table and get yourself something nice. You'll feel better with some good food inside you. You're such a slip of a thing, you'll waste away if you start not eating properly because you's pining away. And you know what they say, sweetheart; breakfast like a king, lunch like a prince…'

'And dine like a pauper,' she carolled with him.

She leant across the table and pointed to the small bowl of fruit and two slices of toast, which was all the food on his tray. 'Like you, you mean!'

It never ceased to amaze her how little the giant West Indian appeared to eat. Six feet four, broad-shouldered and he had to weigh at least eighteen stones, but she couldn't remember ever seeing him tuck into anything other than a modest meal. She had never seen him snacking. Even when she or any of the other passengers offered him sweets, biscuits or any of the local titbits, he always declined.

As expected, everyone made a great fuss of Travis when he

arrived in the reception area ready for the off. He was full of smiles and acting more or less like his old self although Fiona thought she could detect a definite strain around his eyes.

'Could I have your attention, everyone?' It wasn't just to deflect attention from the besieged Travis, she had been tasked with an onerous responsibility and she might as well see to it as soon as possible. 'Please make sure that you have not left your passport or any other valuables in your room safe. While we're on the subject of passports, I'm going to collect those now. It will be easier than when we get to the hotel this evening.'

She hadn't had time to think up any more plausible excuse as to why she was taking them in now, but no one questioned it or appeared to be reluctant to hand them over.

By the time everyone had sorted themselves out it was time to board the coach.

Travis occupied one of the single seats on the left side of the coach almost opposite the side door. The nearest of his fellow passengers was Peter Montgomery-Jones who was hardly likely to pester Travis about his previous day's experiences. Luckily, Rose, who was by far the most likely candidate to want a blow-by-blow account of his interrogation and incarceration, was seated at the front immediately behind Fiona, well out of chatting range with Travis.

Without a local guide, Fiona was free to resume her place at the front where she would be able to use the microphone.

'As you know we have a fairly long drive to get to Meissen. We will be making a short comfort stop on the way. I expect most of you would like to watch one of the programmes on your screens, so I won't keep pestering you, but if anyone would like me to make them a coffee or tea along the way, let me know.'

Although all Super Sun coaches had a drinks station by the side door, the itinerary allowed for regular coffee stops which meant few passengers ever made use of it.

Once they left the outskirts of Berlin and were on the open road, Fiona checked that everyone had settled down. Using the mirror that Winston had adjusted for her before they left Dover, she could see some were quietly chatting with their partners, some watching their screens and others looking out at the countryside. Morris already had his eyes closed.

Despite all David Rushworth's assurances that she need do no research for this trip, Fiona had slipped a couple of guidebooks into her luggage. On days like this, it might be useful to read up on the places they would be visiting. She pulled a copy of the Eyewitness Guide to Germany from her bag and sat back. Inevitably, there was only a short section on Meissen itself. Had things not been so frenetic while they were in Berlin, she might have found time to see what she could find on the internet. She would have to take the Tours Director at his word and hope nobody asked her any questions that she couldn't answer.

A little over an hour later, the coach pulled into a smart-looking service station. As Winston drew up alongside two much larger coaches, Fiona gently tapped the microphone to wake the dozers.

'This is only a short comfort stop.' She glanced at her watch. 'It's coming up to nine-forty. If you would like to get yourself a quick cup of coffee, that will be fine, but please be back on the coach by ten o'clock at the latest. Our visit to the Porcelain Factory is by timed tour so we cannot afford to be late arriving in Meissen.'

Henry was one of the last to the leave the coach. He looked a good deal happier than he had yesterday.

'I'm so sorry I never got back to you yesterday, Henry. Perhaps we could talk now?'

'Not to worry, Fiona. Problem solved.'

As he hurried off after his wife, Fiona shrugged and turned back to help Morris with his stick.

Once everyone had left, Fiona stood waiting while

Winston locked the coach.

'I know they will be secure in the coach, but I must confess I shall be a great deal happier when those passports are locked in the hotel safe this evening.'

'You're not worried that one of them is going to try and steal them?'

'No, not really, but Inspector Bauer put the fear of God into me when he made me responsible for everyone. I can't keep an eye on everyone all the time.'

He put a hand on her shoulder as they walked towards the building. 'You said you'self, he was just trying to bully you because he didn't get his own way. Besides, sweetheart, you do have me to help you.'

'Thank you, Winston. You're right as always. I really can't see any of these people running off into the night, no matter what the Inspector thinks.'

All except Peter Montgomery-Jones and Sonya, she thought. Not because they were responsible for Frederick's death, but for some reason to do with this mysterious mission of theirs.

Everyone crowded into the reception area waiting for the guide. Fiona glanced across at Travis. He stood next to Sol and Anna, listening to their conversation, giving the occasional smile but apparently contributing nothing.

A dark-haired, smartly dressed woman came through the doors. Their guide had arrived. She identified herself as Elsa and gave them a brief history of the porcelain manufacture from 1710 when August the Strong established the first factory in Albrechtsburg Castle to its present location.

'Even today, many of our designs still follow the baroque and rococo styles that were popular in those early days. Now ladies and gentlemen, if you would like to follow me, we will go through to the throwing studio where you can see a demonstration of the first stage in the process.'

As everyone sat around the display table watching the young bearded man moulding the wet clay, Fiona was able to observe her charges. The colour was gradually returning to Travis's face but the strain of the last couple of days was still etched on his features. It was doubtful that he was taking in much of Elsa's explanation of what the potter was doing.

It wasn't surprising that it was the women who asked more questions in the plate painting and figure moulding studios. For once, even Sonya showed an interest in what was going on.

'You can appreciate why Meissen is so expensive when you see what is involved in making it, can't you?' Anna said enthusiastically as Fiona held open the door to the last studio for her.

'Especially when every piece is handmade and hand-painted,' Fiona agreed.

'I asked that lady we saw in the painting studio how long she'd been doing it and she said forty-one years. Fancy that. What are we doing now?'

'I believe Elsa is taking us to the museum.'

Anna and Fiona were the last to join the group waiting at the bottom of an impressive white and gilt double staircase. A stunning ten-foot-high white porcelain tower rose up to the second floor. Several people were already taking photos of the intricate figures at its base and it was several minutes before Elsa could get everyone's attention.

'This area is our museum. It constitutes the most comprehensive collection of Meissen porcelain anywhere. There are 3000 pieces on display dating from 1710 right up to the present day. These are arranged chronologically to illustrate design developments through the ages. You are free to wander through the various rooms at your leisure. Please enjoy and don't forget to take a look in our shop alongside the entrance before you leave.'

Everyone gradually drifted away.

Fiona had a momentary qualm over lunch when she saw Travis had ordered a bottle of wine with his meal. True, he was offering it round to the other two couples on his table, but she had little doubt that he would consume most of it himself. It wasn't as if she grudged him a glass, even two – the man was a hardened drinker – but a whole bottle so early in the day could only lead to trouble. She could only hope that it wasn't the start of a hard day's drinking. There was nothing she could do about it. She could hardly march over and confiscate it.

'When you said we'd be going to the porcelain factory, I thought we'd be going into the actual production area and see them actually making things rather than just demonstrations,' said Barbara Wolf, bringing Fiona's attention back to her own table.

'It is more of a tourist attraction than a factory tour,' she agreed.

'Barbara was particularly keen to see it, weren't you love? She did pottery at night school for years.'

'Nothing like that though,' said his wife shaking her head. 'Our efforts may have been handmade and painted, but out of good old thick clay not fine porcelain.'

'Maybe, but you made some lovely pieces. Everyone remarks on that green vase in the hall. It's just the thing to show off the roses in the late summer.'

Barbara gave an embarrassed grin. 'I confess, I am rather proud of that piece.'

The conversation continued around her. Fiona smiled and nodded in what she hoped was the right places, but her concentration was constantly being drawn back to Travis and what was happening on the other table. It didn't help that the afternoon itinerary included a visit to a brewery.

Chapter 19

The afternoon walk began in the town's main square with its distinct medieval atmosphere. It was here that the party met up with Brigitte, their local guide.

'Let me begin with the most impressive feature here in the Market Square, the Frauenkirche or perhaps I should say its spectacular tower looming above us, displaying the beautiful carillon of handmade porcelain bells. This church was the very first to have a set of bells made of porcelain and they chime a different tune six times a day.'

Everyone craned their necks to look up at the tiers of delicate, white china bells halfway up the tall tower arranged in a shallow arched recess.

'They're very small,' said Rose. 'I was expecting something much bigger.'

'But there are a lot of them,' said Faith.

Several people started to count.

'Thirty-seven,' said Henry triumphantly, pipping the others to the post. There were nods of agreement.

Henry was definitely in a good mood, Fiona decided. She had never seen him as lively as he'd been today. All the time they were in Berlin, he'd been quiet, almost subdued, especially the last few days. Frederick's death had inevitably had a sobering effect on the whole party, but in Henry's case perhaps returning to the city of his birth, with its memories of the trauma suffered by the people he had left behind, had added to the sense of oppression he must have experienced.

Brigitte walked them round the edge of the large open

square, pointing out the well-preserved Renaissance and neo-Renaissance houses until she came to a stop by the Town Hall.

'The Rathaus was built between 1471 and 1486 by the councillors of Meissen. This makes it one of the oldest in Saxony.'

Leaving Berlin may have lifted Henry's spirits, but Travis looked anything but content. Fiona doubted if anything that Brigitte had told them so far had gone in at all. The journalist looked deflated, almost unaware of what was going on around him. He should be the jubilant one – happy to be free from Inspector Bauer's clutches at last – but he looked as though he carried the weight of the world on his shoulders.

The next section of the walk was a relatively steep climb up a series of narrow lanes and steps towards the castle of Albrechtsburg, but Brigitte led them slowly and stopped at frequent intervals to point out particular features. Eventually they came to a halt outside a small, rather insignificant-looking shop.

'If you would all like to wait here for me for a moment while I buy you a cake.'

Eyebrows were raised as Brigitte disappeared inside. A few minutes later, she reappeared balancing a paper bag in one hand.

She removed her gloves very carefully and handed them to Fiona to hold while she opened the bag and slowly eased out its contents.

'It's a loaf of bread,' said Rose, sounding disappointed.

'Oh no,' protested Brigitte. 'This is a flummel.'

She offered it to Rose and said, 'Break a piece off.'

'It's as light as a feather.' As soon as Rose pinched finger and thumb on the shell-like surface of the tortoise-shaped confection, a hole appeared, revealing that there was nothing inside. 'It's empty.'

'Some people compare it to an ostrich egg,' agreed Brigitte. 'King Augustus was very upset about the amount of breakages when his precious porcelain was transported from the castle factory by barge downstream for twenty-five kilometres along the River Elbe to his palace in Dresden. He had the local baker devise this cake. As you see this is quite delicate, so these flummel were packed with the porcelain and if the bargee could not present an unbroken flummel when they arrived in Dresden, he did not get paid.'

The flummel was passed round and everyone broke off a small piece to try.

'If you ask me,' muttered Walter, 'that's about all it's good for. It's pretty tasteless and hardly satisfying, so I can't think why anyone would buy it to eat.'

'I think it's just a novelty,' said Fiona. 'Though I can't imagine many tourists will be able to get them back home in one piece, do you?'

It was still some way up to the castle and the cathedral at the top of the hill, so Brigitte gave everyone the option of either continuing up the steps to the top or walking back down the steep narrow cobblestone Burgstrasse leading down to the market square.

'You will find many small shops along the way selling a variety of local crafts and also wine. Meissen is the centre of the Saxon wine region.'

Though Fiona was not a beer drinker, having been in the job for almost a year now, she was aware that it had become almost as popular a drink for many of her women passengers as it was for the men. Therefore, it came as no surprise that there was a fair amount of excitement as everyone began to gather at the meeting point in front of **the Frauenkirche, waiting for Brigitte to lead them to the brewery.**

The general chatter was brought to a halt as the liquid melody of the carillon in the church tower sounded across the square to mark the hour. Everyone looked up at the rows of porcelain bells as they danced with the tune.

There were cries of approval and spontaneous clapping

when the musical chimes ceased.

The brewery was less than a five-minute walk away. After they had been shown the huge brass vats and listened to the various stages in the process, everyone shuffled through to the tasting hall and found a place on either side of the long trestle table. Fiona had intended to ensure that she sat next to Travis, but a question from Sol as they were leaving the production area held her back and Travis ended up sitting at the far end of the table. She wasn't unduly worried. She had been to enough wine tastings on her trips with Super Sun to appreciate that the thimblefuls of alcohol they were offered were hardly likely to have much effect. Her eyes widened when she saw the three-quarter full tankards placed in front of each of them. The tankards may have been relatively small, but knowing there were two more varieties to come, each stronger than the last, did little to ease her sense of foreboding.

'This is the light beer,' announced their brewery guide.

'You're not going to try it, Fiona?' asked Sol.

Fiona shook her head.

'It would be a pity to waste it.'

With a laugh, she pushed the glass tankard towards him.

In quick time, two more tankards were passed in his direction. Glancing across the table, Fiona could see a couple of the wives taking a sip or two before passing the glasses to their husbands. Travis was too far away for her to see what was happening at his end of the table. All she could do was offer a silent prayer.

Fiona was relieved when the time came to leave. While everyone collected coats and made themselves ready, Fiona decided to pop outside to ring and let Winston know they were on their way.

After her call, she turned to go back inside, almost bumping into someone who burst out of the door.

'I'm so sorry . . .'

He had rushed away before she had a chance to finish her

sentence.

Turning back, she came face to face with Peter, a deep frown on his handsome face.

'Did you notice a man leaving the brewery just now? Middle-aged, average height and wearing a thick padded navy jacket.'

'He almost bumped into me.'

'Have you seen him before?'

'To be honest, Peter, he was gone so quickly I didn't take much notice of what he looked like. Why? Is it important?'

'He was just behind us most of the morning. The thing is, he looks very much like the same man who was following us in Wittenberg yesterday.'

'That's perfectly possible, isn't it? It might be the low season but there must be hundreds of tourists all going to the same places we are.'

'That is true. But what was he doing coming in here?'

'Picking up leaflets on the brewery tours?'

'Possibly, but as soon as he saw me walking towards him, he rushed out of the door?'

'Are you suggesting someone is following our party?' He didn't answer, but he didn't deny it either. 'Can you be sure? There are a great many middle-aged men wearing dark padded jackets wandering round. It's a major tourist region.'

The rest of the party began to crowd into the small entrance area. There was no opportunity to continue their conversation.

He shook his head, gave her a quick smile and said quietly, 'You are correct of course. All the same, if you do notice him again, will you tell me?'

'Of course.'

'Thank you.'

Though he had readily agreed with her suggestion, it was obvious that he was worried that someone was keeping a tail on the party, or more specifically given his line of work, Peter himself and Sonya.

With all that had been going on, she had given little

thought lately to Peter's mission and who his strange companion might be. Fiona had found it difficult to take to the woman and the feeling appeared to be mutual. Quite what she'd done to offend the woman she wasn't sure. Fiona had to admit, after a stuttering start, Sonya had made an effort to ingratiate herself with the other passengers, but there was always a certain tension between the two of them. A definite mutual wariness. How much of that was down to Fiona herself, she wasn't sure.

Once they were all outside, Brigitte led the short distance to the rendezvous for the coach pick up. Fiona fell into step behind Sol and Travis. She only caught snatches of their conversation, but they appeared to be discussing the merits of the various beers they'd just been tasting. If anything, Sol seemed to be the merrier of the two and Travis even managed a smile, which was a definite improvement on his distracted state of that morning.

Everyone said goodbye to Brigitte and Fiona did a double check that no one had been left behind before sinking down into her seat at the front. She closed her eyes momentarily. When she opened them again, she caught Winston smiling at her in his rear-view mirror.

'That bad, was it?' he mouthed at her.

She grinned back and shook her head.

'Then relax, sweetheart. Take the tension out of those shoulders,' he said softly.

She kneaded the back of her neck with her fingers, forcing her whole body to relax. Winston had a point; she really must learn to stop worrying about her passengers. It wasn't good for her own state of health.

Their hotel in Dresden was considerably smaller than the Berlin Hilton. Fiona handed out the room keys, keeping Travis's until last. Most of the others had already picked up their hand luggage and moved off towards the lifts.

'Room 316 which is on the third floor,' she said, deliberately taking time to double-check the number on the small key card envelope with her list, to ensure that no one else was in earshot.

Travis hoisted his rucksack over one shoulder, muttered his thanks, took the envelope and turned to go.

'Just a second, Travis.' Fiona pulled a folded sheet of notepaper from her bag and held it out. 'This is the address of the nearest police station to the hotel for you to check in. I've jotted down the directions as well.'

He scowled, but when he saw the expression on her face, he quickly turned it into a grimace. 'Thanks.'

'I know it's a bind, Travis, but it's a great deal better than the alternative.'

He sighed and nodded. 'Best get it over with, I suppose. I'll dump my stuff in my room and go and find it.'

'Good idea. If anyone does see you, they'll think you've just popped out for some air or to the local shops.'

'You haven't told anyone?' He sounded surprised.

'Of course not. It's your private business. What you choose to tell them is entirely up to you.'

He took a step towards her and put a hand on her shoulder. 'Thanks, Fiona. For everything.'

He hurried away before she had a chance to reply.

Once again, the restaurant had arranged for them to sit in two groups of eight. Two sets of small square tables had been pushed together. As the room was relatively small and their reserved tables could be easily picked out, Fiona decided there was no need for her to wait at the door for everyone to come down and once the first few were seated, she went to join them. There was a place at the end of the table between Gary and Loraine Peters. Rose and Faith were also sitting across the table from one another.

'I'm not sure if it was all those steps up to the cathedral or the beer, but I confess I'm pretty knackered this evening,' said Loraine.

'We didn't bother to go right up to the top. Was it good?' asked Rose.

'Unfortunately, the cathedral was closed, but the view up there was spectacular.'

They were joined by Peter and Sonya. Sonya took the seat next to Faith but unlike the other two couples who had chosen to sit opposite each other, Peter took the chair at the head of the table. Fiona wondered if any of the others noticed how close a rein he liked to keep on his so-called wife.

The waitress was hovering, waiting to take their orders, but there was still an empty place.

'Who is missing?' asked Sonya looking across at the other table.

'It must be Travis. He is the only single in the party,' Rose answered.

'Oh yes,' Sonya gave one of those smiles that never quite reached her eyes. 'I expect he is still getting ready. I saw him coming back into the hotel half an hour ago. I was too far away to ask him where he had been.'

Quite why Sonya was stirring it, Fiona couldn't imagine. Before Sonya could start speculating, Fiona picked up her menu and said, 'Is anyone ready to order? The Saxony pork with potato dumplings sounds interesting.'

Travis eventually arrived after the others had all given their orders.

'Sorry I'm late,' he mumbled as he slid onto the spare seat opposite Sonya. 'Forgot the time.'

His face was flushed though there was nothing in his walk or speech to suggest he was drunk. Fiona's heart sank when he signalled the wine waiter. She was too far away to hear what he had asked for.

Peter caught her eye. He gave her a half smile, glanced at Travis and back at her giving a barely perceptible nod of the head. He knew her too well. He must have realised she was worried about Travis's drinking and was letting her know he would keep an eye on the situation. It was oddly reassuring but disconcerting at the same time. He could read her like a book.

The first half of the meal passed pleasantly enough, and it wasn't until they were all tucking into their apple strudels that the tension began to mount.

'Why do you keep looking at me like that?' Sonya glared across the table at Travis.

Travis sat back in his chair, his hands raised, whether in apology or for protection, it was difficult to tell. 'Sorry, old girl. Didn't mean to upset you. It's only that you remind me of someone, but I can't think who.'

'Do not call me "old girl",' she snapped.

Peter put a steadying hand on her arm.

'Everyone has a double somewhere; don't they say?' Loraine said with a laugh. 'My sister-in-law is the spitting image of that actress who played the girlfriend in Spectre, the James Bond movie. What was the character's name?' She clicked her fingers. 'Madeleine something or other. But don't ask me the actor's name.'

'Swann. Madeleine Swann and the actor's name was Léa Seydoux.' Rose clapped her hands, shaking her fair curls in girlish glee. 'I loved that film.'

Throughout the animated discussion that followed discussing everyone's favourite Bond film and which actor had been the best James Bond, Fiona sensed there was a definite atmosphere at the far end of the table and it didn't help that Travis beckoned to the wine waiter yet again. She watched Travis push away his plate and sit back nursing what she assumed was a glass of whiskey. The only consolation was that he wasn't one of those belligerent drunks eager to pick a fight. Presumably, Peter had decided that trying to stop him drinking would only cause a scene and it was best to let the man drink himself into a stupor.

When the time came for them all to leave, Peter and Gary stood either side of Travis and all but frog-marched him out to the lifts. Sonya did not look happy at being deserted but she followed the others to the lounge for coffee. As if by mutual consent, no one commented on Travis's behaviour. There was something to be said for the natural tendency of the British to avoid unpleasant scenes, Fiona decided.

The rest of the party had settled themselves into the comfortable chairs by the time Gary joined them. It was a good ten minutes later when Peter slipped unobtrusively back into the group. He gave Fiona a brief nod and sat down on the end of the deep settee next to Sonya.

The party broke up not long after they had finished coffee. The early start and the long journey all the way from Berlin had clearly taken their toll. By ten o'clock, there was only a handful of people left in the lounge. Peter, Sonya, Gary and Loraine were discussing some of the porcelain figurines they had seen in the Meissen museum and Gary was showing them all some of the photos he'd taken of his favourite pieces. Fiona was waiting for a lull in the conversation to make her apologies and slip up to her room when Faith rushed back into the room.

'Fiona, may I have a word?'

Putting an arm around the clearly agitated woman, Fiona led her to a quiet corner where they wouldn't be overheard.

'Whatever's the matter?'

'It's my son. There's been an accident. He was involved in a pile-up on the motorway and he's been taken to hospital. I've got to get home as soon as possible.'

It took a few minutes for Fiona to sort out the details. Faith had received a phone call from Frenchay Hospital in Bristol. Her son had been brought in earlier in the evening following an accident on the M32. He was now out of theatre and although stable, was in a serious condition.

'Dresden does have an international airport. Let me go and see how soon I can get you a flight.'

Before Fiona could hurry out to reception, Faith took hold of her arm to hold her back. 'No need. I've already spoken to the young man on the desk and he's arranging that for me now.'

Day 8

Today we will explore Dresden, the "Florence of the north", the glory of the Elbe and one of Germany's most beautiful cities. In the 12th century, the Margraves of Meissen built a fortress to protect the passage across the Elbe and the town soon grew up around it. From 1465 to 1918, the city was ruled by the Albertine dukes of the house of Wettin, all portrayed in the 331-feet-long mosaic of Meissen porcelain which covers the façade of the long walk at the Royal Stables.

With its magnificent baroque buildings built by Augustus the Strong in the 18th century, the city became a cultural capital. Many of these were destroyed by the carpet-bombing of the city in WWII. The city's reconstruction began in the 1950s and the historic centre, including the glorious Frauenkirche (Church of Our Lady) with its 311-feet dome, has been faithfully restored to its former splendour.

This morning we will take a guided walk to admire some of the city's highlights. The Semper Opera House built in the High Renaissance style marks a high point of 19th-century theatre architecture and the Zwinger Palace is considered an outstanding example of baroque fortification construction. After lunch, we will visit the Green Vault founded in 1723 by Augustus the Strong and which contains the largest collection of treasures in Europe.

There will be free time for you to explore Dresden. You may wish to visit one of the city's many museums such as the Gemäldegalerie Alte Meister (the Old Masters Picture Gallery), Hofkirche – the monumental Baroque royal church which contains the heart of Augustus the Strong, the reconstructed Frauenkirche or simply take a stroll through the streets of the Old Town.

Super Sun Executive Travel

Chapter 20

The jarring note of her mobile woke Fiona with a start. It took her a few seconds to work out what was happening. She struggled to her elbow and reached across to the bedside table. It was not quite pitch-black, there was a hint of light under the door from the corridor but not enough to see her phone. Her hand groped about on the small surface cluttered with her book, reading glasses and assorted paraphernalia. Something fell to the floor.

'Damn, damn, damn.'

She found the switch for the bedside light and snapped it on. Her mobile lay half hidden under the bed.

'Hello.'

'Mum! It's Adam.'

Her heart lurched. 'Is everything alright? What on earth is that noise in the background? Where are you?'

'We're at the hospital. We had a bit of a crisis yesterday with Becky. She's a lot better now and the doctor's told us she's going to be fine, but it was touch and go for a while.'

'Thank goodness. What happened?'

'She didn't have a very good day yesterday and when she went to bed, her cough got worse. We had to bring her downstairs again and then she started crying which made things even worse. She was having trouble breathing and making these dreadful whooping noises. We bundled up Adam Junior and rushed her straight here. They put her on oxygen straightaway. Anyway, to cut a long story short, they've decided she has croup. I never realised it could be so serious.'

'It isn't normally.'

'I don't understand why the doctor didn't diagnose it earlier.'

'Well it is a lot more common in babies and in boys rather than girls.'

'That's no excuse. The surgery didn't want to know on Tuesday. The doctor just fobbed us off over the phone.'

'Even if he'd seen her, I doubt he would have been able to diagnose things at that stage. Children go downhill very quickly.'

'I forget sometimes you were a nurse. It's a pity you weren't here. You'd have spotted it earlier.'

'I doubt it, so stop trying to make me feel guilty. What's happening now?'

'They've given her something to reduce the swelling in her throat, but they're keeping her in just in case there are any complications. Not that they've told us what they might be, but the doctor did say that she's definitely over the worst.'

It sounded as though he was yawning. Fiona glanced at the clock.

'You must be exhausted. It's the middle of the night over there. It sounds as though you need to get some sleep. What's happened to Adam Junior?'

'He's here, asleep in his pushchair. Kristie wants to stay here obviously, but I'm about to take him home and grab a few hours' shuteye myself.'

'Sounds like a good idea. Give everyone my love and tell them you're all in my prayers. If you get a moment, give me a ring to let me know how things are going in the morning. Night, darling.'

'Night, Mum.'

Fiona looked at the digital clock by the bedside and groaned. 06.05. It had gone midnight when she'd left Faith's room, but there was no point in trying to go back to sleep now.

Faith would be leaving for the airport in ten minutes. If

she rushed down now, she might just be in time to catch her.

The receptionist had arranged for a taxi to get Faith there in time for the first available flight to Bristol. Quickly she threw on a few clothes and hurried downstairs. She dashed along the short corridor into reception to see Rose coming back inside through the entrance doors.

'You've only just missed her.' Rose gave Fiona a rueful smile.

'At least she had you to see her off.'

'I wanted to go with her to the airport, but Faith insisted that was pointless. I couldn't have got past security.'

'How was she this morning?'

'A lot calmer, but she didn't get much sleep last night.'

'Hardly surprising. I don't suppose you got much either.'

Rose pulled a face. 'Not a lot. I'm going straight back to bed. I've still got my pyjamas on underneath this lot. I'll skip breakfast, but I'll be down in time for the tour.'

Fiona had no such option. Apart from anything else, there was her breakfast meeting with Winston, and she would have to inform Head Office as soon as it was open.

'You don't look a happy bunny, sweetheart. That journalist chap causing problems again?'

Fiona looked up at Winston as he joined her at the breakfast table.

'No. Well sort of, but quite honestly that's the least of my problems.'

She told him about Faith.

'Poor, poor lady.'

'Her plane leaves mid-morning. Unfortunately, it's not a direct flight to Bristol, but at least there is only the one connection to make in Frankfurt. Even so, she won't get there until early evening. There was an earlier flight to Heathrow via Düsseldorf with a shorter stop over but then she'd have had all the hassle of getting a train or a coach all the way across to Bristol.'

Looking uncharacteristically solemn, Winston said, 'There's nothing more you can do to help. No point in you worrying. What's the problem with the reporter chap?'

'Travis? It's nothing really.' She gave a weary sigh and put down the cup she'd been cradling in both hands. 'It's just that he was drinking heavily last evening and had to be put to bed. Heaven knows what state he'll be in this morning. He's probably still sleeping it off. I suppose I'd better check up on him after breakfast. Part of me says, it might make my day a great deal easier if he didn't come out with the rest of us today, but then I'd only worry that without me to keep an eye on him, he'd spend the whole time drinking himself into a stupor and causing even more problems I'd have to sort out later.'

Feeling utterly exhausted, she pushed her plate away, put her elbows on the table and dropped her head in her hands.

A moment or two later, she felt a massive hand on her shoulder.

'Now that don't sound like the Fiona Mason I know. Not one little bit. Somethin's up. Is you stressing about that little granddaughter of yours?'

The waitress chose that moment to approach. 'Tea or coffee, sir?'

'Tea please.'

'Help yourself to cereal or continental breakfast on the cold table under the window and hot dishes are over there, sir.' She waved a hand in the direction of the far wall where a man in whites and a tall chef's hat was preparing omelettes and fried eggs to order at the end of the table laden with a line of large heated silver serving dishes.

'Thank you, miss.' Winston turned back to Fiona, raised a questioning eyebrow and waited. It was clear he was not to be diverted.

She nodded. 'I had a phone call from my son first thing this morning. Becky is in hospital.'

'That's not good.' Winston shook his head. 'Have they said what's wrong with the poor little mite?'

'The doctors have diagnosed croup.'

'Is that serious?'

'Not usually but it can lead to complications such as pneumonia and middle-ear infections, which I presume is why the hospital wants to keep her in for a short while.'

Fiona did her best to manage a smile. That was the trouble with having a medical background. Knowing just what could go wrong didn't always help.

Once the business of the day's arrangements had been confirmed, Winston went to check on the coach. Fiona was in no rush to leave the restaurant. Their tour of Dresden was not due to start until nine-thirty and their local guide would not be at the hotel until half an hour before that. As she poured herself a last cup of tea, a few of more of her passengers began to arrive.

'Good morning. You both slept well I hope.'

'Yes, thank you, Fiona.' Anna and Sol took their seats and began to discuss what they were going to have for breakfast.

Before long they were joined by Loraine and Gary Peters.

'Anyone catch the news before they came down?' asked Gary.

'I make a point of deliberately *not* watching it when I'm on holiday,' said Anna with feeling. 'It never seems to be good news these days. It's always about fighting breaking out as rebels try to take another city or a group of religious fanatics causing mayhem. Either that or some natural disaster like an earthquake or a volcanic eruption and the last thing I want is to feel depressed.'

Not to be deterred, Gary carried on, 'I only turned on the television to get the weather forecast but managed to catch the end of the news. Have any of you been following all this fuss they seem to be making over this Ukrainian politician who they speculate was captured by the separatists?'

'I thought she'd been rescued,' said Anna. 'Wasn't she in a Russian convoy that was attacked on its way to the border?'

'So they say, but there's been no sign of Natalia Shevchenko ever since. If she was rescued by the Ukrainian forces why isn't she back in Kiev denouncing the Russians for all she's worth?' Gary shook his head.

'Well the Russians would hardly have killed their own troops, so presumably it wasn't them either,' said Sol.

'Once the remains of the convoy were found, the Russians could hardly deny she had been in their hands but according to the news report, they're now claiming she was some sort of spy for the West.'

'It all sounds a bit suspect to me.' There were nods of agreement all round.

'Seems that's also the excuse the Russians are using for walking out on the latest international peace talks claiming that the West can't be trusted.'

'I can't see how those talks were achieving anything anyway. As soon as they agree a ceasefire between the Ukrainians and the separatists, one or other side breaks it before the ink is even dry on the paper.' Anna pushed aside her now empty cereal bowl and glanced over to the hot buffet.

'So where do they think this Natalia is now?' Fiona asked Gary.

'That's what they were talking about on the news programme. If she was actually spying for one of the Western powers, the likelihood is that they mounted the rescue and have whisked her out of the country. It explains why the Russians sent so many military units into that area to try to find her before she can pass on valuable info.'

'How would she be able to get hold of anything likely to be of use to any of the Western Powers? It's not as though she was a Kremlin insider or anything,' said Anna. 'I appreciate that there are still pro-Russian elements in the Ukrainian Government they might be interested in but I can't see why the Russians would see her as so great a threat that they'd mount such a major operation.'

'Perhaps it's just an excuse to overrun the area with

Russian troops,' suggested Loraine.

'Possibly,' agreed Gary. 'But don't forget, she was married to that Russian Colonel. Through him she would have moved among some pretty important circles.'

'Wouldn't that information be far too dated to be of any significance now?' said Loraine.

Fiona glanced at her watch. If she was going to check up on Travis, it was time for her to make a move. Making her apologies, she slipped away.

There was no need for Fiona to let the rest of the party know about Faith's return to England. As soon as everyone began to gather in the foyer ready for the morning walk, Rose was quick to pass on the details and the news spread throughout the group.

It was no surprise that they were ten minutes late setting out than planned. Thankfully, once Fiona explained the situation, their local guide, a dumpy middle-aged woman, was understanding. Ludwiga was dressed in an over-long bulky navy coat with a multi-coloured Andean-style knitted woollen cap complete with earmuffs and flapping tassels. Despite her somewhat strange appearance, Ludwiga had a pleasing voice with little accent.

Much as Fiona enjoyed the walk up to the massive circular Opera House and on to the ornate **Zwinger Palace** with its extensive grounds, she found her thoughts constantly returning to the plight of her eldest grandchild. Her hand clutched her mobile inside her coat pocket, willing it to ring.

They made a stop at one of the cafés for coffee and as everyone filed in and found themselves places to sit; Fiona hovered in the doorway. Should she take the opportunity to ring Adam? She caught the eye of the guide who gave her a beaming smile. Ludwiga clearly expected Fiona to join her, so Fiona made her way over.

Fiona let the guide do most of the talking and she had almost finished her coffee when her phone began to burble. Dropping her cup back in its saucer with a clatter, Fiona jumped to her feet.

'Please forgive me. This call is probably important.' Without waiting for a reply, she rushed outside. 'Hello.'

'Mrs Mason, it's David Rushworth. Is it convenient to talk at the moment?'

Fiona took a deep breath and tried to steady her jangling nerves. Obviously, the message she'd left at Head Office had been picked up, but it was still a surprise that the Tours Director himself should phone her.

'Certainly, sir. We're on a coffee break at the moment.'

'Good, good. Firstly, thank you for your message about Mrs Reynolds having to return home and I was pleased to hear that Mr Everest has been released from custody. That's all sorted now, I hope?'

'Yes, sir,' she lied. Little point in telling him about Travis's drunken display last night, especially as the reporter had made a point of coming to apologise for his behaviour and giving her his assurance that he would not let it happen again.

'We are back on schedule. In the end, having to stay another night in Berlin didn't cause us too many problems, but we've moved on to Dresden and things are going well.'

'Good, good. Let's hope things run a little more smoothly from now on.'

She had wondered if he would complain about the extra expense, but he didn't sound annoyed. 'Thank you again for arranging for a solicitor to represent Mr Everest. I doubt we'd have been able to get Travis out of police custody without his help.'

'I did nothing.' He sounded surprised. 'I assumed you were the one who engaged him.'

'It wasn't me.' Fiona frowned. 'The first thing I knew was when the Inspector rang to say Dieter Jäger was already at the police station. I took it for granted that someone at Head Office had arranged for him to act for Mr Everest. That's why I left the message to thank you.'

'I see. Well, I can assure you no one here knows anything

about it.'

Fiona was lost for words.

'Perhaps Mr Everest hired him directly. No matter. All's well that ends well, as they say. I'll let you get on. If you do solve the mystery, do let me know, won't you?'

'Certainly, sir.'

The phone went dead, leaving Fiona standing staring into space. It wasn't until she realised her un-gloved hands were starting to hurt with the cold that she shook herself from her reverie and went back into the warmth of the café.

Chapter 21

Ludwiga, their local guide, had promised them a true treasure chamber in the Green Vault and from the oohs and aahs as they wandered from the Amber Cabinet, through the Ivory, White Silver and Jewel Rooms to the Hall of Precious Objects, her audience was not disappointed.

'That is truly amazing.' Anna Stein wasn't the only one to be transfixed by the model they were now all clustered around.

'Created by the court goldsmith Johann Dinglinger, it depicts the Royal Household at Delhi celebrating the Grand Mogul's birthday,' their guide informed them.

'The figures are so tiny but each one is absolutely perfect. The detail is amazing,' said Elsie Danby. 'And all those jewels. It must be priceless.'

Ludwiga nodded. 'It contains 4,909 diamonds, 164 emeralds, 160 rubies, a sapphire and 16 pearls. Augustus the Strong paid more for this single artwork than he did for the construction of Moritzburg Castle.'

Fiona was so absorbed in admiring the model that she had failed to keep an eye on those members of the group who had wandered off. After an initial tour of the most prominent pieces in the collection, Ludwiga had given them time to explore on their own to look in more detail at the objects that had interested them.

She looked around for Travis and her heart gave a small flip when she realised that he had left the room. It wasn't just the chance of him absconding, not that she considered that a serious possibility no matter what Inspector Bauer might think, it was Travis's drinking that concerned her. First thing this morning, he had promised faithfully he would not get drunk again for the rest of the tour. However, she had made a mental note that he had not actually said anything about abstaining altogether. To expect him to do that was probably akin to asking a child not to eat sweets. Telling herself there was no cause for alarm, that this was hardly a place where Travis would find an opportunity to start hitting the bottle again, she strode towards the next room.

When she reached the doorway, she spotted Travis talking with Henry in the far corner. Travis had his back to her, so she couldn't read his expression but from his rigid stance Henry did not appear happy. If they were arguing, as Fiona suspected, they were keeping their voices low. Neither man appeared to want to make a scene. Suddenly, she saw Henry bunch his fist. He obviously thought better of it and turned away sharply. Fiona found herself having to jump out of his way and Henry stormed through the doorway back to his wife who was still admiring the golden coffee service by the master craftsman Dinglinger in the previous room.

Was there no end to Travis's propensity for causing trouble? Today wasn't the first time he'd managed to upset someone in the party. His snide comments were getting out of hand. Much more of this and she'd have to ask him to leave the group altogether. It had never happened to her before, but there was a clause in the small print about the penalty of unreasonable behaviour in the terms and conditions that all passengers were asked to sign.

Ludwiga led the party back to the main square. Before leaving them, she made sure they all had copies of the town map and pointed out the way to the main sites. As Ludwiga said her goodbyes, Fiona was still debating with herself about whether or not to read the riot act to Travis before they all departed to go their own way for the rest of the afternoon. In the event, by the time Fiona had finished thanking the guide, Travis was long gone. Best not to think about where, and mother hen she might be, but she had no intention of spending the rest of her afternoon searching the town's bars.

Fiona had had little time to consider her own plans for the next few hours. The Frauenkirche was a definite possibility and it was only a relatively short distance away. Ludwiga had told them something of the church's reconstruction as a symbol of Saxony's rebirth following reunification but they had only spent a few minutes inside. Far too little time to appreciate its full magnificence. Besides which, a few quiet words with the Almighty on Becky's behalf would not come amiss.

Fiona was not the only one heading for the church. Some fifty yards ahead, she spotted Peter and Sonya strolling in the same direction.

A thought suddenly struck her. The phone call she had earlier from David Rushworth about arranging the lawyer for Travis. Apart from Head Office, the only person who had known Travis was in custody was Peter. He had been adamant that he was in no position to help but who else could it be? He'd said he was not prepared to intervene with the police or arrange for official pressure from his department but a discreet arrangement with a local lawyer was unlikely to jeopardise his mission whatever that might be. The more she thought about it, the more it made sense.

She'd been so angry with him at the time and had made her displeasure obvious ever since by having as little to do with him as possible. She'd hardly exchanged more than a few words in the last couple of days. He had wished her good morning when they were within ten feet of each other at the breakfast bar this morning, but she had pretended she hadn't even seen him and turned the other way. It was bad enough that she was still nurturing a grudge but to find out that he had gone out of his way to help the situation made her realise just how petty her behaviour had been. He was probably paying for Dieter Jäger out of his own pocket and presumably, the lawyer had not come cheap.

Her mobile started burbling as she stood in the main aisle looking up at the tiers of balconies that drew the eye to the impressive altarpiece and crowning organ. Quickly backtracking to the main door, she prayed that Adam would not ring off before she got outside.

'Mrs Mason.' Not Adam, but not a voice she immediately recognised. 'This is Detective Inspector Bauer.'

She waited for him to continue.

'I hope I have not disturbed your afternoon. I checked the itinerary you gave me, and I see your party have been given some free time to do as they wish.'

'Yes, Inspector.' Presumably then, his call was not urgent. 'If you are ringing to check that Travis is still with us, the answer is yes. I did promise that I would inform you immediately if he disappeared.'

'I am glad to hear Mr Everest is with you.' For once, the man sounded quite chipper. 'I wanted to let you know that we are close to making an arrest.'

'I am pleased to hear it. Perhaps then, my party will be allowed to enjoy the rest of our tour. Does that mean that you no longer require Travis to check in with the local station?'

'I am afraid not. You should not assume that my investigations into the members of your party are at an end. That must continue. I merely wished to confirm that *all* your passengers are still with you.'

'They are, Inspector. Do you wish to enquire about anyone in particular?'

The Inspector actually gave a chuckle. 'That I am not prepared to say, Mrs Mason. Not at this stage.'

'You are being very enigmatic, Inspector. Is there a point to this call, or are you simply trying to annoy me?'

'Why would I wish to do that, Mrs Mason?' He sounded

affronted at the suggestion and much as she would have liked to tell him that it was in his nature, there was little point in antagonising the man. 'Our investigations have discovered that not all your passengers are necessarily quite who they say they are.'

Her heart gave a little flip. 'What is that supposed to mean?'

'Let us just say that it has been impossible to verify details about their backgrounds. You are still in possession of all the passports, are you?'

'I am, Inspector.'

'Good, good. I may need to come and verify certain details, so we may be seeing each other again in the next day or so.'

'Thank you for letting me know, Inspector.'

'Please make sure that no one leaves the group before I get there.'

'I will do my best, Inspector.'

Fiona slipped her mobile back in her bag. She would need to speak to Montgomery-Jones as soon as possible. Was it worth trying to ring him now or would it make things more difficult if he was with any of the others and had to explain away the call? Perhaps she should wait until they were all back in the hotel. As if she didn't have enough of her own problems to worry about without the prospect of Montgomery-Jones's mission being uncovered.

Much as she tried to push all the problems to the back of her mind and lose herself in the sheer splendour of the church's sumptuous soaring architecture, her efforts failed miserably.

By the time Fiona returned to the hotel, she had still not heard from Adam. She tried to tell herself that there were all sorts of reasons for that. He could be catching up on some much-needed sleep or in the hospital at Becky's bedside and prevented from using his phone on the ward. Besides which, there was something else she needed to sort out.

Up in her room, she shrugged out of her coat and changed her shoes. It was still relatively early. There was a strong possibility that Peter and Sonya had not yet returned to the hotel. She tried ringing their hotel room number. No reply. There was a chance that they were in the café area. Even if they weren't, she could do with a cup of tea.

Walter and Elsie Danby were already sitting at one of the small tables and it would have been churlish not to join them. They weren't the easiest of people to talk to. Walter rarely said more than two consecutive sentences and Elsie struck Fiona as one of those faintly disapproving people who preferred to keep the world at a distance. It was hard going making conversation until Morris and Drina arrived. After five minutes, Fiona was able to make her excuses and leave.

As she walked through the lobby on her way to the stairs to go back up to her room, she spotted Peter and Sonya coming through the main entrance doors.

'I hope you had a pleasant afternoon,' she said.

'Yes, thank you, Fiona.' Sonya's answer was polite, but she had no intention of stopping for small talk and turned away heading for the lifts.

It gave Fiona the opportunity to signal to Peter that they needed to talk.

'You go ahead, my dear. I will be up in a minute or two. There is something I need to ask Fiona.'

Sonya didn't even bother to turn her head, merely raising a hand in acknowledgement as she continued walking.

With hotel guests arriving back after their day's activities, the hotel entrance was much too public a place for what Fiona had to say, so they walked to a more secluded area at the rear of the lobby.

'How secure are the cover stories for Peter and Sonya Adams?'

'More than adequate I would have thought. Why? Is there a problem?'

'I had the impression you were still making changes to your mission plans right up to the last minute and I wondered if it gave enough time to ensure adequate backup should anyone choose to check up. I've just had a strange phone call from Inspector Bauer. Seems he's been looking into the backgrounds of all the passengers and hinting that his investigations have uncovered some anomalies. He said something about people not being who they say they are.'

'Did he mention anyone specifically?'

'No. He was extremely cagey. He intimated that it may be necessary for him to come down here to ask some more questions.'

'That sounds ominous.' Montgomery-Jones lowered himself onto one of the settees furthest from the main doors and the lift area. Fiona sank down beside him.

'He was very vague. I'm not certain he really has anything at all. It's just as likely that he's trying to wind me up. I wouldn't put it past him. He takes great delight in goading me.'

Montgomery-Jones turned to look at her, shaking his head with a wry smile. 'Much as I respect your judgement, Mrs Mason,' He put a hand over one of hers and gave it a gentle squeeze. 'You do have this amazing blind spot when it comes to authority figures. I am certain a psychologist would come up with an explanation for this almost pathological antagonism to anyone in charge.'

Recalling the many spats the two of them had had in the past, she had the grace to give him a sheepish grin of acknowledgement.

'It doesn't take a psychologist. If you had to deal with as many petty officials intent on playing God as I did when fighting for my husband's rights all that time he was ill, you'd have a healthy distrust of people who stand in the way of justice.'

'Justice as you see it perhaps. Regulations have to be followed and sometimes one has to acknowledge that there is a bigger picture. One that you may not be privy to.'

Fiona sighed. 'Point taken.'

'I must be going. Thank you for the warning.'

She watched him make his way to the stairs. At least he didn't seem to be harbouring any grudge against her for cold-shouldering him all day.

Travis kept his head down over dinner. He contributed little to the general conversation, but he was perfectly amiable and did nothing to draw undue attention to himself. As long as he stuck to drinking only water with his meal, Fiona was happy enough.

Fiona wasn't the only one to notice Travis's sudden sobriety.

'That talk Peter had with friend Travis last night seems to have been effective, don't you think?' said Gary quietly to her as they all got up from the table.

'Sorry?'

'You have to admit, Fiona, Travis hasn't put a foot out of line today.'

On reflection, Travis had been on his best behaviour. He'd been on time at all the meeting places, been gracious to everyone and never tried to hog the conversation as he'd been prone to do at the start of the tour.

'Up to a point,' she agreed. 'Though he still managed to upset Henry in the Green Vault this afternoon. Quite what all that was about, I have no idea.'

Gary shook his head. 'I'm not sure you can blame Travis for that. He made a seemingly innocent remark and for some reason, Henry took umbrage. Mind you, Henry's a bit of an oddball if you ask me. Takes offence at the slightest thing. Look at the way he reacted in Berlin that time when someone asked him about his childhood.'

'I don't think I remember that.'

'He nearly knocked you over when you came back with a cup of coffee.'

'Oh yes. Although I didn't know what upset him. Did you hear what Travis said to him to make Henry storm out of the room at the Vault?'

'We were all talking about the looting of art treasures by the Nazis during the war and by the Russians during the Soviet occupation in Berlin. The subject of the Wall came up and Travis asked Henry if he knew any of the people who were shot trying to escape.'

'Why should that have upset Henry?'

'Heaven knows. It seemed a pretty innocuous question given the conversation we were having at the time. Henry told him to mind his own business in rather choice language and stormed off.'

Gary turned to follow the others who were already making for the door. Fiona put a hand on his arm. 'Changing the subject, what were you saying about Peter earlier?'

'Didn't he tell you? You know Peter and I helped carry Travis back to his room after dinner last night? When we'd got him onto the bed, Peter read him the riot act. Laid it on good and proper! Said if it wasn't for you, he'd still be languishing in a cell in some Berlin police station and the least he could do was show a bit of gratitude by not causing any more problems for you. Carrying on that way, he was in dire danger of not only getting himself thrown out of the hotel, but getting you sacked in the process for not keeping your passengers in line.'

'Really?' Perhaps that explained why Travis had appeared in the foyer before they all set off first thing this morning looking contrite and had apologised profusely for his behaviour of the night before.

As they made their way to the lounge to join the others for coffee, Fiona felt more guilty than ever for the way she'd treated Peter. Perhaps it was time to make an apology of her own.

It was relatively late by the time Fiona had retired to her room. Adam still hadn't phoned, and it was difficult to concentrate on anything else. She had done her best to feign interest in the general conversation because she felt it was important to socialise with her passengers and never liked to leave until the bulk of the party had already gone up.

She perched on the side of the bed and tapped in the number. It was several minutes before Adam picked up.

'Hi, Mum. Look, do you think I could ring you back in half an hour? I'm in the middle of giving Adam Junior his bath.'

'Of course, darling. Speak to you later.'

Fiona gave a sigh of relief. It didn't mean that the problems were over but the very fact that he was home, and he didn't sound unduly anxious, just a trifle harassed coping with a normal lively toddler, was a good sign.

Time for a nice relaxing shower.

It was as she stood under the water, tilting her head forward to let its full force pound on her shoulders and upper back to ease away the tension, that a thought struck her. She jerked upright, soaking her hair in the process.

'Damn, damn, damn!'

She turned off the water, stepped out of the shower and wrapped herself in a fluffy, white towel. Earlier, when the Inspector had asked her if she still had all her passengers, she forgotten completely about Faith. It probably wasn't important. Even Inspector Bauer could hardly suspect Faith of being involved in Frederick's death. It was too late now to phone him now in any case. Best to leave it.

Day 9

Our journey today takes us into the area known as the Saxon Switzerland. This beautiful area of sandstone mountains towering above the River Elbe was designated a National Park in 1990. It is popular with walkers and climbers and has over 1,000 climbing peaks.

Our first stop will be in the small town of Pirna, known as the Gateway to Saxon Switzerland. The town grew up at an easy river crossing and by the 13th century was the most important trading centre along this stretch of the River Elbe between Magdeburg, west of Berlin and Litoměřice in the Czech Republic. A guided walk will take us through the chequerboard pattern of streets of the old town to the Marienkirche, a late-Gothic hall-church built in 1545.

Other interesting buildings include the Rathaus (Town Hall) and the picturesque old houses in the town square. Towering above the old town is Schloss Sonnestein which was extended in the 17th and 18th centuries.

We will arrive in Bad Schandau in time for lunch in the hotel where we will be staying for the next two nights. Bad means spa in German and Bad Schandau is on one of the oldest spa resorts in Saxon Switzerland. This beautiful city lies nestled in a picturesque valley among lush hills and deep gorges.

Our afternoon excursion will take us to explore the

natural beauty of the region. We will enjoy spectacular views of the river, narrow valleys and deep gorges from the 656-feet-high Bastei — bizarre tower-like rock formations that rise abruptly and are connected by footbridges.

Super Sun Executive Travel

Chapter 22

Fiona was down to breakfast earlier than usual on Sunday morning. She even beat Winston, but it was a surprise to see Travis already sitting there. He wasn't the world's earliest riser and by his own admission, frequently missed breakfast altogether.

There were so few people in the restaurant that it would have seemed rude not to join him.

They exchanged pleasantries, then lapsed into silence.

As he stirred his tea pensively, she said, 'Is anything wrong, Travis?

'Just thinking.'

When he didn't elaborate, she said, 'You're not still brooding about Inspector Bauer, are you?'

Travis slumped forward; arms folded on the table. 'Not really.'

'For goodness' sake, Travis.' It was difficult to stop herself from being sharp with him. 'If the Inspector had any evidence against you, you would still be in Berlin. Besides you now have one of the best lawyers in the city acting for you.'

He shook his head and said quickly, 'It's not that. It's what he told me. You know the main grounds for holding me were my notes about Frederick being a border guard?'

Fiona nodded.

'I genuinely believed he was,' he went on. 'That's what the stupid man implied in order to make out he was a hell of a lot more important than some two-bit factory worker which according to Inspector Bauer, is all he was.' There was a long pause.

'Why is that bothering you now?'

'Because that's what I told all the others. The Inspector is convinced one of us killed him. If that's true, then don't you see? Frederick is dead because of something that I said.'

'Travis, I really can't see why. Even if one of the other passengers believed your story that Frederick was a border guard, it's hardly a reason to kill him. Despise him, yes. But you'd have to have a pretty strong incentive to take someone's life and can you really see any of our party capable of that?'

'I can think of at least one person who might have a damn good motive,' he said bitterly.

'Who, for goodness' sake?'

He shook his head vigorously. 'I shouldn't have said anything.' He got to his feet and hurried away, almost bumping into Winston who was coming through the restaurant doors.

'Morning, sweetheart. Someone's in a hurry. Something wrong?'

'I hope not, but I'm beginning to have serious doubts about Travis's state of mind. He's heading for a nervous breakdown the way he's going.'

Rose was the first one to join Fiona, waiting for everyone to gather for the tour. She came bursting through the lift doors and raced across the foyer, her lips pinched and two fiery red spots on her cheeks.

'I've just had a call from Faith.'

As she paused for breath, Fiona asked, 'How is her son? Is there any news?'

'That's the point,' Rose said, eyes flashing, and fists clenched. 'He's absolutely fine. When she got to the hospital, they hadn't even heard of a Colin Reynolds. There was no such patient, and no one had been brought in from a traffic incident in the last fortnight, let alone the previous day.'

'I don't understand.'

'Faith phoned Colin and he was at work as usual. He hadn't been in any accident.'

'So who sent the message?'

'Faith went back through her phone history to check and the number was nothing to do with Frenchay Hospital. She tried ringing it, but all she got was number discontinued.'

'But that doesn't make sense.'

'It's someone's idea of a sick joke. I'd like to wring their ruddy neck, causing all that grief.'

'But who on earth would do such a thing?'

Another late start as the news spread throughout the group.

'Is everyone ready?'

There was a flurry of movement as people slipped on their coats and collected up hats, scarves and last-minute hand-luggage. Fiona moved towards the hotel doors where she could do a quick head count.

Winston waited patiently for everyone to settle down in the coach. It always took some time removing coats and finding places to put everything up on the luggage rack, but today everyone was still expressing their indignation at what had happened to Faith.

A sudden cold shiver ran down Fiona's spine. She tried to tell herself she was being ridiculous. How could anyone possibly suspect the friendly likable widow of being involved in Frederick's death? Anyone less like a murderer, it would be hard to imagine. But as Fiona of all people, knew only too well, there was no such thing as a recognisable murdering type. In the last year, she had rubbed shoulders with several murderers. Not one of them had stood out or seemed anything other than ordinary – the sort of people you could meet anywhere.

The more she thought about it, the more uneasy Fiona became. That hoax call about a non-existent accident, was a mighty convenient way to escape back to England. And she only had Faith's word that there had been a phone call in the first place.

There was nothing for it. She would have to inform the Inspector now. The man would be furious that she had failed to let him know the moment things started to swing into action on Friday night. And who could blame him? This tour was just one disaster on the heels of another. She'd hardly had time to stop and take stock.

Despite the sun, the temperatures had dropped even lower now they were in the mountains and everyone was happy to get into the warm for their coffee stop in one of the local cafés after their short walk around the town.

Sonya sat rubbing her hands vigorously to get back the circulation and Fiona was glad to be able to wrap her hands around the hot mug of steaming coffee.

'I bought a pair of thermal gloves especially for this holiday,' Fiona said. 'But I wish I'd brought another pair to put inside.'

Travis came to join them at the spare seat at their table.

'That story the guide told us about Sonnenstein Castle was pretty horrific, wasn't it? Fifteen thousand people gassed just because they were disabled,' Rose said, shaking her head.

'That's the Nazis for you,' said Travis offhandedly.

'I thought the buildings in the market square were very pretty,' Fiona said, quickly changing the subject. 'Did any of you get any nice photos?'

'Peter did,' replied Sonya. 'You will have to give him your email address so he can send you some copies.'

There was something in the way that she said it and the penetrating look she gave that made Fiona think there was more behind the remark than a simple friendly gesture. It was as if the woman was testing her out. She must know that Peter had known Fiona before the trip even though none of the others did. Was Sonya as curious about the relationship Fiona had with Peter as she was about that which existed between him and Sonya?

'I got some decent ones too, Fiona. If you're interested, I can email you the jpegs.'

'Thank you, Travis. That's very kind.' She could hardly refuse, and he was trying very hard to be the perfect passenger. Though she wasn't sure she really wanted to give him her email address. At the end of the holiday it often happened that she was asked to collate everyone's email and print off copies for each of them, but she never added her own address. If she did that every trip, she'd end up being besieged by emails.

It was as they were all getting up to leave that the atmosphere suddenly became frosty.

'Why are you staring at me like that? It is very rude.'

Sonya's outburst was directed at Travis. The reporter raised his hands in mock apology and gave the angry woman a smile.

'A cat can look at a queen.'

The look she threw him would have frozen the steam from a boiling kettle, but before Sonya had a chance to reply, Peter cut in, 'Come along, my dear. We don't want to be late back to the coach.'

There was little chance of that given that at least half the party were still sitting down, but Peter had hold of Sonya's arm and was already guiding her away.

Travis shrugged his shoulders and continued to sit nonchalantly finishing his coffee. Fiona bit back the instinct to tell Travis to behave and stop antagonising the woman. It was probably not a good idea to draw more attention to the incident than need be.

Everyone enjoyed the drive to Bad Schandau. The rugged scenery was truly spectacular, and the bare trees were made magical by their light dusting of snow. Winston made frequent stops so that everyone could take photos and what should have been a relatively short journey took some time. Not that it was a problem, Fiona decided. No one appeared eager to leave the pleasant warmth of the coach and there was still plenty of time before lunch.

Their hotel was well located alongside the river.

'It would be good if everyone's been given a room with a view,' Fiona said to Winston as she passed him to go down the steps. 'I know the place isn't full.'

Leaving Winston to see to her passengers, Fiona hurried inside to check everyone in.

'I'm not sure how long it will take to get your main luggage to your rooms, but in any case, I doubt you will have time to unpack now. The restaurant is just along the corridor and lunch will be at one o'clock. Please be on time because we'll be leaving straight after we've eaten for our trip up to the Bastei rock formations.'

Lunch was set on a single long table. The meal provided by the hotel was a full meal and not the usual help-yourself cold buffet that Fiona had been expecting. Pleasant though it was to be brought a bowl of appetising hot vegetable soup on such a cold day, Fiona had misgivings that lunch might drag on and the start of their afternoon tour be delayed. The last thing she needed was Winston having to drive back down from the heights of Bastei along those perilous roads in the dark. She trusted his driving implicitly, but her passengers could not be expected to have the same confidence in their driver.

At least after her little pep talk, no one was late coming into the restaurant.

One major advantage of the seating arrangements was the ease and speed with which they could all be served. As one waiter carried a large tray of plates along the line, another served them out.

Travis was sitting at the head of the table, looking very pleased with himself. He was chatting away merrily to Morris and his wife on his left and Barbara who was sitting at the end of the row on his other side. Henry busied himself talking to Walter and Elsie Danby. Fiona couldn't swear that

Henry had been deliberately avoiding Travis since the incident in the Green Vault, but she certainly had her suspicions.

Halfway through the meal, a great guffaw of laughter from the top of the table got everyone's attention. Travis was back to the jocular assertive man he'd been at the start of the trip.

'What's put you in such a good mood, Travis?' someone called out.

Travis tapped the side of his nose. 'The old journalist's instinct, old boy. Got the sniff of a great story. My future is looking up.'

'What's it about, Travis?' asked Sol Sachs.

'Now that would be telling.' He wagged a finger.

'You can tell us,' Sol protested. 'We're hardly likely to pinch it, now are we?'

'Watch the headlines in a couple of days.' Travis laughed and raised his glass, thankfully full of water Fiona thought, and toasted the group. 'Here's to a bright future for us all.'

Joining in the spirit of the thing, Sol raised his glass of red wine and repeated the toast. One by one the others joined in, a couple of them with obvious reluctance. And it wasn't only Henry Wolf who had a face like thunder.

Thanks to the restaurant's speedy service, everyone was on the coach and ready to go at the planned time. The journey was not nearly as perilous as Fiona had feared. It turned out to be a perfectly reasonable road, clinging to the valley side and not the series of sharp hairpin bends with precipitous drops that she had been expecting.

The snow gave everything a fairy tale quality and Fiona lost count of the number of picturesque frozen waterfalls they had passed.

At the top, the coach pulled into the car park and they all made their way to the main building. Once Fiona had pointed out the meeting place, they each made their separate ways. There was a small exhibition hall but almost everyone went straight to the viewpoint.

Fiona hung back with Walter and Elsie Danby who were being very tentative about walking on the snow-covered uneven surface. Morris had his stick and he seemed confident enough and knowing how Drina fussed over him, Fiona had no qualms as she watched the two ease ahead and out of sight, leaving her to give her attention to the elderly couple.

By the time Fiona and the Danbys reached the viewing area, the rest of the party were all spread out.

'Those craggy pillars are quite breath-taking, aren't they?' said Fiona.

'Never seen anything like it,' agreed Walter. 'Like great towers rising out of nowhere. There are pictures in the guidebook, but somehow covered in snow like that makes them even more dramatic.'

A small group was gathered at the end of a short bridge across to one of the other rocks. Gary tentatively took a few steps. He'd only gone a couple of paces before a foot slipped from under him and his other knee collapsed. It was only by holding onto the high rails on either side that he managed to stay upright.

Loraine gave a little scream and there was a sharp intake of breath from all those watching.

'It's very icy,' Gary said, looking back up at everyone with a sheepish grin.

Very slowly, he backed towards solid ground.

Several of the others lined up to have a go, but no one succeeded in going any further than a couple of yards.

Fiona decided to leave them all to their macho games trying to outdo each other and moved further along the barrier to see more of the spectacular landscape.

'Pity the sun's gone in, isn't it?'

She turned to see Anna who had come up behind her.

'Yes, it is. It's quite grey now and getting a bit misty but it's still a fantastic view of the river, isn't it?'

'Definitely worth a few photos.' Anna lifted her small

camera and fired off a quick succession of shots.

'Sol not with you?'

'He's busy taking photos but he takes forever getting the best possible picture. I haven't got the patience.' She shrugged. 'You know me, point-and-click lady. Sol won't agree of course, but I think my pictures are just as good as his.'

Some half an hour later, Fiona was inside looking at the exhibition when she heard her name being called urgently. She turned to see Loraine hurrying towards her.

'Come quick, there's been a terrible accident.'

Fiona froze. She opened her lips to ask what had happened but not a sound came.

Together the two women ran outside.

The story came in short bursts. 'It's Travis. He fell . . .'

'Is he alright?'

'We don't know. The rescue team are getting ready to go down to him.'

Fiona stopped in her tracks and stared at Loraine. 'You mean he fell into the ravine?'

'He's not far down. Onto a ledge. Not at the very bottom.'

The icy surface made it impossible to hurry. Slipping and sliding, Fiona reached the crowd gathered around the viewpoint. It was with some difficulty that she managed to edge her way through to the front. A man in a uniform of some kind was holding everyone back with outstretched arms.

'Move away please.'

Fiona eased her way over to him. 'The man who fell. He's one of my party. I'm the tour manager for Super Sun Tours. Can you tell me what's happening?'

Chapter 23

'So how is he now?'

'He's being kept in an induced coma but apparently that's the usual treatment for severe head injuries these days. All the doctor at the hospital will tell me is that he has a great number of broken bones, including a badly fractured leg, and that he's still "very poorly". Whether that means he's critical, I really don't know. Unfortunately, the doctor didn't speak English that well and because I'm not a relative, there's a limit to what he'll tell me anyway. When the hospital asked me for details of his next of kin, I told them you would be able to give them the relevant information and gave them the Head Office number.'

Fiona heard what sounded like a snort at the other end of the line.

'Something wrong, Mr Rushworth?'

'We haven't been able to get hold of William Everest. Travis's brother lives up in the wilds of Scotland somewhere. It could be that he is Travis Everest's only remaining relative because the second name he gave on his emergency contacts list turned out to be his landlady. We've spoken to her and she seemed to think the two brothers didn't have much to do with each other.'

'Not very helpful.' Fiona gave a deep sigh. 'That doesn't make my position any easier.'

'How come?'

'We are all due to leave Germany first thing the day after tomorrow and I really don't like the thought of leaving

Travis in the state he's in, in a strange country and without anyone he knows.'

'It's hardly your responsibility!' David Rushworth sounded none too pleased. Fiona winced. It had been a stupid thing to say to the Tours Director. The last thing she needed was for him to think her unprofessional. 'You have the rest of the party to think about. How are they taking all this?'

'They are obviously still very shocked. Especially those who saw him fall.'

'What happened exactly?'

'As I said, I wasn't actually there. In fact, speaking to those who were, no one actually saw how Travis slipped in the first place. There was quite a crowd standing there by the railing. Some of them said there was a bit of a kerfuffle, a bit of shoving and pushing but quite how he managed to slip under the rail or tip over it or whatever, no one seems to know.'

'Well we'll keep trying to contact this brother of his. Mr Everest is in the best place for the time being, so you get back to the hotel and see to the others. I take it you're still at the hospital?'

'Yes, sir. I'm waiting for a taxi. You're right about Travis being in the best place. This is a major climbing area so the doctors here are very experienced in dealing with accidents of this kind. In fact, surprisingly for such a small town, it has two hospitals. There was a bit of confusion when I asked the taxi to bring me here.'

She rang off and walked to the main doors to look out to see if the taxi had arrived. There were no waiting vehicles. For the next fifteen minutes, she watched the approaching cars, their headlights distorted by the steady drizzle, gearing herself ready to rush out the moment the taxi pulled up. The hotel was only a short distance away. At this rate it would have been quicker to walk. It was only the dark and the rain that stopped her. A miserable end to a miserable day.

Dinner was over by the time Fiona got back to the hotel. At this time of year, when the hotel was only half-full, the restaurant closed early. Not that she was bothered. The bar sold hot snacks and there was probably some sort of room service, but food was the last thing on her mind. She had asked the taxi to drop her off at the side door from where she could use the back stairs to get up to her room.

It was tempting to stay up there, but she knew it wasn't an option. The rest of the party would be waiting for news in the lounge. There was no way of avoiding the barrage of questions, but there was little she could tell them. Feeling utterly drained, it took all her effort to steel herself to face them.

Apart from the Super Sun party, there were only half a dozen other guests in the lounge. None of her party were missing. They were all huddled together in one corner, talking earnestly.

'Fiona!' It was Anna Sachs who spotted her hovering in the doorway.

Immediately, everyone shuffled around to make room for another chair to be pulled into the tight circle.

'What's the news about Travis?'

'How's Travis?'

'Will he be okay?'

The questions all came at once.

She did her best to make the prognosis sound as hopeful as possible. As far as they were concerned, though his condition was serious, it would only be a matter of time before he made a full recovery. The doctors had given her no such assurances. All she could get from the harassed-looking junior doctor was that they would know better if he made it through the night. Her own experience from working in what had been called the Casualty department had taught her that brain injuries were unpredictable. Medical science had moved on considerably in the last thirty or so years, but nonetheless all they could do was hope and pray.

'What I don't understand is how it could have happened.' Sol scratched his beard, half muttering to himself. It was a question that had been worrying Fiona all those hours she'd spent pacing up and down in the family room in the hospital waiting for news. 'Surely the fence was too high for someone to fall over?'

'I seem to remember Travis was leaning right over it, taking photos,' said Rose.

'Even so,' Fiona protested. 'It was almost chest high.'

'Well yes, but he was standing on the bottom rail and reaching out for a better shot of the bridge. I suppose if he was pushed suddenly . . .'

'What do you mean "pushed"?' Fiona leant forward in her chair. 'Are you saying it was deliberate?'

'No, no! That's not what I meant at all.' Rose waved her hands frantically in front of her face as though trying to ward off such a dreadful suggestion. 'Just that there was quite a bit of jostling and elbowing as people tried to squeeze through to the front to take photos. We were all so tightly packed.'

'Travis was rather hogging the best position,' Gary said with some feeling.

'But I still don't see how Travis could get pushed over.' Fiona protested.

'It happened when all the commotion came from behind,' said Rose. 'Someone slipped on the ice knocking other people over. We all got jostled around. Everyone at the front turned round to see what was happening. Someone could easily have knocked against him causing him to lose his balance.'

'That's right,' agreed Loraine. 'I had a job keeping my balance. I would have fallen if Gary hadn't grabbed my arm.'

'So no one actually saw Travis go over?' Fiona asked.

There was a sea of shaking heads.

'I was standing not far from him, but I'd turned to see what was going on behind,' said Barbara. 'I heard him scream above all the noise that was going on, but when I looked back, he was already falling.'

'We saw him land. It was horrible!' Rose shivered and covered her face with her hands. Loraine put a consoling arm around her shoulder.

'I think several of us might have a few nightmares tonight,' Loraine said softly.

'Time for another round of drinks, I think. On me. What's everyone having?' Peter was on his feet.

'Just coffee for me,' said Fiona.

'Me too. Doesn't seem right when poor Travis is lying there in hospital,' said Anna. 'I'll help fetch them.'

In the end, Peter had few takers. Whether by choice or because of Anna's comment, most people opted for more coffee.

While they were waiting for them to return, Fiona's mobile began to burble. The muted hum of conversation stopped, and all eyes turned to watch as Fiona lifted her shoulder bag and retrieved her phone. Everyone held his or her breath in anticipation.

Fiona glanced at the caller number and shook her head. 'It's not the hospital.' There was an audible collective exhalation. Fiona got to her feet. 'It's a private call. If you don't mind, I'll take it outside.'

'Hello.'

'Mrs Mason. It was our agreement that you would keep me informed of all that is happening.' DI Bauer was not in the best of moods. 'Mr Everest has not reported to the local police station as requested. I do hope you can account for his whereabouts.'

'I apologise for not contacting you before, Detective Inspector . . .'

He calmed down a little once Fiona had explained the situation. He was still full of questions. She could hardly continue to stand in the middle of the lobby, so she made her way to a quiet corner and slumped down on one of the long couches.

The Inspector gave a snort. 'I suppose he was being

reckless.'

'Not at all,' she said more sharply than she'd intended. 'He was in the main viewing area with a whole crowd of others.'

'I cannot say that I know the area well and it is a few years since I was up at Bastei, but I seem to remember the viewing areas were all protected by chest high iron railings.'

'They are. No one knows exactly what happened. It was incredibly icy, and people were slipping all over the place.'

There was a long silence. 'Are you certain that it was not deliberate? Could he have jumped?'

'What are you suggesting, Inspector? That he was trying to take his own life?' Her left hand was clenched so tightly that she could feel the nails pressing into her palm. 'That's a ridiculous suggestion. Why on earth would he?'

'If you had told him of our conversation last evening and he thought we were closing in on . . .'

'That would suggest Travis is guilty,' Fiona snapped. 'Which he most definitely is not. And for your information, Inspector, I never told him we spoke last night. Good night, Inspector.'

She broke off the call, dropped the phone to her lap and leant back in the seat, and closed her eyes.

When she opened them again, she saw Peter standing a few feet away, looking down on her. The thick carpet had masked the sound of his approaching footsteps.

'How long have you been here?'

He smiled, walked over and sat down beside her.

'I assure you; I was not trying to overhear your conversation.'

'You'd be hard pushed to miss it!' Her voice betrayed her lingering sense of outrage.

He struggled to suppress a grin. 'It was a little difficult when you started shouting, I confess.'

Fiona gave a long sigh. 'It's a good job there's no one else in the lobby.'

'Our good Inspector is causing you problems, I take it?'

She gave him a sheepish grin. 'As you so kindly pointed

out the other day, I do have a problem with authority figures.'

His only answer was a low chuckle.

'Unlike you, he isn't so forgiving when I fly off the handle.'

He raised an eyebrow, trying to look disapproving. When this failed, he grinned and said, 'The Inspector does not know you like I do.'

'I'm sorry, I know I haven't been exactly appreciative of all your help lately. Thank you for what you did for Travis the other night.'

'Someone had to help put him to bed.'

'Well, yes. Thank you for that too, and the pep talk I hear you gave him afterwards. But that wasn't what I was thinking of.'

'Oh?'

'I meant Dieter Jäger.' He turned his head to look at her. For a moment it looked as though he was about to deny it.

She didn't give him time. 'If it wasn't for him, Inspector Bauer would still have Travis locked away in a cell. I do appreciate it.'

'Let us say it was very much in my interest to leave Berlin. Keep reminding yourself that the day after tomorrow when we cross the border, we will be out of Detective Inspector Bauer's jurisdiction and he will not be able to trouble you anymore.'

Fiona suddenly looked thoughtful.

'What is it?' Peter asked.

'Something the Inspector said just now has got me thinking.'

'Oh?'

'Peter, you were there when Travis went over? Did you notice who was behind him?

He sat back, puckering his forehead as he tried to recall. 'Rose was standing on his right, and we were behind her. I believe Loraine Peters was on his other side, standing next to her husband.' He was silent for a few moments, still lost in thought. 'I would not swear to the fact but to the best of my memory, I think Barbara Wolf was next to Sonya. When the commotion came from behind, we were all pushed and started sliding on the icy surface. Things were somewhat chaotic to say the least. Plus, everything happened so quickly. After that, I was busy looking to see what had happened to Travis and I really cannot say I noticed where anyone was. Does it matter? What are you thinking?'

Fiona sat back, folded her arms and sat lost in thought.

'Is it possible for someone to have deliberately pushed him?'

'Are you serious?'

'Is it anymore silly an idea than Travis deciding to jump?'

Peter looked at her with a deep frown. 'In as much as I very much doubt that it would be physically possible for Travis to jump from that position without first climbing up on the rail, which there was no time for him to do, then I suppose the literal answer is no. However, the likelihood of Everest being pushed would seem to be extremely remote.'

'Doesn't it strike you as something of a coincidence that both Frederick and Travis fell over barriers and we know that Frederick at least was pushed?'

'I will admit that our reporter friend could be annoying in the extreme, even obnoxious on occasions, but can you think of any serious reason why anyone would wish to attempt to murder him?'

'Possibly.'

'What!' He turned sharply, giving her an incredulous glare.

When she lapsed into silence again, staring into space, he added, 'Would you care to illuminate that statement?'

She turned to him and smiled. 'Not yet. I need to think it through first.'

'You suspect someone?'

'Not specifically.'

He shook his head and gave a wry smile. 'There are times, Fiona Mason, when you are the most infuriating woman on God's earth!'

She sat up, gave a bubbling laugh and on impulse leant towards him and kissed him lightly on the cheek before leaping to her feet and hurrying to the stairs and up to her room.

Chapter 24

Fiona was already on the second floor when she realised that she had not informed the hotel about Travis. It was probably best to see to that now. It would only cause confusion if the hospital rang with any information.

Back at reception, Fiona asked if she could speak to the manager. She didn't have to wait long. A tall, fair-haired man who looked far too young to be holding such a responsible position came through from a side door, gave her a firm handshake and led her through to his office.

'I did hear that there had been an accident up at Bastei,' he said after she'd told him what had happened. 'I take it that the gentleman will be in hospital for some time.'

'I would imagine so. I imagine we will know more in a few days.'

'Will anyone else be staying on when the rest of your party leave Bad Schandau?'

Fiona shook her head. 'Mr Everest was travelling on his own.'

'In which case, would you like one of my staff to pack up his things?'

'Thank you, but I can do that.' For some reason, Fiona did not like the idea of leaving the task to a stranger.

He smiled. 'Then I will arrange a key for you straight away. When you have finished, leave his case in his room and I will have someone collect it. We can put it in storage until it is needed.'

'That's very good of you.' The hospital was unlikely to

want to take responsibility for it. 'My company is trying to get hold of his brother. I will let them know you have it here.'

They walked together back to reception where he gave instructions to the attractive girl behind the desk.

'Thank you for your help.' Fiona shook his hand and turned back to wait while the receptionist programmed a new key card.

The digital clock on the wall behind the desk showed 21.47. Too late to start sorting out his things now, Fiona decided.

'Room 206,' said the girl handing it over.

When she reached the second floor, Fiona realised that she would pass 206 on the way to her own room further along the corridor. Despite her earlier resolution, she found herself slipping the card into the lock. After all, she reasoned, it wouldn't hurt to just take a look at what needed to be done tomorrow.

Travis was clearly not the tidiest of people. His suitcase was on the floor with its lid thrown back against the wall, revealing a jumble of clothes. He obviously hadn't bothered to unpack anything other than bare essentials. It was hardly any wonder that the man always had a slightly dishevelled look. Anything that might once have been neatly folded was by now crumpled. With everything jumbled together, how did he ever know what was clean and what was not?

Glancing round the rest of the room, she noticed half a dozen loose pages torn from the spiral-topped reporter's notepad lying on the bedside table. She went over to tidy them up and began shuffling the sheets together, ready to tuck them back into the notepad lying alongside.

The pages had all been crumpled up, then smoothed out again. It looked as though Travis had been writing some pointers for an article and then abandoned the idea, screwed up his notes ready to throw away and then thought better of it. She hadn't intended to read them, but she couldn't fail to notice that scrawled sideways over the top of the closely written notes, in enormous letters, were the words Frederick NOT GDR!!!

All the loose sheets appeared to be about Frederick. Notes on the things the guide had apparently told Travis at their interview and given the number of question marks after every point, another couple of pages of Travis's speculations. Presumably, these notes formed part of the evidence that Inspector Bauer had used to hold Travis for questioning in the first place. It was perfectly understandable that once his property was returned after his release, Travis would want to rip them out and throw them away. But he hadn't. He seemed to have had a change of heart. But why?

Curiosity got the better of her. She sat down on the bed and began to flick through the notebook itself. There was a page headed Konstantin Belousov. Where had she heard that name before? Very recently. Possibly in the last day or so. It had been on the television in the news. Had it been in relation to the Peace Talks? But why had Travis made notes on the man's biography?

There were several pages devoted to the missing Ukrainian politician, Natalia Shevchenko. The two names seemed to be connected. It was difficult to see what angle Travis might have been planning for an article, which his extensive notes suggested, on a current topic taking place nowhere near their present location.

The majority of the remaining pages appeared to be little more than lists of odd jottings plus several diagrams covered in initials that in all likelihood made sense only to Travis himself. She remembered Travis saying that it was his way of organising his thoughts. Were they possible ideas for an article he was working on? Could they have anything to do with the niggling suspicion that she had about the possibility that Travis might have been pushed?

It seemed so absurd that she hadn't even been prepared to voice those suspicions out loud to Peter Montgomery-Jones. He would probably have allayed her fears, but if there was any truth in the idea, the motive might just lay in one of these jottings.

She was about to leave when she spotted what looked like another thick spiral-bound notebook half-hidden under a guidebook tucked into the space beneath the bedside table. It turned out to be a diary, a page-a-day A5 size version. She sat down on the bed and started thumbing through. Most entries were a simple record of the day's events. Although the daily entries for the preceding few months were mostly short, some only two or three line efforts, those for the holiday were full of observations, not only of the places they had visited, but comments about his fellow travellers. She wasn't surprised to see that few were complimentary. The first day's entry was particularly scathing. It seemed even by the evening when they had the overnight stop in Cologne, Travis was no happier than when she'd spoken to him a few hours earlier at the comfort break.

He bewailed his lot at being stuck with "a bunch of senile, doddery old farts". At 53, if she remembered correctly from his passport, Travis was far from the youngest member of the party, but even his juniors – Barbara and Henry Wolf, Loraine and Gary Peters and Sonya he collectively dismissed as lacking in a single original thought between them and therefore incapable of any meaningful conversation. Which seemed particularly harsh, given that he'd had so little time to talk to any of them, having spent the whole of that first-day travelling.

His most unpleasant comment concerned poor Faith whom he described as having boobs so large she had to lean back all the time to stop herself from falling forward. It couldn't be denied that Faith was well-endowed and that she did have a tendency to tilt her head back lifting her chin but that hardly justified such a snide comment.

Fiona had a sudden thought. Could Travis have been the one to play that cruel joke on her? She shook her head. Whatever private notes he may have made, even he would never be so cruel.

Faith wasn't the only passenger who came in for Travis's cruel observations. Elsie was accused of looking as though she constantly sucked lemons and even Anna's dyed black hair came in for ridicule. His description of Fiona herself as "a faded blonde pixie eager to please" could have been worse she decided, even if she was sensitive to comments about her height. Travis appeared to have reserved his caustic comments for the women in the party. The man was a complete misogynist.

Her only hope was that Travis had confined his observations to the diary. If he'd made snide comments in public, then it was hardly a surprise that he had made himself unpopular.

Fiona turned to the entry for the day of Frederick's death. There were brief details about the morning tour, a comment about Frederick being East German and the afternoon walk. There was mention of an interview followed by a stark line halfway down the page about Frederick being found dead, having fallen from the first floor into the lobby. Apart from the fact that there was a line space immediately before and after, it was a totally unemotional, matter-of-fact account. Nothing to indicate how Travis had felt about the incident or how it had affected him. The only thing that appeared to have troubled him at all was when his laptop was confiscated after his police interview, which had prompted a furious diatribe against the Inspector.

If the police had read his diary at the time when they had decided to confiscate his laptop, there would have been no reference to Frederick, which was presumably why Travis had been allowed to keep it. To judge from the next day's entry, it seemed that without his laptop, Travis had decided to put all his notes in his diary.

The sound of people talking loudly as they walked down the corridor made Fiona realise how late it was getting. It was Sunday and the boys would start to worry if she didn't call them soon.

She picked up the notebook and the diary, tucked them

under her arm and walked to the door. After a quick look up and down the corridor to check no one else was around; she slipped out and hurried to her own room. Quite why she was acting like some spy, she wasn't sure. She had a perfectly legitimate reason for being in Travis's room, nevertheless she preferred no one should know. Perhaps it was the guilt she felt at reading someone else's private papers. But this wasn't idle curiosity. If, by any remote chance she was right, Travis could still be in danger.

They might even help her to identify Frederick's killer.

'Hi, Mum. What's the latest news on Becky?'

'I haven't actually spoken to Adam today. I tried ringing the house just before phoning you, but the line was engaged. As far as I know, she's still in hospital but out of danger. The doctors want to make absolutely sure before letting her go home.'

'That's what Adam told me when we last spoke. So how's your trip going? Where are you now?'

It always made Fiona guilty talking about her tours. It was not in her nature to hold things back, but it would serve no purpose to tell either of her boys about what had happened to Travis.

It wasn't a long conversation but after listening to his account of a weekend jolly with a couple of his close friends, she felt far more relaxed than she'd been all day by the time she'd finished the call. Of her two sons, Martin was always the easier to talk to these days. He was more easygoing than his older brother and didn't attempt to take control of her life as Adam so often seemed to want to do in the eighteen months since Bill's death. She knew it was for the best of motives, but she didn't need protecting although convincing Adam that she was quite capable of making decisions for herself proved difficult at times.

It wasn't until much later that she was able to curl up in bed and study Travis's jottings in more detail. As far as Fiona could tell, Travis was collecting material and trying out ideas for several different articles. Some pages were little more than gibberish as far as she was concerned.

There were seventeen pages in all but the only other names she could find at the top were unrelated to any other of her passengers. There was a long screed covering several pages about the Ukrainian politician Natalia Shevchenko, prompted no doubt by the fact that the woman had featured so prominently in the news over the last few weeks. If Travis was following up on that story, it might explain why he'd also been researching Konstantin Belousov. Scanning down the substantial biographical notes which seemed to be taken from the internet, Fiona confirmed that he was Natalia's ex-husband. Whether that was why Travis was interested in the man or because Colonel Belousov was a major figure in Russia's current military strategy on the Ukrainian borders, there was no way of knowing.

It was tempting to return to Travis's room and collect his laptop to see if he'd typed up any of these scribbled jottings into something more decipherable. Apart from the fact that it was a step too far encroaching on Travis's privacy, the machine was probably password-protected anyway.

Her only course of action was to attempt to establish which pages were related. Some notes were so cryptic that she had no idea what they could refer to. Three of the pages were not so much notes as spider maps or line diagrams. The problem with these was that all the key points were in initials rather than decipherable words.

One she was certain was related to Natalia and Belousov. The initials NS and KB were written in two squares on either side of the sheet connected by a series of lines, some with dates alongside and others with cryptic abbreviations. However, from the notes in the two biographies, she was able to work out that Travis was attempting to establish when the two met, married and separated, and possibly, if she was interpreting the various questions and exclamation marks correctly, what if anything was their current relationship. Travis had written, "2005 div???? Amical??" Was he uncertain of the date or did it have some other significance? It was something she thought she might research herself at a later date, though not when it was fast approaching midnight and she had another busy day ahead of her tomorrow.

As she turned to put out the light, a thought struck her. In his diary, Travis had written screeds of notes about his fellow passengers. Was there anything to explain the obvious rift between him and Henry Wolf? It was no good. The thought would keep going round her head, keeping her awake until she knew the answer. Reluctantly, she sat up, leant over and retrieved the second pillow from the floor where she'd dropped it minutes before and using it as a backrest, propped herself up. She fished the diary from under Travis's notebook and turned to the day of the visit to the Green Vault.

Much to her surprise, there was no mention of the incident. She flicked through the previous pages to see if Henry's name was mentioned. The first entry came on the second day of the tour. It was little more than a throw-away about Barbara and Henry having Yorkshire accents and a reference to Henry being a bit of a cold fish and a later one noting that he was born in Berlin. There was a further entry about Henry being very cagey about his early life.

Fiona was aware that Travis had apparently pressed Henry on the subject of his family and whether he had any relatives left behind in Berlin. According to Gary Peters, when Travis had asked Henry what it was like growing up in Germany in the 1950s and 60s, Henry had said that it was a period of his life he'd rather forget. Perhaps Travis's further attempt to press Henry on the subject a day or so later in the Green Vault explained why Henry had been so rude to him and stormed off.

What had prompted Travis's interest in the German-born Yorkshireman? Why had he been so keen to pursue his questioning? Did he suspect him of Frederick's murder?

How was the story suggested by Travis that their guide had been a border guard relevant as far as Henry was concerned? Had Travis suggested as much to Henry? There was definitely some kind of friction between the two men, but it would be a mistake to start leaping to conclusions, she told herself sharply.

Day 10

Bad Schandau has retained much of the splendour of bygone days. Established in the 15th century, the town was an important trading centre; however, the discovery of iron-rich springs and the building of a spa house in the mid-18th century led to it becoming a popular tourist resort. The National Park was established not long after. In 2002, the town suffered a disastrous flood, although much of the town is now restored.

This morning we will explore the old town with its medieval buildings. Our guided walk will begin in the Market square at the beautiful Sendig Fountain. Dominating the square is the 17th-century Lutheran church of St. John with its impressive tower. The highlight of the interior is the stunning altar, originally made for the church of the Holy Cross in Dresden and moved to Bad Schandau in 1927. The altar is a major work of the famous sculptor Hans Walther II. The church - like the town – was severely damaged by a major flood in 2002 but has been beautifully restored. Our guide will show us the marker plaques to show the height of the many floods that have covered the town.

Another notable building is the "Brauhof", a former brewery built in 1680, which is now a restaurant with an attractive courtyard. We will end our walk with a stroll along the cobbled alleys north of the Market square after which you will have free time to explore further, to shop or maybe to make use of the hotel spa.

After lunch, we drive back along the beautiful river Elbe to visit the spectacular Königstein Fortress which rises dramatically from the rock. The construction of this formidable building began in 1250 when it was established as a border fortress between the Kingdom of Bohemia and the Margraviate or Bishopric of Meissen. Over the years, it was enlarged to 30 separate buildings spread across 9.5 hectares, to become Germany's largest intact fortress.

For a short time, the fortress also served as a monastery, but it is as a jail for many prominent figures that it is best remembered. These include Johann Böttger, the inventor of Meissen porcelain, the social democrat August Bebel and the poet Frank Wedekind. During WWII, it served as a POW camp and also as a refuge for Dresden's art treasures.

Highlights of our tour will include the seemingly bottomless well dug 500 feet down into rock, a remarkable collection of weapons and the Georgenburg or jailhouse.

Super Sun Executive Travel

Chapter 25

For the first time in over a week, Fiona's waking thoughts were not about Becky. Travis's notebook and diary were uppermost in her mind.

Propping herself on one elbow, she reached for her watch on the bedside table. A good half hour before the restaurant would be open for breakfast. If she didn't linger in the shower, there was just enough time to do a quick bit of research on her laptop.

Googling the name of the captured Ukrainian politician, she discovered several pages of references. She clicked through the first few until she came to a news article dated less than two weeks ago, soon after the story of her release from capture hit the world headlines. It confirmed the facts that Travis had noted that Natalia Shevchenko was married to Konstantin Belousov, now Colonel Belousov, who was an important figure in Russia's current military strategy.

Fiona clicked through to some of the older news items. She was so engrossed in her research that time slipped away. Winston would be wondering where she had got to.

Fiona finished her cup of tea and was about to leave when a shadow fell across the table.

'May I have a word, Fiona?'

Fiona could only hope that the mixture of surprise and guilt that she was feeling was not revealed in her expression as she turned to see Henry who had been hovering behind her. Guilt because she had been wondering if he had anything to do with Travis's fall, and surprise because the man appeared to spend the majority of his time avoiding company rather than seeking it out.

'Sorry. Did I make you jump?'

'No need to apologise, Henry. I was lost in thought and I didn't see you there. What can I do for you?'

'Has there been any news about Travis this morning? Do you know how he's doing?'

'I was about to go and phone the hospital. I was told not to ring before eight o'clock. The last I heard he was making good progress.'

'That's what they always say, isn't it? I can't say I liked the man, always prying into everyone's business, but you wouldn't wish that on anyone would you?'

'True.'

Fiona got to her feet but from the way Henry was hovering, there was clearly still something troubling him.

'Is there anything else I can do for you, Henry?'

'I was wondering,' he hesitated, then rushed on, 'As we'll be in the Czech Republic tomorrow, I was wondering if you'd heard any more about the investigation into the murder of our Berlin guide.' He must have seen her surprise at the sudden change of subject. 'I know it must seem a strange question to ask but I haven't seen anything on the news and once we leave Germany, I don't suppose we'll ever know.'

'I presume the investigation is still ongoing.'

'The police haven't contacted you at all?'

'Is there any reason that they should?'

He shook his head. 'I suppose not. It was just something that Travis said yesterday.'

'And what was that?'

'It doesn't matter. It's not important.' He hurried away to where Barbara was sitting on the other side of the restaurant, before Fiona had a chance to quiz him further.

There was little time for Fiona to puzzle over what was worrying Henry. She glanced at her watch. Although she'd been told not to ring the hospital until the day shift came on duty, it was probably best to wait until things had settled down a little. This morning's guided walk was not until nine-thirty and the guide was unlikely to be at the hotel much before nine-fifteen. Nonetheless, it was probably best to take a quick look at the itinerary and check on the places to recommend for those who planned to do more exploring during the day's free time.

'For sure, this beautiful pulpit was built in 1615 and you see here Moses and the evangelists.'

To judge from the muttering, it wasn't only the guide's poor English that was causing problems. The acoustics in the echoey old church were not good and standing at the back of the semi-circle gathered in front of the wooden Baroque pulpit, Fiona found it difficult to concentrate on what the softly-spoken woman was saying. It didn't help that Helga had her back to them all as she kept turning to point out the carved figures.

They were outside again when Fiona received the call.

'Inspector Bauer here. I am coming to Bad Schandau. I should be at your hotel in about an hour. Will it be possible for you to meet me there?'

The temptation to invent a previous engagement was strong, but the annoying man had her itinerary and he must know that it would be their free time by then. 'Yes, Inspector. I'll be there. Can you give me any idea why you want to speak to me?'

'In good time, Mrs Mason. All in good time.'

Though she had hung back as she'd taken the call, she caught Peter Montgomery-Jones's glance. He raised an eyebrow. As the others trailed after Helga, Peter slowed his pace, waiting for her to join him.

'More problems?'

'I really don't know. The Inspector is on his way to see me about something, but he won't say what.'

He looked grim. 'To make an arrest presumably.'

'I assume so.'

'Any ideas who that might be?'

She turned to look up at him directly. 'Honest answer. I do have two possible candidates.'

His eyebrows shot up. Montgomery-Jones rarely revealed what he was thinking but there was no hiding his surprise. 'I do not suppose you would care to share your suspicions?'

'Not here.'

'Hotel after we finish the walk?'

Fiona debated with herself for only a second. It might be a good idea to get Peter's take on things before her interview with the Inspector. She nodded. 'Assuming the Inspector doesn't beat us to it.'

'It might be better if we joined the rest of the party before anyone starts wondering what we are discussing,' he said, quickening his pace.

Helga gathered the group in front of another building.

'For sure, this is Church of St. John builded in the 18th century.'

'Not another flipping church.' This from Sol who was usually the most patient of men.

Fiona stifled a grin. It appeared she was not the only one eager for the walk to finish. Helga was by no means a bad guide, she certainly knew a great deal about every place they had visited, but she was easily the least engaging of the local guides they had had so far, and her poor command of English didn't make things any easier.

Most of the party headed towards one of the many cafés in the town centre as soon as the walk was over, but there were more people who opted to return to the hotel on the coach than Fiona had expected. Rose, Sonya and Loraine all had plans to try out the hotel spa and Peter was not the only man as Gary had decided to come back with his wife; although in his case, he was still undecided about joining his wife in the spa.

As they stood in the lobby waiting for the lift, Fiona said,

'Enjoy your dip, ladies. As soon as I've dumped my things, I'm heading for the café for a well-deserved coffee and quiet sit down.'

Peter laughed. 'That sounds like an excellent idea. Do you mind if I join you?'

'Please do.'

Peter was already sitting at a corner table by the time Fiona had made her way back down.

'I have ordered a cappuccino for you. I hope that is satisfactory,' he said, picking up his own tiny cup of expresso.

'Perfect,' she said, settling herself into the chair next to him. He knew her preferences.

'No sign of the Inspector, I take it?'

Fiona glanced at her watch. 'Not yet, but he did say he hoped to be here by half past so it shouldn't be too long.'

'Then let us get straight to the point. Assuming the Inspector is here to interview one of us if not to make an actual arrest, you said you have some thoughts.'

Fiona stirred her coffee thoughtfully. 'Inspector Bauer has made it very clear from the start that he is convinced that Frederick Schumacher was murdered by one of the Super Sun Party. It seems our guide had no close family and according to Klaus who worked with him in the agency, he only had a small circle of friends. His best friend was apparently his dog and he led something of a solitary existence. His life revolved around his work, taking his golden retriever for long walks and watching television. There was nothing in the man's background to suggest he had any enemies, which probably explains the Inspector's obsession with one of us. Today is Inspector Bauer's last opportunity to question us. By tomorrow, we'll be out of his jurisdiction. All, that is except for Travis, and the Inspector is hardly likely to come all this way to arrest a man lying in a coma with only a fifty-fifty chance of recovery.'

Peter's eyes widened. 'Is the situation as bad as that?'

'Honest answer, I don't know, but the prognosis is not good.'

'You hinted that you had a couple of possible suspects in mind.'

'Not for Frederick's murder as such. As you know, I let my temper get the better of me last night when the Inspector phoned. But thinking about it later, when he asked me if I thought it was deliberate, I jumped to the conclusion that the Inspector was implying Travis jumped. I cut him off before he had a chance to explain. He could just as easily have been asking if I thought Travis had been pushed.'

'Is that why you were asking me who was standing behind him just before he fell?'

Fiona nodded. 'The obvious motive for getting rid of Travis is that the culprit believed that he had worked out who killed Frederick and was about to reveal it to the world at large.'

'If that were the case, surely it would be more logical for Everest to go straight to the police with the information, if only to clear his own name.'

'Possibly. I do know that Travis felt guilty that he had spread the story about Frederick being a border guard. He admitted that he should have realised that Frederick's boasting about what he had done in the past was all make-believe, trying to imply he was far more important than he really was.'

Peter gave a derisive snort. 'I find that somewhat ironic, given that Everest possessed the self-same tendency. Do you think there is any substance to this big exposé he claimed he was about to write? His visions of it making front-page news would appear to be as much a fantasy as Frederick's claims to have been decorated for playing a significant role during the Soviet occupation.'

'I think he may well have had a story, though I'm not sure that it's the one that Travis was concerned about when he spoke to me. Travis was genuinely upset at the prospect of what he'd said about Frederick and felt responsible for the man's death. He reasoned that if someone believed Frederick was given those medals for shooting escapees, then it might have given them a motive.'

'Did Travis say whom he suspected?'

'No.' Fiona shook her head. 'But I think he may have had someone in mind. The person he believed was not only born in Berlin but spent his childhood behind the Wall.'

'Are we talking about Henry Wolf?'

'It's a possibility.'

'Is that why you asked me if background checks had been done on all the passengers the other day?'

She nodded.

'I seem to remember Wolf saying he left Berlin in his infancy.' Montgomery-Jones looked pensive. 'Why would Everest think otherwise?'

'I don't know, but I'm certain Travis was convinced Henry was lying about his time in Berlin. Travis was a master at giving subtle digs. Saying seemingly innocuous things, suggesting he knew more than he did, just to see if he could get some sort of response. At first, I thought he did it simply to antagonise people, but now I think there was more to it.'

'If they reacted then he knew he was on the right track.'

'Something like that. He's a journalist through and through, always on the lookout for a story.'

Peter replaced his cup back in its saucer and sat back, looking thoughtful. 'You said you had another suspect.'

'For who pushed Travis, not for killing Frederick.'

Peter turned to her and smiled. 'I was standing behind him. Do I feature in your shortlist?'

Fiona stared back at him; her face expressionless.

'Fiona?' He looked shocked.

After a long pause she smiled and shook her head. 'No. But I think you might be capable of such an act if you thought it necessary for your mission.'

He drew in a sharp breath. 'Whatever you may have heard

to the contrary, the British Secret Service operates within the bounds of human decency. It might bend the law on occasions, but it does not kill innocent people,' he said, pausing for emphasis between each of the last few words.

'I'm glad to hear it. Does Sonya operate by the same code of ethics?'

His jaw dropped visibly, but Fiona held his gaze. There was a long silence. 'Is this what it is all about?'

'I think it may well be. Is it not at least a possibility that Sonya was afraid that Travis's boast that he was about to hit the headlines with a startling revelation might just reveal her true identity? Your whole mission would be in tatters if it all came out.'

'You are on dangerous ground, Fiona.' His tone was neutral, but the warning was all too clear.

'Surely you know me well enough to know I'm not going to say anything. By the same token, I wouldn't dream of asking you to confirm it. But assuming my suspicions about Sonya's true identity are correct, I very much doubt that the same thought hasn't crossed your mind.'

His face was neutral. As ever, he was giving nothing away.

Fiona leant forward and picked up her coffee cup and sat back, cradling it in her hands. The silence continued for some time.

'How long have you known?'

'I realised early on that the woman with the so-called bad cold who left England posing as your wife is not the same Sonya we have all got to know here in Germany. I presume the cold was a ploy so that she could isolate herself from everyone else.'

'How astute of you. What gave it away?'

'The original Sonya had blue eyes, not grey, and was an inch or so shorter. She didn't reach your shoulder. The new Sonya does. I'll admit it took me quite a while longer before I worked out who she might be. The glasses and the new hairstyle change the shape of her face considerably. Plus, the change from blonde to that rich chestnut colour.'

'Has anyone else made any comment?'

'Not to me. She looks very different from all the media pictures. I doubt it would ever have crossed my mind without knowing you were on a mission of some kind. Travis did once mention she reminded him of someone. He is a journalist and may have kept digging, trying to find out more information on the internet. As far as the others are concerned, I doubt it. I'm sure they would have mentioned it and I haven't heard any rumours.'

'That is something I suppose.'

'I have a feeling Faith Reynolds was close to putting two and two together and may well have done had she remained here with the group.' When he made no comment she continued, 'Strange that hoax that was played on her, wasn't it? And how convenient for your mission. I wonder if we'll ever discover who engineered it.'

There was no point in antagonising him further by making a direct accusation. It was enough to let him know she had worked it out. She could only hope that poor Faith would be recompensed for the heartache she'd been caused, let alone the loss of the rest of her holiday. Quite how that might be done, Fiona had no idea but if there was a way, she had enough faith in Montgomery-Jones to believe he would find it.

Time to move on. 'I decided I was jumping to conclusions at first. Natalia Shevchenko is a well-known figure. Her picture has been plastered over the world media for weeks. Why risk bringing her all this way and spending so much time travelling through Germany on a coach tour when you could have flown her to Britain straight away?'

He gave her a rueful smile. 'That is precisely what she demanded, and I will tell you what I told her. The original plan to take her out of the area by helicopter before anyone realised what was happening was thwarted by bad weather and a series of unforeseen events. Had we made any attempt to do so later, it would have been quickly detected. Modern monitoring technology is now so advanced that all flights are immediately detected and anything without officially recognised flight plans would alert suspicion straight away. I doubt that the Russians would have any compunction about shooting any such suspicious aircraft out of the skies, claiming it was hostile and a threat to their security.'

'Couldn't you have used a military plane?'

'It was considered but rejected on the grounds too many people would know that something highly unusual was happening. Word would have got out somehow. Officially, the British Government knows nothing. The Foreign Minister refused to sanction the operation on the grounds that the whole operation could be denied should it fail. If there is the remotest hint that the British are involved in any of this, the Peace Talks will be at an end. At this point in time, we cannot afford to let that happen.'

'But surely taking so long to get her back increases the risk of detection?'

'Admittedly.' He shook his head. 'As plans go, it was far from ideal, but after every other possibility had been thwarted, this was what you might call a last-ditch effort. It was the only way that she could be brought into the country undetected.'

'But as long as the names and passports of returning coach passengers tally with those going out, there is no problem. Security is far less rigorous than at airports.'

'Certainly, more difficult for Russians to infiltrate.'

'So what happened to the original Sonya?'

'She left as soon as we arrived at the Berlin Hilton. Shevchenko was waiting in another room in the hotel and they swapped places. My agent then made her own way back to Britain using her own passport.'

'So that was the letter waiting for you when we got to the hotel, saying which room she was in?' His eyebrows lifted as he gave her a surprised wide-eyed look. 'I saw you collecting it from reception.'

'How observant of you.' The slight edge in his voice intimated that he hadn't intended the remark as a compliment.

Fiona lifted her coffee cup. She was surprised to see it was already empty. She couldn't remember drinking it. Her mouth felt dry, but there was no going back now.

'What I don't understand is why a Ukrainian Politician is so important. Please don't pretend this is a humanitarian mission. What does Natalia know that merits this complex operation we're all now embroiled in? I know you won't give me an answer, but I can only assume that all this has something to do with Colonel Belousov.'

His eyebrows lifted just a fraction but enough for Fiona to judge that there was a definite connection. 'My, my! You have been doing your research.'

'And I'm not the only one. Travis made the connection too. He made quite a few notes. I haven't looked at his laptop but there is a strong possibility that this breakthrough article he was talking about may well be related.'

His body suddenly stiffened. 'What did the notes say? Do you have them with you now?'

'I put them in the safe in my room. I thought it best not to leave them lying around. Most of what I can decipher is background stuff. However, from what I can make out despite all the reports of the very public acrimony between Natalia and Belousov that followed their divorce, Travis seems to suggest that the two have kept in touch. There are even hints that there may have been secret meetings between the two of them.'

'What are you saying?'

'I'm simply wondering if the divorce is merely a front. That the two of them could still be working together. I'm sure you know the answers even if you can't tell me. To my way of thinking, if these Peace Talks are so vital to the British Government, why would they jeopardise the negotiation process and risk the Russian delegate walking out over the rescue of a politician for a minor power with no world clout who the majority of the world had probably never heard of until her dramatic rescue? What possible information can she be privy to that would justify such an operation? Now if she were a senior Russian strategist who had the ear of the President himself it would be a different matter.'

'Is that what Travis has written?' Montgomery-Jones leant forward in his chair.

'No. At least not in his notes. Nothing to suggest he was thinking along those lines. Though as I said, I haven't looked at his laptop. I'm just thinking out loud.'

Montgomery-Jones did not look pleased. 'You are jumping to a great many conclusions.'

'Possibly.' Fiona couldn't hold back her satisfied smile.

'What do you intend to say to Inspector Bauer?'

'I see no reason to volunteer any information that Travis's fall was anything more than a dreadful accident. As you say, all I have about Henry Wolf is supposition, nothing more. About Sonya? Don't worry, I have no intention of jeopardising your mission. I assume that is why you asked for me to act as tour manager at the last minute, to smooth over any sticky moments that might arise. My being here can hardly be a coincidence.'

He didn't deny it.

'But why? You've held me at arm's length ever since day one. In fact, you've gone out of your way to distance yourself from me.'

'As you have just pointed out, it was a very risky operation. I thought it might have been useful for backup. To help deflect attention if needed. If things had gone smoothly, you would have known nothing about it. My becoming personally involved at the lastminute complicated things.'

'I see.' She glanced at her watch. 'The Inspector should be here soon.'

'Will you let me know what he says?'

She turned and smiled. 'Of course.'

Chapter 26

There was little point in her hanging around the lobby waiting for the Inspector's arrival. He had her mobile number, so there was no reason she should not make a start on packing up Travis's belongings.

The room was as she had left it last night. As she had anticipated, there was nothing in any of the drawers, and the wardrobe was empty apart from a pair of shoes. He'd been wearing his thick jacket and walking shoes. The only other thing was his laptop sitting on the top shelf. She could only reach it by standing on the stool tucked in the cubbyhole beneath the television. It was still not quite high enough for her to see if there was anything else pushed to the very back but Travis was not a particularly tall man so the chance that he'd hidden anything back there was remote. Perhaps later, she could ask one of the taller men, Peter or Gary, if they would check for her.

The door to the small safe was open, so either he hadn't bothered to use it or had taken all his valuables with him. At least it saved her another trip to reception to get them to open it for her.

As she put Travis's toothbrush and shaving things into the sponge bag, it occurred to her that he would need these when he came out of his coma. Perhaps she ought to see if she could get these to the hospital before they all left. She would also have to decide what to do about his laptop. It might be better to ask if it could be kept in the hotel safe until he was ready for it rather than be left in storage in his case. In the meantime, she would take it to her room.

The Inspector had obviously been delayed but it didn't seem worth starting anything else. She had plenty of paperwork to do. The downside of the job, one of her fellow tour managers had once called it. If only, Fiona thought as she sank down on her bed still clutching Travis's laptop.

Almost without thinking, she opened it up and switched it on. To her surprise, it wasn't even password-protected. Perhaps Travis had been asked to unlock it so the police could inspect it and had not got round to putting it back in its former state. Looking at the last date modified column, it was the day he had had it confiscated.

The last file he'd been working on was called Book Project. She clicked onto it. After all the trauma of the last nine days, the most recent one was definitely not what she expected. It was headed Child Abuse. Surely, he didn't suspect someone on the trip was involved in any such thing.

The file she'd opened was a collection of notes of interviews he'd conducted with individuals over a period of several years. Scanning through the notes, it appeared to have nothing to do with what had been going on during the trip. It was a lengthy document. From what she could make out, it looked as though Travis was planning on putting together a book about people who had suffered child abuse. It seemed to be concerned less with the abuse itself than how it had affected the victim's adult lives. It made interesting reading.

Some of those he'd spoken to were badly affected as one might expect, but the majority appeared to have managed to put it behind them. Fiona was engrossed in the story of one woman, now a very successful lawyer, who had been raped by a family friend at the age of fifteen but was determined not to let her whole life be blighted by it. Travis had asked if she considered that her choice of career had been as a response to the incident. Fiona was only half-way through the woman's answer when her mobile rang.

Inspector Bauer was waiting in the main lounge, accompanied by Sergeant Hase. Both men got to their feet and shook her hand. The Inspector waved in the direction of the coffee pot and cups on the table in front of them.

'May I get one for you?'

'No thank you, Inspector. I've just had one.'

She sat in the chair opposite and waited as they settled themselves. Sergeant Hase gave her a quick smile then dropped his gaze, burying his nose in his coffee cup.

'I understand Mr Everest is still in a coma.' When she made no comment, the Inspector continued. 'A bad business. You have no more information as to how the accident occurred?'

'As I explained before, Inspector, I wasn't there. It would seem that none of my party actually saw exactly what happened. And before you ask, I did try to find out who was closest to him immediately before he fell. Bearing in mind that it may be an inaccurate list, do you wish to interrogate those half dozen people or all those who were there? It might take some time and we are due to leave at two, but I can arrange that for you when we get back. The area was crowded but obviously I have had no contact with all those who were not with Super Sun.'

He waved a hand. 'I doubt that will be necessary at this stage, though I may get back to you.'

'So why are you here, Inspector?'

'My concern is still with the murder of Frederick Schumacher. Our enquiries have progressed since I saw you last, Mrs Mason. I am sure you will be pleased to know that we have decided to eliminate Mr Everest from our list of suspects.'

'I'm sure that will be a great comfort to Travis if or when he recovers.'

'Indeed. However, as you so rightly surmised, I did not come all this way to relay that information. I would like to interview two of your other passengers.'

'I see. They should all be returning to the hotel in time for lunch at one o'clock, although some are here already. If you give me their names, I could go and check for you.'

'In good time, Mrs Mason.' He crossed his legs and sat back in the chair. 'Have you had any further thoughts on the matter since leaving Berlin?'

'If I had any evidence, I would have contacted you straightaway, Inspector.'

He smiled. 'I do appreciate that, Mrs Mason, but that is not the question I asked.'

Damn the man. Dieter Jäger had said he was no fool. His English was now so good he was beginning to appreciate the subtleties of the language.

'I'm not quite sure I know what you're referring to, Inspector.'

'Let us dispense with the prevarication, Mrs Mason,' he said more sharply, 'It has been a week now since Schumacher was murdered; you have lived in close proximity with these people ever since. You are clearly an astute woman and I am asking if you have noticed anything out of the ordinary, any changes in behaviour, comments that are at odds with things said earlier, anything at all that may have struck you.'

'What happened was a shock for us all, Inspector. Naturally, everyone was very upset. People react in different ways as I'm sure you are aware. As I believe I mentioned before, Frederick did not endear himself to the group but . . .'

The sound of approaching footsteps made her stop and turn round.

'Forgive me for interrupting,' One of the hotel staff stood hovering several feet away. 'Inspector, you asked for a room you could use for interrogation purposes. We have arranged for the Albert Suite, one of our meeting rooms, to be made available. If you would like to come with me, I will show you. Or I can come back later if you prefer.'

'Now will be fine.'

The two policemen got to their feet and picked up their briefcases. The Inspector signalled for the Sergeant to follow their guide and hung back until the two were out of earshot.

'We appear to have no records for anyone called Henry Wolf either in Berlin or in the Hamburg area. In fact, nothing until he arrived in England in 1983. There may be a simple explanation. But it is an issue we would like to clarify. Perhaps you could ask him to join us when you see him.'

'Certainly, Inspector.'

Although Fiona always kept a record of the room allocation for each hotel, it was quicker to go to reception and ask for Henry's room number. As she crossed the lobby, she saw several of the group coming in.

'Either I'm getting used to this cold outside or it's a lot warmer today,' Sol called out as he and Anna pulled off gloves and hats.

Fiona laughed. 'The altitude is a great deal lower here than where we were yesterday, but you might find the temperature will drop again this afternoon when we go up to the Fortress. It's on top of a high rock, so I wouldn't leave off any layers just yet.'

Fiona was about to ask if either of them had seen Barbara and Henry when they were out but decided against it. Best to be discreet.

It was no surprise when there was no answer to her knock on the door of room 215. As two of the younger and fitter members of the party, they always liked to make the most of their free time to explore for as long as possible.

It was a very worried looking Barbara who rushed over to Fiona who was standing at the reception desk.

'Henry hasn't come back on his own, has he?'

Fiona led her over to one of the settees and made the frantic woman sit down.

'Tell me what's happened.'

'Henry wanted to go up into that iron tower at the end of the town. After yesterday, I'd had enough of heights, so I said I'd take a wander round the shops and we'd meet up later. When he didn't turn up at the café, I got worried. I tried a couple of others in case he'd got the wrong place, but he was nowhere to be seen. I went back to the lift, but he wasn't there either. He forgot to take his damned mobile this morning, so I can't ring him.'

'I'm sure there's a simple explanation. He's probably wandering around the town trying to find you. When he realises he's missed you, he'll come back here for lunch.'

'But what if he's had an accident . . .'

'If he's not back soon, I'll let the police know.'

It took all of Fiona's powers of persuasion to stop Barbara rushing out again to look for him.

'There is no point in you wandering aimlessly around the town.' Fiona bent down and retrieved one of Barbara's woollen gloves that had fallen to the floor. 'Or standing around here, come to that. Let's go up to your room and you can get out of your outdoor things. You'll swelter in that thick coat. I'll come with you.'

Fiona took the padded jacket and hung it on the back of the door, then helped pull off Barbara's knee-high fur-lined boots.

'I don't know what's got into Henry this holiday. He's been like a different person since we got to Berlin.'

'Different how?'

'He's been so withdrawn. Not like himself at all. I know he wasn't really that keen when I suggested this holiday. I thought he'd jump at the chance to see the city where he was born. He nearly always leaves the choice of where we go to me, so I suppose I just thought he'd enjoy it when we got here.'

'He has seemed a bit preoccupied. Is there something worrying him, do you know?'

'I asked him that very question, and he said not. I'm not saying he's ever the life and soul of the party so to speak, but he's always been sociable. It all started with that guide Frederick. He never had a good word to say about him. And that really isn't like Henry. He usually gets on with most people. And now these last few days, he's taken against Travis too for some reason.'

'Did he say why?'

Barbara shook her head. 'The other day he had a real go at Travis. Called him a bloody liar and said it served him right getting himself locked up in a police cell overnight for spreading all sorts of malicious gossip without a shred of evidence to back it up. When I asked Henry what it was all about, he wouldn't tell me. Just said the man was a menace and deserved all he got. But this last day or so, I've hardly got a word out of him. I know he's brooding about something, but he just won't discuss it.'

She sniffed back the tears, then pulled a tissue from her pocket and blew her nose.

After a moment or two, she turned to Fiona. 'You don't think he's done anything stupid, do you?'

'Such as?'

'He's so depressed at the moment. The rate he's going, he's heading for a nervous breakdown.' She gave Fiona a pleading look. 'He did go up that tower and over that bridge onto the rocks.'

Barbara broke down in shuddering sobs. Fiona put her arms around her and held her tight.

'I know you're worried, Barbara, but you mustn't think like that. We all tend to think the worst when someone is missing but everything will turn out fine. I'm sure it will. There's no point in torturing yourself like this. There's probably a very innocent explanation. If he went looking for you, he could have got lost or, most likely, he's simply forgotten the time.'

'Would you like me to get room service to send something

up for you?' Fiona asked some ten minutes later.

Barbara shook her head. 'I'm really not hungry.'

She felt guilty about leaving Barbara alone upstairs but there were things she needed to do. The first thing was to check the dining room. She hadn't expected to find Henry there but there was no point in telling the Inspector that Henry was missing if he was sitting down to eat with everyone else. And she would have to tell him. And soon.

Outside the Albert Suite, Fiona waited a moment or two before knocking, trying to think of how to word what she was going to say. There was no way she could put a gloss on things, she decided. All she could do was tell him straight out.

Both men were halfway through their meal. The Inspector looked none too pleased at the interruption. But once she had explained the reason, he pushed away his plate, giving her his full attention. 'When did his wife last see him?'

'A couple of hours ago. Henry told his wife he intended to go up the tower. When he didn't turn up at the café at their prearranged time she went back and asked the attendant, but no one remembered seeing him. She is desperately worried that he may have crossed the bridge onto the rocks and fallen.'

'I will contact the local force immediately and ask for a search to be made. Can you describe the clothes the man was wearing?'

'A bright red padded jacket and a navy woollen hat and scarf.'

'That should help to make him stand out from the crowd.' He turned to the Sergeant and spoke rapidly in German.

As Sergeant Hase passed her on the way to the door, he patted her arm and said, 'Tell his wife not to worry. We will find him soon.'

When the door closed, Fiona turned back to the Inspector who was already busy tapping a number into his mobile. He looked up when he realised that she was still there.

'Was there something else?'

Fiona shook her head. 'Are you going to have him arrested?'

He looked surprised at her suggestion. 'On what charge? It is true I have some questions to put to Mr Wolf, but if he has fallen, the man will need help.'

Fiona was halfway to the restaurant but changed her mind. Instead, she hurried to the stairs and back up to her room.

She opened her room safe and took out Travis's diary. There was little chance of anyone else reading it, but nonetheless she preferred to keep it hidden. She opened it on the first day of the tour and went through every entry looking for any mention of Henry. Although Travis had made no mention of the scene in the Green Vault, there may be an earlier reference that might explain what was going on.

Apart from a single reference to Henry having no sense of humour at the beginning, Fiona found nothing. Travis appeared to have his own pet name for everyone. Little and Large were presumably Rose and Faith, Lord and Lady Snooty obviously Peter and Sonya and from the context, she guessed that Travis's name for her must be Tinkerbell. Another reference to her as a little fairy flitting around, waving her wand to spread good cheer to everyone confirmed it. She went through each page more carefully, stopping at anything that might possibly refer to Henry.

Mr Spiky. That must be it. The entry was made almost a week ago on the Wednesday. There was a reference to them all having coffee in the lounge at the end of the day. "Mr Spiky refused to talk about his family or his childhood. Was he a victim?"

Is that what had caused the bust-up Barbara had referred to? Travis asking searching questions. If he suspected Henry had been abused when he was a child, Travis might see him as another prospective interviewee for the book he was planning. The fact that Henry resented any form of intrusion into his private life would never deter someone like Travis. He had the hide of a rhinoceros. And the sensitivity.

Replacing the diary in her safe, Fiona looked at her watch. The afternoon tour was due to start in less than an hour. Would they have found Henry by then?

Downstairs, she saw one of the staff walking towards the Albert Suite carrying a tray of coffee. Fiona quickened her pace and hovered in the open doorway.

Sergeant Hase shook his head. 'No news yet.'

It was only what she had expected, but she couldn't just wait around.

After half an hour searching the streets, Fiona decided that attempting to find Henry was not one of her better ideas. Why should she have any more luck than Barbara? Nonetheless, if it was at all possible, she needed to speak to him before the Inspector was able to get his hands on him.

As she approached the tower, she saw two uniformed policemen talking to someone she presumed was one of the attendants. Inspector Bauer hadn't wasted much time. Despite what he had said, Fiona wasn't convinced that Henry wouldn't be taken straight into custody. What reasons had the Inspector given to the local police for searching for Henry, given that he'd been missing for so short a time. Back home, it would surely take far more than concern for his safety to get the police to swing into action so quickly.

She glanced again at her watch. If she didn't head back to the hotel soon, she would be late for the afternoon tour.

Chapter 27

Fiona had almost given up hope when she saw a figure in a red jacket slumped on a bench in the distance. He seemed to be lost in his own world when she slipped onto the bench beside him.

It was several minutes before he turned his head to look at her.

'Hello, Henry.'

He gave a faint smile of acknowledgement before turning back to stare across the river, saying nothing.

Fiona decided it would be a mistake to rush him. By rights, she should at least phone Barbara and let her know her husband was safe, if far from well. She resisted the temptation to look at her watch.

After five minutes, he gave a great sigh. 'I didn't mean it to happen, you know.'

Softly, trying not to break the mood, she asked, 'Would you like to tell me about it?'

'I saw red. Seeing him standing there with a great smirk on his face. I just exploded inside and the next thing I knew he went over. I don't even remember pushing him.'

Who was he talking about, Travis or Frederick?

'I was going to own up. I'd never have let Travis take the blame for what I did.' He turned to her; anguish written all over his face. 'You have to believe that.'

She put a hand on his arm. 'I know. That's what you were going to tell me that day in the café at Wittenberg, wasn't it?'

He gave a barely perceptible nod. 'Then when they let us all go, I thought I'd got away with it, but I don't think I can live with it anymore.' He sat forward, his elbows on his knees, gazing down at his hands, lost in some world of his own. She wasn't sure he even remembered she was there anymore. He gave a deep sigh and slowly shook his head. 'We should never have come here. I knew it would be a mistake, but Barbara was so keen.'

They sat in silence for what seemed a long time. 'I overheard them talking. As they were speaking in German, they didn't bother to keep it quiet. He was making out what a big man he was back then. How much he was valued and what an important role he had to play. He boasted about his medal. The bastard even bragged about being in on a black-market racket. Said he could have anything he wanted. That reporter kept egging him on. Started asking questions about those who tried to go over the Wall. And that bloody man laughed. He actually laughed.' Henry's whole body went rigid with anger at the memory. He clenched his fists and sat up straight. 'Said it was their own stupid fault if they got shot.'

Just as suddenly, he leant forward and broke down in heart-rending sobs. Fiona felt at a loss, but he regained control within minutes.

She took a wild stab in the dark. 'Who was it who was shot, Henry? Who did you lose?'

For a long minute, she thought he wasn't going to answer.

'My father. He made me go over first. There were five of us altogether. We all started running and suddenly the searchlights swung in our direction and the shots rang out. I was the youngest and the fittest, so I was in the lead. I heard a scream but the rest of us kept running. I thought Dad was still just behind me. It wasn't till we reached cover that I realised he was the one who'd been hit.' His voice broke as he continued, 'In the space of two years, I'd lost them both.'

Anything she could think to say would sound banal, so

instead she put a hand on his and gave a gentle squeeze. Even through her glove, she could feel the cold of his hands. Without gloves, his must be frozen, but she doubted he was aware of it.

He sighed. 'At seventeen, I was alone. No family. No home. Nothing.'

They sat in silence for a few minutes. This time, it was Fiona who spoke first. 'We need to let Barbara know you are safe. She is worried that you may have gone over to the rocks and fallen.'

He looked befuddled as though she'd woken him from some dream, which in a sense, she realised, she had. He'd been reliving every moment of that dreadful past.

He shook his head. 'I left my phone behind.'

'I have mine. Would you like to speak to her, or would you like me to?'

His pleading look was all the answer she needed.

'You'll need to give me her number.'

Once she'd reassured Barbara that Henry was safe and they were about to head back to the hotel, she rang Winston.

'I'm not going to make it back in time for the afternoon tour. Can you hold the fort for me? The Königstein tour is with one of their guides anyway so it's just a question of checking everyone on and off the coach really.'

'No problem, sweetheart.' Anyone else would have demanded an explanation there and then but she could always rely on Winston not to make a fuss.

'I'll explain when I see you. Give everyone my apologies and say I'll be with them all at dinner.'

'Will do. Take care.'

She returned to the bench, but Henry was still clearly not yet ready to return. He was sitting slumped forward, hands between his knees. There was a question she still needed to put to him.

'What about Travis?'

Henry sat up, quickly turning his head to look at her directly, fury burning in his eyes. 'Don't talk to me about that man. If it wasn't for him, none of this would have happened. He was the one who said that Frederick must have been a border guard and like a damned fool, I believed him.'

The anger dissipated as quickly as it had risen. 'And it was all for nothing. Frederick was never in the military. He was nothing but a factory worker with delusions of grandeur.'

'That must have made you pretty angry with Travis.'

'You can say that again.'

'Enough to push him too?'

Henry turned and looked at her. 'What do you mean?'

'Like Frederick, Travis fell over a railing.'

'True, but that was an accident.'

'Was it?'

He frowned and as far as Fiona could judge, his bewilderment was genuine. 'Are you asking if I tried to kill Travis?'

'You have to admit, Henry, the two events are very similar. Quite a coincidence, wouldn't you say?'

'I've never thought about it before but yes, I suppose they are. I confess I disliked the man intensely; nonetheless, Fiona, I can assure you that I had nothing whatsoever to do with his fall.'

'You were saying at breakfast that he asked you some pretty intrusive questions. Was that when you two had that argument in the Green Vault in Dresden?'

Henry frowned as if trying to remember and shook his head. 'No. It wasn't an argument exactly. The day before, when he got nothing out of me, he started pestering Barbara. Asking if she'd ever met my aunt in Hamburg or any other of my German relations. You see, I told everyone I left Berlin as a toddler, but as you know, that wasn't true. It just seemed the easiest way to avoid talking about the deaths of my parents. Then in Dresden he started making pointed comments in my hearing, trying to get some reaction out of me.' He sighed. 'I foolishly rose to the bait.'

'You thought he suspected you were the one who'd killed

Frederick?'

'It flashed through my mind, but on reflection I think it was just me being paranoid. That or a guilty conscience. The trouble was, he kept going on about this big story he was going to write that would make him famous again, but let's face it, "Tourist kills Berlin Guide," isn't really international front-page material is it?'

'Hardly.'

Henry sighed. 'It was probably nothing more than him working it out that I lied about where I'd spent my childhood. I wonder if there really was a story or just some figment of Travis's imagination.'

'As to that, I doubt we'll ever know, but I think he had something else in mind when he kept asking about your childhood. Nothing to do with the fact that you grew up in Germany.'

'Oh?'

'When you refused to talk about any of your family, he might well have jumped to the conclusion that you were the subject of some form of abuse.'

'What!' Henry gave a snort of derisive laughter. 'Hardly. Nothing could be further from the truth. Mine were the best parents a boy could have. It was just that having to watch them both die so needlessly at that young age is not something you want to talk about. Not to men like Travis.'

'That I can understand.' She pushed herself up from the bench. 'I suppose we'd better get back to the hotel.'

'I'd like to speak to Barbara before we go to the police station to hand myself in or do you think I should phone that Inspector in charge of the case in Berlin?'

'But there's no need to phone the Inspector. He's already here in Bad Schandau. He's waiting at the hotel. And speaking of the Inspector; I'd better ring him and let him know I've found you. He has half the local police force out looking for you.'

'To arrest me?' He stopped walking and turned to stare at her.

'No,' she said quickly. 'I told him that Barbara was worried you might have fallen from the rocks and could be lying badly injured somewhere. However, he does want to speak to you. But as far as I know, that's only because he can't find any records for you in Germany at all. Nothing before you came to Britain.'

'He wouldn't.' Henry sighed. 'My father's name was Drechler. I changed it as soon as I arrived. I didn't want anyone to make the connection with a man shot going over the Wall. Not because I wasn't proud of Dad, but Drechler sounded too German. I didn't want to talk about my past to anyone. I wanted to forget that life. Not my parents, I'll always remember them, but those last few years especially. My mother's maiden name was Wolff, so I dropped the last letter and Henrik became Henry. I worked hard at losing my German accent. Don't get me wrong, I never pretended that I wasn't born in Germany, but I was happier when the subject didn't come up.'

'I can understand that.'

By now, they had reached the hotel. Everything appeared quiet and normal. No police presence. In fact, little sign of anyone. All the guests had left for whatever afternoon's activities they had planned and inside there was no one on the reception desk. Nothing to suggest that it was anything other than an ordinary peaceful afternoon in the low season.

Henry turned to her and said, 'Thanks, Fiona. I'd like to speak to Barbara before I speak to Inspector Bauer, if that's alright with you?'

'I don't see a problem with that.'

'I'm not going to run away.' He gave her a weak smile.

'I'll tell him you're on your way.'

An hour or so later, Fiona had packed her own case and was sitting at the narrow shelf over the drawers that acted as the room's only table, writing up some of her paperwork when there was a ring on the bedside phone.

'Mrs Mason, this is reception. If it is convenient, Inspector

Bauer has asked if you would join him downstairs. He is waiting for you here in reception.'

'Certainly. Tell him I'll come straight down.'

She put down the receiver and headed for the door.

'There's no one in the lounge, shall we sit over there?' the Inspector said as she joined him.

He was looking rather pleased with himself as they made their way across the lobby and through into the deserted lounge. They sat in two of the comfortable armchairs on the far side of the room by the window from where he would have a good view of anyone approaching.

She could hear the satisfied gloat in his voice as he informed her, 'Henry Wolf, or to give him his birth name, Henrik Drechler, has just confessed to causing the death of Friedrich Schumacher.'

He looked disappointed when she gave no reaction to his portentous revelation. His expression ranged from surprise to annoyance. After a moment or two, he frowned and said accusingly, 'You knew.'

'He told me he was going to as we came back to the hotel.'

'Oh!'

She smiled. 'So, your case is now solved, Inspector.'

'Indeed. You and your party will be able to continue on your journey.'

'Presumably you will be taking Henry Wolf back to Berlin.' Fiona eased herself forward in the chair. 'I will need to help Barbara make arrangements to travel back there to be with him . . .'

The Inspector put out a hand. 'No need. His wife can travel back with us. We will find a hotel for her to stay until matters are arranged.'

'Thank you, Inspector. That is good of you. I do appreciate it.'

He waved away her thanks as they both got their feet.

She asked, 'Have you any idea what will happen to him. I don't think he set out to kill him.'

The expression on the Inspector's face softened. 'I agree. In all likelihood, there will be a plea of manslaughter. If it is up to me, the police will not oppose it, though that will be a matter for my superiors. With a competent lawyer, he should not receive too harsh a sentence.'

'Thank you, Inspector.'

They shook hands as they parted in the lobby. As she made her way up the stairs back to her room, she wondered if she had misjudged Inspector Bauer after all. Perhaps in Berlin he had only been doing his job. Just now, she had seen a more human side of the man, but then the pressure of solving the case before the chief suspects could disappear back to their own country was now lifted. Her only concern now was what she should say to the rest of her charges when they returned from **Königstein**.

Chapter 28

It was too cold to wait outside so Fiona positioned herself at the large picture window near the main doors where she had a good view of the approach road. As soon as she spotted the coach, she pulled on her coat hurried out to meet it.

Winston drew up several feet from the entrance door so as not to impede any other vehicles dropping off or collecting hotel guests. The door swished open and Fiona jumped on, taking the microphone that Winston was already holding out for her.

'If you would all just stay in your seats a minute. I'm not going to keep you long, but it's easier to talk here where I know you can all hear me than in the hotel. First of all, my apologies for not being able to be with you this afternoon, but I'm sure you have all had a good time at the fortress in Winston's capable hands.'

'We had a great trip and thanks, Winston.'

Sol's acclamation was greeted by shouts of 'Hear, hear,' and 'Thanks, Winston,' and a spontaneous burst of applause.

The big man waved a hand in acknowledgement.

'Just to let you all know that Henry and Barbara have had to leave a day or two early. Sad to say Henry has had some bad news and has had to return home.'

Above the hubbub, Rose's voice could be heard calling out, 'What's happened?'

'I'm sorry, but I can't go into details. However,' she said

firmly stilling the muttering, 'I do need to remind you that this evening you will need to pack an overnight bag for tomorrow. As you all know, we won't be arriving until the evening at our hotel at Aachen and your main cases will remain securely locked in the coach overnight so that we can be off again first thing. Now I'm sure you would all like to get to your rooms, so I won't keep you any longer. Winston is going to drive forward right up to the entrance, so you won't have so far to walk and then if you'd all like to collect your things, we can get off.'

'It's not one of their children like Rose's poor friend, is it?' demanded Elsie as Fiona helped her down the front steps.

'I really couldn't say. Do watch the step, won't you?'

She could hear her muttering to Walter as they moved away. Elsie wasn't the only one full of questions. This evening might prove quite a trial. It was bound to be the main topic of conversation over dinner and when they all moved into the lounge for coffee.

As usual, Morris was the last to leave the coach and once she'd handed him his stick, she waved to Winston and stood for a moment or two watching the coach draw away. As she turned to go back into the hotel, she saw Peter waiting for her.

'What's that smirk for?'

'It is not a smirk. I am impressed, Mrs Mason, you are beginning to lie like a true politician.'

She pretended to be affronted. 'I don't know what you're talking about.'

'I presume Henry Wolf has been arrested and the Inspector has taken him back to Berlin.'

'If that is not bad news then I don't know what is and you may recall, Henry was born in Berlin so in a very real sense, he *is* on the way home. You may claim that I was being somewhat economical with the truth, but I have had an expert teacher.'

Peter laughed out loud. 'Is that a jibe at me?'

'If the cap fits.'

'Let us talk later.'

He held open the door for her. Sonya was standing a few feet away.

'I wondered where you'd got to.' She turned to glare at Fiona.

'I'm here now,' Peter took Sonya's elbow and steered her towards the lifts.

At least Fiona had one thing to be grateful for. Henry had been taken away before the coach returned. Even though he was not in handcuffs and was being driven back in the unmarked car, seeing him leave with the Inspector and Sergeant whom the rest of the party would instantly have recognised would have been more than she could have explained away.

With the group dwindling rapidly, there were plenty of empty chairs at their two tables in the hotel restaurant that evening. Their ever-decreasing numbers appeared to bring the group closer together as though they needed the support of each other. Telling herself she was imagining it or simply getting more sentimental in her old age, she made for an empty chair on the far side of the table and sat down.

Much to her relief, her fellow diners were Peter, Sonya, Loraine and Gary. They were the least likely members of the party to pry.

'You missed an excellent trip, Fiona.' Loraine proceeded to give an enthusiastic account of the afternoon's highlights.

For once, Sonya also seemed to have enjoyed the visit, commenting on their guide and how he had made the history come alive. Fiona had never seen, Peter's so-called wife looking quite so relaxed and at ease. For once, she was actually being sociable.

'I thought the weaponry display was pretty impressive,' Gary said.

'Oh, you men!' protested his wife. 'Talk about boys with their toys.'

Throughout the banter, Fiona was able to sit back and relax. The crunch would come when they all adjourned for coffee in the lounge. The likes of Rose, Drina and Anna would pester her until she came up with some sort of explanation and even if she pleaded ignorance of Henry and Barbara's problems, she would have to account for her own absence this afternoon. Necessary paperwork before they left the country or something to do with Travis and the hospital perhaps?

As she savoured a particularly delicious rum-trüffel, she tried hard to come up with a ploy that would allow her to escape.

'Our little group is getting smaller by the minute. Shall we all sit together?' suggested Rose as they left the dining room.

'A good idea,' agreed Anna.

Once they reached the lounge, a couple of the men began shifting the chairs into a more sociable group while the rest queued at the coffee station.

'What do you think could have happened to make Barbara and Henry leave like that? It was all a bit sudden, wasn't it?' said Drina.

'I told you something else bad was going to happen when we were all waiting to go on the walk this morning,' said Elsie, frowning as she plonked herself heavily into an armchair next to Drina. 'Didn't I point out we were down to unlucky thirteen.'

Sonya gave a snort of derisive laughter and several of the others tried to hide their smirks.

'Then you must be very relieved that there are now only eleven of us,' said Sol in mock solemnity. 'Twelve if you count Fiona.'

Realising that she was being sent up, Elsie withdrew herself into the back of her chair, a pinched expression on her face.

'I'm afraid I can't stop for long,' Fiona cut in quickly before the situation got out of hand. 'As soon as I've drunk my coffee, I'm going to have to run this evening, I'm afraid.

As well as my own packing, I need to pack all Travis's things. The hotel has kindly agreed to store his case until he comes out of hospital.'

'How is poor Travis?' asked Anna. 'Have you had any more news?'

'I spoke to the sister on his ward late this afternoon and she said he's making excellent progress.'

'Is he conscious yet?' It was not like Sonya to show concern. Of all the group, she had made no secret of her dislike of the intrusive reporter.

'The doctors have said all along that they wanted to keep him in an induced coma for at least twenty-four hours to help the brain recover. It is normal procedure after a serious fall. The ward sister said that they would review the situation tomorrow morning.'

'It's a pity that there will be no one there whom he knows when they bring him round.' Anna shook her head. 'If we'd still been here, perhaps some of us could have popped in just to wish him well. Tomorrow we're not only leaving the town, we'll be halfway across the country by lunchtime.'

'Travis does have a brother, so let's hope he will be over soon,' said Fiona. The likelihood of that sounded pretty remote, given that Head Office still hadn't managed to track the man down, but it was still early days.

Fiona finished her coffee and leant forward to put her cup on the small table in front of her.

'That was quick, Fiona,' said Sol. 'You'll burn your insides drinking it that quickly.'

Fiona laughed and got to her feet. 'I do need to get on.'

Fiona had only been in her room five minutes when there was a soft knock on her door. She wasn't surprised to see Peter standing there.

'Come on in.'

'I cannot stop long.'

Fiona gave him the gist of the afternoon's events. 'I can't help feeling guilty.'

'Why, for goodness' sake?'

'I should have realised something was wrong with Henry a good deal sooner. If I hadn't been so preoccupied with my grand-daughter and made time to listen to him, it might have saved a lot of anguish. He was all ready to confess at one point, but I had a phone call and the moment passed.' She shook her head. 'I confess, I felt sorry for Henry in the end.'

'Now why does that not surprise me?'

She pulled a face at him. 'I know you think I'm far too much of a soft touch when it comes to hard-luck stories, but even our hard-bitten Inspector Bauer expressed sympathy for him. Said he was a man taken over by circumstances. It was bad enough growing up in an environment where you had to watch everything you said. The Stasi could knock on your door any minute and take another of your family away on some trumped-up charge. Poor Henry had to watch his mother die of grief when her two brothers were taken away, and then see his father shot in front of him. What kind of childhood was that? Listening to Frederick going on about how wonderful life was back then, not to mention Travis's claims that the man had been a border guard, must have brought back all that trauma with a vengeance.'

'With a good lawyer, he may be able to plead diminished responsibility while the balance of his mind was disturbed.'

'The Inspector said much the same thing. He also said it will go in his favour that he handed himself in, even if it was a week later.'

'So, contrary to your expectations, our good Inspector Bauer does have a heart after all.'

'I have to admit that I was surprised when he came to reassure me before they all left.'

'Perhaps now you can relax and enjoy the rest of the tour.'

'I suppose so, but I do feel a bit guilty having to leave Travis here in Germany to wake up surrounded by strangers.'

'Fiona!' He raised an eyebrow and gave her an indulgent smile. 'I must get back before anyone starts asking awkward questions.'

Once he'd left, she sat thoughtfully on the bed. It was all very well for Peter to glibly say she could sit back and relax. It wasn't just the thought of leaving Travis that was troubling her. There was something far more serious. She would dearly have loved to talk it through with Peter, but she knew that it would only end in the two of them arguing. Not that Peter ever argued. That was part of the problem. His intransigent cold reasoning drove her to distraction. It would only end in her losing her temper and she couldn't face that right now. She was too mentally and physically drained.

Day 11

Sadly, this morning we leave the Elbe Valley and head for home. We will stop for lunch just outside Bad Hersfeld. Dinner will be at the Mercure Hotel in Aachen where we will make our overnight stop.
Super Sun Executive Travel

Chapter 29

As she lay in bed the next morning, Fiona mentally ran through her to-do list for the day. She mustn't forget to tell reception that Travis's case was ready for collection to be taken for storage when she went down to breakfast.

With their departure planned for eight o'clock, there was no point in even ringing the hospital before they left. In normal circumstances, as she wasn't a relative, the hospital would be very reticent about telling her anything about Travis's condition, but Fiona had built up a rapport with one of the nurses. It turned out that the woman had spent some years in England. Not only had she learnt to speak excellent English, she had trained in one of the hospitals where Fiona had worked, albeit some ten years earlier. There was a possibility Fiona might discover more from her. Perhaps she would try just before they left.

Fiona went to hand in her key card at reception to find Elsie talking earnestly with one of the young men behind the desk with a very sheepish-looking Walter standing beside her.

'I am sorry, madam, but no one has handed them in.'

'Is there a problem, Elsie?'

'Walter's lost his spectacles.'

'We've looked everywhere. Several times,' Elsie insisted when Fiona returned with the flustered woman to their room.

Fiona double-checked drawers, cupboards and the bathroom to no avail. She even checked the bedding.

'We've already looked in all the hand luggage,' said Elsie as she tipped out the contents of a voluminous holdall onto the bed.

Fiona turned to Walter. 'When were you wearing them last?'

'I must have had them on at breakfast,' he replied, 'but I can't remember taking them off.'

'Have you checked in the restaurant?'

'Elsie has but I'm sure I had them coming back up because I can't see too well without them.'

'Which means they must be here,' Fiona said soothingly, trying to calm the elderly man who was getting more and more agitated.

Fiona picked up the washbag lying on the bed and undid the zipper. 'Here we are.'

'Thank you, Fiona.' Walter beamed, taking charge of his glasses. 'Now I remember. I took them off when I cleaned my teeth.'

'So why put them in the washbag, you silly man?' snapped his wife.

'I didn't pack the toothbrushes and stuff,' Walter protested. 'You always insist on doing that. According to you, I can't be trusted.'

'And this just proves it . . .'

'I think we better hurry and get downstairs. The others will all be waiting.'

The couple were still sniping at one another all the way down in the lift.

'You two go and take your seats in the coach. I'll be there in a minute.'

It was already ten minutes past the time set to leave, but there was something she needed to do first. She dialled the number of her friendly nurse.

'Mr Everest is responding well. The doctor checked on him last evening and was pleased with his progress.'

'That's good. Have you any idea when they expect to bring him out of the coma?'

'That I cannot tell you. If he continues to make good progress and there are no unforeseen setbacks, it might even be late today.'

'That's good to know.'

'No guarantees,' the nurse said quickly.

'I appreciate that.'

'Would it be possible to keep me informed if there are any changes?' Fiona asked tentatively.

'Of course. We have your mobile number and I will let you know as soon as Mr Everest regains consciousness.'

'Thank you.'

Fiona slipped her phone into her bag and hurried outside.

'Sorry about the delay, Winston.'

'Not to worry, sweetheart. We can make it up on the journey, no problem.'

If she shaved five minutes off the comfort stop and they were lucky with traffic, there shouldn't be a problem about being well in time for the lunch arrangements.

The journey passed uneventfully. Most people slept or watched films on their individual screens. Despite spending most of the day sitting in the coach, no one seemed to be particularly anxious to leap up from their seats when the coach pulled up outside their overnight hotel in Aachen.

'As you can see our hotel is located right in the heart of the historic part of the city. Some of you may like to take a stroll around the centre after dinner. The cathedral is only a ten-minute walk away and I'm sure the staff at reception will point you in the right direction.'

'Does this hotel have free internet access?' Gary asked.

'I believe so. And all the rooms have satellite TV, and tea and coffee making facilities as you've had everywhere else.'

'Are you going out to see the sights after you've eaten, Fiona?' asked Loraine at dinner.

'I was intending to if I can summon up the energy.'

'Travelling can be amazingly tiring,' agreed Anna who was

also sitting at their table. 'But it might be a good idea to stretch the old legs and get a bit of fresh air. Aachen is supposed to be quite a beautiful city. It would be a shame to miss it.'

'Well you can count me out,' said her husband. 'I'm going to make use of that free internet and send some of the photos to the family.'

In the end, Fiona felt obliged to accompany Anna on a stroll to see the city hall and the other attractive old buildings.

'I enjoyed that, thank you, Anna.'

The older woman gave a wry laugh. 'You sound as though you weren't expecting to.'

'What I meant was that if you hadn't dragged me out, I probably wouldn't have bothered. Tonight was fun. Sol doesn't know what he missed.'

'Oh, I shall tell him, don't you worry,' said Anna, hitting the button for the lift.

Fiona laughed.

She was still chuckling to herself as she walked along the corridor to her room. She turned the corner and almost collided with someone coming the other way.

'Peter, I'm so sorry.'

'No problem. I was just going down to the bar for a drink. Would you care to join me?'

She was all set to refuse, then changed her mind. 'Why not? I was about to turn in, but after all that fresh air, I confess I don't feel in the least bit sleepy. Thank you, Peter, that would be very nice. If you wouldn't mind, first I just need to pop to my room and get rid of my coat?'

'By all means.'

He walked with her and waited as she sat on the bed to pull off her boots.

'You sound cheerful. I have not seen you looking so carefree the whole trip. It has not been an easy one for you. It must be a relief that it is almost over.'

'Yes and no. There are still one or two questions I'd like the answers to.'

'Oh?'

'Henry denied that he had anything to do with Travis's fall.'

'Of course not. It was an accident.'

'That barrier was too high to simply fall over.'

He sank down on the bed next to her. 'Everest was trying to balance on the bottom rail and leaning out to take a photo. It is more than possible, that in all the confusion when people began slipping over on the ice, somebody knocked against him and he toppled over.

Fiona scowled. 'I'm not convinced.'

Peter stared at her and she could feel the rapidly widening gap between them as the tension mounted.

Nonetheless, his voice was calm, almost reasonable, when he said, 'I did not appreciate that you were serious when you hinted that someone might have deliberately pushed Everest onto the rocks.'

'Would I joke about something as serious as that?'

He shook his head. 'That is not what I meant. You were upset, and I thought with more time you would come to appreciate how unlikely the idea must be. What possible reason could anyone have? You have already said Henry Wolf denied it and surely, he is the only one with a credible motive. Are you saying he was lying?'

'Not at all. I believe him.'

'Then who else?' Now there was a definite edge to his voice.

'I think we both know the answer to that, Peter.' She paused to let her words sink in. 'Travis was telling anyone who would listen that he had got hold of a breakthrough story. A revelation that would hit the headlines big time. There is one person in our party who might be anxious about that boast and ruthless enough to do something about it.'

Peter's whole body stiffened. 'Mrs Mason. Fiona. You are

seeing conspiracy theories where they do not exist. Why can you not accept that Everest's fall was a simple accident?'

She could feel her pulse beginning to race, but her voice remained icily calm. 'Look me in the eye, Peter, and tell me you don't have at a least of smidgen of doubt. You could always ask her of course. Is it because you're afraid of the answer if you do?'

'My feelings are irrelevant. I have a job to do.'

'So why is this woman so important? What possible information can she have that justifies all this? Assuming that as I hinted the other day and you didn't deny, your real informant is Colonel Belousov, Natalia is merely a conduit. Once you get her to London, she'll be of no further use to you.'

For a split second, she saw a flicker of an eyebrow, but he regained his composure instantly. 'I am neither admitting nor denying anything.'

'So why go to all this trouble to get her out?'

He shook his head and made as if to go but she put a hand on his arm to hold him back. 'I can understand why you would prefer her not to be in Russian hands. There is always the risk she might give away Belousov's involvement under duress, but she is no use to you now. Give me a good reason why I shouldn't go straight to the local police and voice my concerns that she was responsible for Travis's attempted murder.'

He turned and said sharply, 'You would not do that.'

'Then tell me why it's so imperative that Natalia gets to Britain.'

She put a hand softly on his cheek, looking deep into his eyes. Her voice was barely more than a whisper. 'How far would you go to stop me?' She smiled and shook her head very slowly.

There was a long silence. He took her hand from his face and laid it back in her lap, gently distancing himself from her.

'It was part of the bargain we made with Belousov. His

continued cooperation in return for her safety.'

'My goodness, Peter. Until now, I never realised just how ruthless you can be. That false message that sent Faith scurrying back home was no coincidence, was it? You may not have had her eliminated or whatever euphemistic term you like to use, but you still ruined her holiday. I am prepared to believe you were not the one who actually pushed Travis over the railing, but would you really let Natalia get away with it?'

'Neither of us have proof that she did any such thing,' he said. His voice was uncharacteristically sharp.

'But you're not prepared to find out! Doesn't Travis Everest deserve justice?'

Montgomery-Jones got to his feet and started walking to the door.

Her anger spilled over. 'I thought you were better than that, Peter. I always believed that you were a man of integrity. But you're a straw man, a man without feeling. I trusted you.'

The door closed quietly, and she listened to the sound of his steady footfalls gradually fade away.

Day 12

We will make an early start this morning in order to arrive at Calais for a midday crossing.

At the terminal, you will bid a fond farewell to your fellow passengers and transfer to your feeder coach for the last leg of the journey home.

Here at Super Sun Executive Travel, we trust you had a magnificent holiday and we hope to see you all again in the near future on another of our exciting itineraries.

Super Sun Executive Travel

Chapter 30

It took all her effort to drag herself to the shower. Her spat with Peter Montgomery-Jones the night before had left her feeling deeply depressed. She hated it when they were on bad terms, but this time she really had gone overboard. Would she ever be able to look him in the eye again? Even at the time, she doubted that she meant those words. She shuddered at the memory. Why was it he could drive her to such levels of frustration? No one else was able to provoke her as he did. There were times when she just wanted to get hold of him and shake him until he showed some sort of real emotion.

He was right of course. He did have a job to do. Whatever he felt about it, even if he was as convinced as she was that Natalia had something to do with what had happened to Travis, there was nothing he could do about it. This whole affair wasn't about justice. It was about the national interest.

But that didn't make it right! She wrenched the shower curtain, almost tearing the fabric from its rail. She may have been the one in the wrong, but if he was waiting for an apology, he could think again.

She stood in the shower and gave a deep sigh. Closing her eyes, she lifted her head to the full force of the water. The hotel shower gel, shampoo and conditioner were all heavily perfumed. Almond and jojoba. The lingering smell left her feeling as is if she'd smothered herself in some exotic dessert rather than with what, according to the labels, were supposed to be refreshing toiletries.

Telling herself sharply to pull herself together, she dressed and turned to pick up her watch from the bedside table when a pinging sound on her mobile indicated that someone had just sent her a text message.

'Happy birthday, Mum. Card and present waiting for you back home. Call you this evening. Love, Martin. XXX.'

Her birthday! She'd forgotten all about it. Even when Bill was alive, birthdays were always low key. She always made a cake and prepared a special meal for his birthday, but in the latter years, when Bill was more or less confined to the house there was no chance of going out or doing anything special on hers. But it gave her a warm glow to know that Martin had remembered and was thinking of her. No doubt, Adam would phone later. She may have lost her beloved Bill, but she was lucky to have two sons like hers.

It would be a long time before she finally got back home to Guildford, so Fiona decided to treat herself to the full English cooked breakfast rather than her usual fare of fruit and toast. The majority of her passengers appeared to have had the same idea she decided, as she glanced around the restaurant.

It wasn't long before she was joined at her table by Loraine and Gary Peters.

'Do you have far to go when we get back to Dover?' Fiona asked.

'Far enough. We get dropped off in Coventry and then we'll get a taxi to our village just outside Rugby. What about you? I expect you will be pleased when this tour is over one way or another.'

'It has been somewhat eventful,' Fiona said with a grimace. 'I do hope that despite all the upset, you have enjoyed your holiday.'

'Oh yes!' Loraine's enthusiasm was genuine. 'All the places we've seen have been wonderful. Much better than we anticipated actually. Berlin was wonderful. We've decided that at some point in the future we'll come back and spend more time there. There is so much to see.'

'That's good to hear.'

Thinking about her conversation with Loraine and Gary and their onward journey as she made her way back up to her room after breakfast, she wondered how many more of her passengers she would be saying goodbye to at Calais. She had travelled to Dover on a feeder coach directly from Guildford but on the return journey she would have to report to the London office. That meant she would be staying with Winston until Victoria Coach Station. In all likelihood, so too would Peter and Sonya. If Peter worked in the MI6 building, Vauxhall Cross, presumably he lived somewhere near.

She seemed to remember him saying something about rushing to the port in a taxi, but because all the changeovers were made in Calais, once they arrived at Dover, all the coaches would join the streams of traffic heading up the hill and out of the port without stopping.

There were several people at the reception desk, including Sol and Anna at the front of the small queue. When Sol had paid his drinks bill and had disappeared off in the direction of the lifts, Fiona caught the receptionist's eye and pushed her room key card across the counter and turned to move away.

'Mrs Mason! Just a moment.' She turned back. 'I have something for you.'

Fiona gave an apologetic smile to the three people still waiting while the receptionist dived under the counter and brought out a large bouquet of flowers wrapped in cellophane.

'These arrived for you ten minutes ago.'

'Are you sure they're for me? I'm not expecting anything.'

Not only was her name clearly printed on the delivery label, it was on the small envelope clipped to the wrapping. Moving further along the desk and out of everyone's way, she pulled off the envelope and took out the card.

All it said was *Happy Birthday*. There was no name. No indication of who had sent it.

One of the boys must have ordered them. Martin hadn't mentioned it, so it must be from Adam. But how did he know where she was staying? No one here knew it was her birthday.

Any minute now, her passengers would be coming down ready for the off. The last thing she wanted was for them to know it was her birthday. She hurried out to see if Winston was ready with the coach. She could hardly hide such a large bouquet, but the flowers might not be noticed on a spare seat at the back of the coach.

Fiona glanced back to check all was well with her passengers, then settled herself into her seat. It wasn't until then that she noticed a white envelope tucked into the mesh pocket in front of her.

She opened it to find a card with a picture of a kitten on the front. Inside, in large letters were the words, "Happy Birthday to my favourite tour guide, love W XXX.'

Slipping the card into her tote bag before any of the passengers could see it, she undid her seatbelt and eased forward.

'Thank you, Winston. You shouldn't have.'

He chuckled, 'I's only a card, sweetheart.'

'How did you know?'

He tapped the side of his nose. 'Let's just say, a little bird told me.'

She gave him a pretend punch on his arm.

He laughed again. 'Sylvia in the office noticed it in your records. She mentioned it when I went in to collect the paperwork before we left.'

'Don't you dare tell the passengers or I'll never speak to you again.'

With a big smile, she settled back in her seat. If they realised at Head Office she was away on her birthday, could the flowers be from David Rushworth as an attempt to make up for strong-arming her into agreeing to take on the tour and make up for all the problems she'd had?

It didn't seem likely, somehow. Who had sent the bouquet and why was there no signature?

The sound of her mobile made her start. She must have dozed off in the warm coach.

'Fiona Mason.'

'This is Nurse Weiss. I promised to let you know when Herr Everest regained consciousness. He is doing well.'

'That is good news! Do give him our regards. Tell him we are all thinking of him. I hope he's being a good patient.'

'Hmm. I have had easier patients to deal with,' she said with a rueful laugh. 'Once the doctor said he could be taken off the drugs he came round quite quickly. He slept for the first half hour and then he began to make his presence felt.'

'Oh?'

'He is complaining about his broken leg and demanding more pain relief.'

'Tell him he's very lucky to be alive at all after a fall like that.'

'He does not remember anything about it. He remembers being with you all at Bastei and standing by the railings taking photos, but he has no explanation of how he came to fall.'

'I see. Thank you for letting me know.'

She rang off and sat pensively for a few moments. It looked as if the mystery might never be solved. Perhaps it was best that way, but for her own peace of mind she would have liked a definitive answer.

Time to be honest with herself. There was no evidence that Travis's fall was other than an accident. She was the only one who thought it in any way suspicious. And how much of that was because of her prejudice against the woman posing as Peter's wife?

She picked up the microphone.

'Good news, everyone.'

The coach made a comfort stop at the motorway station. They were just finishing coffee when Fiona's mobile started buzzing again. She checked the caller ID. It was Adam. It was probably only to wish her a happy birthday and she was tempted to let it go to voice-mail as she was sitting with some of the passengers.

'I'm sorry about this but if you'll excuse me, I need to answer this.'

She slipped out of her chair and hurried outside.

'Hello, darling.'

Two high voices began singing 'Happy birthday to you,' followed by shouts of 'love you Grandma,' from Becky and Adam Junior.

'Hi, Mum. Hope I haven't caught you in the middle of something. The kids have been pestering to ring you as soon as they woke up.' Fiona could hear their mother in the background shooing them upstairs with instructions to hurry and get dressed before they were late for school.

'Becky seems to have recovered quickly. Is she back to school already?

'This will be her first day. She's been demanding to go back ever since she got home, and the doctor says it's okay.'

'That is good news.'

'So where are you now? Are you still in Berlin?'

'No, darling. We left there nearly a week ago.'

They talked for a few more minutes. Fiona stood holding her phone lost in thought. Obviously, Adam hadn't ordered the mystery flowers.

There was only one possible candidate. Someone in a position to have all her details. Someone who knew far too much about her for her own comfort.

Damn, damn, damn. She was still annoyed with him and they had managed to avoid each other all morning, but now she was going to have to find to Peter and thank him.

And not just thank him. She owed him an apology. Why did she keep letting him provoke her to such outbursts?

Peter Montgomery-Jones really was the most infuriating man she knew!

There was no time left during their mid-morning coffee comfort stop. Everyone was already making their way back to the coach. Her only consolation was that she'd have a couple of hours to think what she was going to say.

The coach arrived at the terminal and as Winston slowly drove to the Super Sun assembly area, Sol made his way to the front and asked the driver for the microphone.

'This is the point where we all split up and go our separate ways but before we do on behalf of all of us, I'd like to say a big thank you to Winston for his excellent driving.'

Cries of, 'Hear, hear!' and spontaneous clapping broke out.

Winston acknowledged their tributes with a wave of his hand.

'And what can I say about this lovely lady who has been our mentor . . .'

The rest of his words were drowned out by the cheers and applause. There may have been far fewer passengers on their return journey than at the beginning, but they made enough noise to attract the attention of passers-by.

Even the ever-critical Elsie was enthusiastic in her goodbyes as they left the coach. Peter and Sonya were at the end of the line. Fiona could not quite look him in the eye, but he behaved like any other passenger, thanking her for an excellent tour, shaking her hand leaving what she had no doubt was a very generous tip in her palm before following the others.

The biggest surprise was Sonya waiting patiently behind him. For once, the woman's smile reached her eyes. 'Thank you. Thank you for everything.' Fiona found herself embraced in an affectionate hug. 'I know I have not been the easiest passenger you have ever had to deal with and for that I apologise. You have never been anything but kind and tolerant and for that I thank you.'

She turned away quickly and hurried after Peter who was already some fifty yards away, talking with Morris and Drina.

Officially her duties were now at an end which meant that she could dispense with the regulation uniform she was obliged to wear on the outgoing and homecoming journeys. Back on the coach, she untied the bright yellow scarf and stuffed it into her tote bag and laid her navy-blue jacket carefully on the luggage rack. For the rest of the journey, she would be just another passenger.

There was just one more thing to do.

The café area at the terminal was vast and trying to find a specific person was a tall order. She had almost given up hope until following the signs to the washrooms, she turned down the corridor and noticed a familiar figure ahead of her.

'Peter!'

He turned and waited for her to catch up. At least he hadn't pretended not to hear. Although it did cross her mind that perhaps it was because he had not recognised her voice.

Without waiting for him to speak, she said in a rush, 'I owe you an apology. I should never have said those things. It was unforgivable. If it's any consolation, I've been worrying ever since.'

There was a sudden burst of raucous laughter and a group of young women turned into the corridor, talking noisily.

Peter took Fiona's arm and steered her back out into the café area. They made their way over to a quieter section of the vast seating area where they found an empty table against a wall where they would not be overheard.

'I fully accept I was overreacting. As I said, I've been giving it a lot of thought. I realise how much I let my prejudice against Natalia colour my judgement. She must have been under a terrible strain, having to play tourist all that time knowing that any minute she might be tracked down and killed. I don't suppose any of us would be at our best under those circumstances.' Her words came tumbling out and she barely paused for breath.

'You said on the coach that Everest has regained consciousness.'

She nodded. 'The doctors seem to think he'll make a full recovery.'

'That is good news. Was he able to tell them what happened at Bastei?'

'He remembers the fall but not in any detail.'

'He is not claiming he was pushed?'

'No.'

'Does that mean you are no longer accusing me of covering up an attempted murder?'

'Make me squirm, why don't you?'

He laughed. 'I think we might both need a good holiday after these last two weeks.'

'It has been a somewhat stressful tour.'

'Are you travelling back to Guildford this evening?'

'I'm catching the first train home as soon as I've dropped off all the paperwork at the office.'

'Would you consider catching a later one and letting me take you out to dinner to celebrate your birthday?'

'I'd like that. Very much.'

ABOUT THE AUTHOR

Judith has three passions in life – writing, travel and ancient history. Her novels are the product of those passions. Her Fiona Mason Mysteries are each set on coach tours to different European countries and her history lecturer Aunt Jessica, accompanies travel tours to more exotic parts of the world.

Born and brought up in Norwich, she now lives with her husband in Wiltshire. Though she wrote her first novel (now languishing in the back of a drawer somewhere) when her two children were toddlers. There was little time for writing when she returned to work teaching Geography in a large comprehensive. It was only after retiring from her headship, that she was able to take up writing again in earnest.

Life is still busy. She spends her mornings teaching Tai Chi and yoga or at line dancing, Pilates and Zumba classes. That's when she's not at sea as a cruise lecturer giving talks on ancient history, writing and writers or running writing workshops.

***

Find out more about Judith at www.judithcranswick.co.uk

Printed in Great Britain
by Amazon